Advance Praise

"An allegorical novel that seems eerily contemporary. Thoreau meets Ballard, meets Huysmans and many more."

~ Tom McCarthy, author of *Remainder* and C

"With *The Bee-Loud Glade*, Steve Himmer has written a hypnotic and heartfelt debut novel, interweaving naturalistic beauty and postmodern complexity within this compulsively readable parable. Whether the story's hermit-for-hire is a man approaching some form of enlightenment or merely the whim of an eccentric billionaire remains up for debate, but the novel itself is unambiguously ingenious and very clearly announces a shining new talent."

~ Frederick Reiken, author of *Day For Night*, *The Lost Legends of New Jersey*, and *The Odd Sea*

"Meet Finch: 10 years into his job as Assistant to the Director of Brand Awareness at Second Nature Modern Greenery, writer of dozens of blogs where he creates imaginary lives for himself— none as surreal as the life he'll soon lead as a hermit. Enter Himmer's humorous, carefully imagined world. Watch his skillful hand transform Finch into a postmodern Thoreau before your eyes. Sit still. Pay attention. Do all this, and you, too, will fall under this novel's wondrous spell. I promise."

~ Peter Grandbois, author of *The Gravedigger*, *The Arsenic Lobster*, and *Nahoonkara*

"Featuring a faceless drone from the world of corporate America and an eccentric millionaire whose whims change by the week, Steve Himmer's *The Bee-Loud Glade* is a wonderful novel that's hard to describe, but that's a good thing. Just go where this stunning book takes you and enjoy the story, the characters, and the language."

~ Michael Kindness, host of *Books on the Nightstand*

"In *The Bee-Loud Glade,* Steve Himmer examines the charm of inertia. He professionalizes hermitry, making it a spectacle that is equal parts sitcom and documentary. The premise is wild but the execution is contemplative, making this novel funny two ways: funny ha-ha and funny strange. "

~ William Walsh, author of *Questionstruck* and *Ampersand, Mass.*

the bee-loud glade

the
bee-loud
glade

steve
himmer

An Atticus Trade Paperback Original

Atticus Books LLC
3766 Howard Avenue, Suite 202
Kensington MD 20895
http://atticusbooksonline.com

Excerpts of *The Bee-Loud Glade* have appeared previously in *Pindeldyboz*,
PANK Magazine, *Emprise Review*, *Everyday Genius*, *The Collagist*, *Monkeybicycle*, and
Hawk & Handsaw.

ISBN-13: 978-0-9845105-8-0
ISBN-10: 0-9845105-8-3

Typeset in Berling
Cover design by Jamie Keenan

for my parents

1

Last night's storm rolled through like it meant something, crackling and snarling and snapping down branches, howling outside the mouth of my cave like the coyotes I sometimes hear far away in these hills (they've never come close, and I've never known why). It was the loudest storm I've heard in the years I've lived here, or maybe it was only the first big one to pass since my eyes began failing and forced me to listen more deeply than I did before. There's no way of measuring that sort of thing. I can't return to when my eyes worked to find out. I can't compare a storm known with five senses to a storm known only through four. Or four and a half, I suppose; I can still see, just not as well as I could. I can make out the flash of lightning but never the shape of its bolt. Some mornings it's better and others it's worse; some days I can see almost as clearly as I ever could, only to wake up the next morning to find my eyes are worse than ever. It's like there's a loose lens in my head that sometimes, by chance, slides into place for a while. But despite those day-to-day fluctuations in its decline, I've had to accept that my eyesight is fading from blurry to black and is taking the bright, green world around me down with it. It's getting harder and harder to be on my own, and in this line of work—not that it is really work, though it started that way—being on your own is more or less the whole job.

This morning I stepped out of my cave into a world that still smelled like fresh rain and burnt air. Something was different—a feeling, an itch at the back of awareness—and the left-behind lightning scent made me think of those old monster movies in which the scientist waits to see if his creature has been brought to life, and the audience waits along with him. Those crackling moments of anticipation, the knowledge that something has happened, but what? The same birds were singing as sing any day, the same treetops rustling in a light breeze as their leaves sprayed a shower of rain down onto my body. It was the same as any one of my mornings, except for that nagging feeling it wasn't.

I checked on my crops, to be sure they were safe and not torn up by wind or flooded too deep to survive, and to my relief the informal fence of blackberry bushes had once again done its job. Berries were scattered all over the ground, slipping and squishing between my bare toes as I circled the potatoes and carrots and beans with the stoop and squint it now takes me to get a good view, but the crops themselves were unharmed. I pulled a bright yellow squash from its vine, washed it off on the wet grass, and crunched through its crisp skin as I felt my way back to the gap in the bushes and set off to inspect the rest of my world. And for once, for some reason, I walked away from the river. I went against my usual route and my long-standing habit of starting each day in its waters.

And that's how I got into trouble: wandering away from routine, relying on an ever more obsolete image of what my home acres look like to guide me. As long as everything stays where I expect it to be, I can find it; as long as trees don't walk off and my cave doesn't move and crops grow where I plant their seeds, I can get by with only this foggy tunnel of vision. But last night's storm shifted things; it laid branches across my familiar paths and uprooted bushes I've used as landmarks for ages. It knocked over the cairn of stones I'd stacked up a long time ago to mark the edge of my regular ambling, but I only realized it had fallen down later, on the way back to my cave, after wandering past the downed marker and into the tangled part of the forest where I don't go very often with these failing eyes.

I must have wandered for hours, long enough for the angle of sunlight to rise and fall as the day dragged on, and as I dragged myself through the forest. I may have crossed my own hidden trail dozens or hundreds of times, whipped in the face and legs by the same eager branches again and again, and I may have been on the edge of the woods, on the edge of the glade by my cave, for most of the day—how would I have known when all I could see was the green veil of forest before my eyes, hanging always a few inches ahead with all the world blurry behind it?

Sometime in late afternoon, long after the sweet-smelling wild grapes I found for lunch had stopped filling my stomach, I was still out there walking. And that's when I got an even bigger surprise than getting lost in my own landscape: two hikers, tramping between trees and pushing aside brambles and branches, snapping twigs and crushing pinecones and acorns with heavy boots, and squashing shy mushrooms with a heavy hiss under their soles. Every once in a very, very long while someone passes this way, proves persistent enough to climb a rock face or hop over a ditch into my secret world. Every so often I hear someone nearby, but I've never been so close to any of them and they've never come so close to me; they pass through and pass on, out of my forest and out of my life, leaving nothing but a temporary tear that the resettled quiet soon stitches.

I heard the hikers coming in time to crawl under some thick, dripping bushes, to slide my nude self off their crackling path. Lying on my belly and balls in wet leaves and cool mud, I watched as the brown blurs of their boots passed within the small sphere of my sight. They weren't speaking, but they were breathing hard and sniffing and spitting and making all of the sounds humans make when they think they're being silent, sounds I must make myself all the time without knowing because there's no one around me to notice. The legs in the first boots were thick with muscles and hair, but the second pair was smooth and slender.

My nose burned and I nearly coughed with the sudden rush of their smells—shampoo and soap, factory-made fabrics and leather and sweat from a body that was human but for the first time in years wasn't mine—and for a moment I thought I might retch, but I held it down as they passed.

They moved quickly out of my limited sight, though I could still hear the crackle and snap of their steps. And that's when one hiker, the woman—the more slender and sleek pair of legs, I supposed— spoke a word. "Here," she said, or maybe she asked it; the sound of a voice was such a surprise that I missed its tone altogether, and though no answer was given and she said nothing else, that syllable boomed in my mind and my garden so much more loudly than the storm had last night. The first word I'd heard spoken in so many years, long after I made peace with knowing I wouldn't hear words again. I was stunned like lightning had struck me, and the hikers kept walking until they were out of earshot but their word stayed behind, echoing across unsettled canyons of quiet.

I might have sprung out of my bush before it was too late. Before they had passed, I might have asked them to help me find the way back to my cave, to lead a nearly blind man to his home, but how on earth would I have done it? If they didn't run from a nude, filthy mute leaping out of the scrub, it would only be because they'd cracked my skull with one of their walking sticks and so knew they had nothing to fear. For the first time in forever I had occasion to wonder how I might look to somebody else, calloused and tanned on parts of my body that no one would have any desire to see, a shaggy skeleton or a dirty old mop stood on end. I realized that if I saw myself bursting out of the woods, I might not offer help either. And if they knew I was here they might wonder why, they might find my cave and my crops. The less I disturbed them, I thought, the less chance that they'd disturb me.

And if I asked for help, if I did it by speaking and breaking my vow or simply by signing my needs in some manner of gesture and dance, I would be giving up all that I've gained in this garden, all the faith the Old Man has rewarded so well, for a weak moment's aid from a stranger. Better to be left behind in my blindness, waiting for silence to reseal the rent left by that hiker's word, so I waited beneath the wet bush until their breathing and boots were long gone. I knew the Old Man would get me out of the woods in his own good time, and in the end—at the end of a very long day—I was right. He guided me out not long after the hikers had passed, pulling me from the forest right at the downed cairn so I could stop to rebuild it and avoid getting lost the next time I go walking, a task that needed doing before I could head to the river for a slow evening swim and to repent for my lapse in routine.

I crouched at the base of the cairn, feeling around in the tall grass and downed twigs for displaced stones to restack, working slowly with care because one of the hazards of naked living is that even the most mundane tasks become dangerous to some delicate part of the body, and some of those stones were rough and all of them weighed enough to cause harm, and who knew what snakes and sharp sticks I might kneel upon in the grass.

I was glad for the work, glad to keep my hands busy and to settle my fluttering thoughts after spotting those hikers and hearing that word. The adrenaline of surprise still shook in my bones, and my heart beat so hard I could hear rushing blood in my ears. I wondered where they were headed and how long it had been since I'd seen, heard, or smelled other people (the memory of their strong odors made my nose itch again), and that made me wonder how long ago this estate was abandoned to me. How long I'd spent happily here on my own.

Given my chance to be spotted, I chose to hide in the scrub. I gave in to the same habit of disappearing that brought me here in the first place, but this time—unlike the last—I have something worth keeping to lose.

2

I knew I was about to be fired when the new submanager asked, "So what is it you do here, Mr. Finch?" Almost ten years in my job, nearly that many submanagers come and gone over time, and he was the first one to open my file or notice me working in his department. I'd had a long run of good luck.

"Brand awareness," I said. "I'm assistant to the director of brand—"

"I know your title. But what do you actually *do*?" He tapped a fingertip hard on the manila folder spread open on his desk, and it made a sharp crack because there were only two or three sheets in my file including the résumé I'd applied with years earlier, when résumés were still sent on paper. My résumé looked almost as old as the new submanager, but if I updated it—*when* I updated it, the way that meeting appeared to be going—it wouldn't change very much. There was only my current (for the moment) position to add, along with its start and end dates. A decade of my life would be condensed into a couple of lines aimed at convincing some other submanager in some other office to lay claim to my remaining years.

What could I tell him that he didn't know, that it didn't say in my slim file? I'd been charged by one of his predecessors with making our plastic plants (we preferred "hyperefficient" to "artificial") into household names. My employers at Second Nature Modern Greenery envisioned a world in which trees and rosebushes reminded consumers of our reproductions and comparisons were made in our favor. "Look at the spots on those leaves," we wanted the plant-buying public to say. "My Second Nature trees never have spots."

When I'd started with the company, I spent my days writing letters to newspapers and trade magazines, sowing word of our products wherever I could. A letter to *Paper Products Quarterly*, for instance, about how breathtaking the new corporate headquarters of some company was, might mention in passing a potted plant spotted on the mezzanine level and refer to it as one of ours. Even if the actual plants in the actual building weren't Second Nature, even if there weren't any plants or mezzanines in the building at all, the brand might take root in the readers of that magazine.

Over time the arrows in my quiver changed. I frequented newsgroups about business and gardening and home decoration, trolling for any topic I could connect our greenery to, however tenuous that connection might be. A science fiction forum on which some green moon arose in conversation allowed me to mention our greenest of greens, and an argument about urban planning in some city I'd never been to became fertile ground on which to suggest hyperefficient trees for its traffic islands.

Later I kept dozens of weblogs, and post after post shared intimate memories of the imaginary lives I'd created. Sometimes my bloggers left comments on each other's sites, and they commented on other sites, too, drawing more traffic and potential plant buyers into my marketing web. Unless those commenters weren't actual people, but the inventions of others with jobs just like mine, the whole blogosphere a soapbox for a few busy schemers selling plastic palm trees and flavored milk drinks and guides to selling products online. Each of my imaginary bloggers had a backstory, a family or else an explainable absence of one; each had his or her own history of successes and failures. Second Nature's viral campaign spanned the gamut of human behavior from borderline psychotic to contemplative, fractured English to erudition, and all of those voices and vices were mine.

And the more I said through my ciphers, the less I spoke in real life. My cube was in a far corner of the department, near some filing cabinets to which the keys had been lost, so apart from occasional walks to the bathroom and my twice-daily route between front door and desk, I was easy to miss. The faces changed around me without introduction, and in time no one knew who I was. There was no director of brand awareness for me to assist, and no one asked what I was doing. I'd been forgotten, become furniture in my far corner, and that's how I held onto the job for as long as I did even after I'd stopped writing about Second Nature and had let my online shills take on lives of their own. Their weblogs grew longer, spanned months and then years as they made projects for high school and graduated from college, grumbled or raved about various jobs, and enjoyed visits from growing grandchildren. They took trips to Hawaii and endured bouts with cancer, enjoyed good days at work and suffered through awful blind dates. Some gave birth and others died, their comment inboxes filling with sympathy notes they would never read, but I read them all. Commenters asked where flowers could be sent, and others suggested—success!—Second Nature's own hyperefficient arrangements.

Years went by offline, too. Computers and carpets upgraded around me, but always at night so I never saw how or by whom. The restaurant across the street from our office changed from sub shop to low-carb to noodles to salads, then back to sub shop again, and I ate whatever it sold. I gave up my newspaper subscription and read only the headlines from my browser's home page, then I stopped reading news altogether because the headlines were the same ones they'd been all my life.

Sometimes I postdated a batch of blog posts so they'd appear across upcoming days, then I let my computer sleep as I sat at my desk doing nothing. I spent days watching a trickle of water rise up and wash over the cairn of reconstituted brown stone in my desktop fountain (a decoration I'd claimed after its owner, the woman in the cubicle beside me years earlier, never returned from vacation). The same few cubic inches of liquid flowed by me again and again, until the soft sound of water and the whir of the fountain's electric pump carried my mind away from Second Nature and plastic plants to more or less nothing at all.

So for this new submanager to notice my name in his files, to ask himself what, exactly, I was being paid for out of his budget... it was less of a shock to be fired than to hear someone speaking my name, and to hear my telephone ring when he called me into his office. The shock was being reminded that I had a job so long since I'd actually done it.

First he took a stab at small talk, speculating about the year's Wimbledon prospects for a player who had been retired a decade at least. Years earlier, before I had been forgotten, before this particular submanager's time, a rumor had somehow started that I was a big tennis fan, which I wasn't and never had been. One of the best things about being forgotten at work was the cessation of tennis-themed holiday cards and questions about tournaments and players I'd never heard of but felt obliged to offer cryptic opinions on each time I was asked. I had even taken to reading up on the world of tennis so I wouldn't let down my side of those forced conversations, and pretending to have insider knowledge I wasn't able to share. My co-workers seemed to enjoy that I knew things they didn't, so they deferred to whatever I told them even though I made it all up. Maybe it had been more satisfying to know me as "the tennis guy" than to wonder who I actually was, and then it became easier not to know me at all.

Once he had exhausted the tennis chat I'm sure he'd planned out in advance, the submanager asked about my role at Second Nature, and I knew where the conversation was headed.

We sat for a moment, neither one of us speaking, and perhaps he was hoping as hard as I was for silence to carry the message. I couldn't tell him what I did at Second Nature because I didn't do much of anything, not anymore, and the file wouldn't say otherwise. He might have been hoping to avoid firing me in his own voice. So we played our game of silent chicken, avoiding each other's eyes until the awkwardness had done its job and I grew tired of waiting to be told what I already knew.

"Ah," I said, and rose from my chair.

The submanager spoke without showing a hint of surprise or acknowledging that a long silence had passed. "You have two weeks of vacation pay coming, and a generous...," he paused to shuffle some papers and find the one he was looking for, "a not unreasonable severance package." He stood and reached a hand toward me across his desk, and his forearm knocked over a framed photograph of an ugly little girl who, for some reason, was facing the visitor's chair instead of his own.

"It's not you, of course, Finch. Tough times. You know how it is. And you should be proud that you've done such a fine job with...," he scanned his papers again, "at brand awareness. You should interpret this... *readjustment* as testimony to how valuable you've been to the Second Nature family. How effectively you've fulfilled our goals. And if there's anything we can do for you in the future, naturally..."

I nodded as the submanager pumped away at my hand, grinding my knuckles against one another like a fistful of marbles. Then I walked back to my cube, past co-workers intensely interested in computer screens flickering with meaningless spreadsheets, conspicuous in their casual attempts to avoid looking at me as I passed. I sat in my chair for a moment, rolling back and forth on the semiopaque plastic carpet protector, wondering if there was a way I could steal it. It was, in fact, a very comfortable chair; the carpet protector I could do without. Of the things in the cube I might actually be able to take out of the building, there wasn't much I wanted to keep. There weren't any photographs tacked to my walls, no figurines, statuettes, or novelty trophies standing on the desk or on the adjustable shelves. Not a single piece of promotional swag from the sales conferences I never attended, not even a tote bag or obscenely outsized golf umbrella. I kept no extra shoes under my desk and no spare sweater for days when the office was cold—and the office had never *been* cold, I realized then for the first time, and it had never been hot for that matter; it was always generically, uncomfortably tepid. There was just the computer, not actually mine, and a filing cabinet overstuffed long ago with paper versions of all the same documents stored on the computer and backed up in several locations both on-site and off. And there was a plastic model of the company logo, which I suppose was some sort of plant but had always looked to me like a Martian.

In the end I took only my miniature fountain, in its gray basin made to look like concrete, whatever the material actually was. I pulled the fountain's plug from the overcrowded power strip under my desk, and the whir of the electric motor had never seemed so loud as when it went quiet. The water flowed for a split-second longer due to leftover force from the tiny vacuum the pump had created, then settled into the basin, becalmed.

The computer had fallen asleep during my meeting with the submanager, but I bumped the mouse while moving the fountain and the monitor came to life with a ping. I might have made final postings for each of my online personas, bringing their imaginary lives to some closure, but the idea of dozens of people who had never existed simply vanishing all over the web had an appeal I couldn't resist. And all of those voices falling silent at once, having said everything they had to say, remains—even all these years later—the most satisfying accomplishment of my tenure at Second Nature. So I set the fountain down on the desk and went online one more time to erase all my records of usernames and their passwords, removing bookmarks to those many sites created by me but belonging, most likely, most legally, to Second Nature. I didn't know then if anyone would replace me, and I don't know if anyone did, but I know they were never able to make my congregation of characters speak to sell plastic plants or to celebrate birthdays or just to vent about a bad day at work. All the lives I'd created and lived in those years went into stasis for as long as they stayed on their servers. For as long as their archives existed and their permalinks worked.

When I had finished erasing my online tracks, I lifted the fountain in both hands and wove through the cubicle maze toward the exit, trailing a dark thread of water across gray industrial carpet. As I walked to my car, I smiled to think that the trail, too, would vanish within a few minutes, and I would go back to being forgotten.

3

The first weekend of my unemployment passed like any other: I watched reruns of shows I couldn't remember from when they were new, and I went grocery shopping in the middle of the night and washed clothes in the quiet hours of morning when the laundry room of my apartment complex was otherwise empty.

Saturday night I went to the movies; I bought my ticket online then fed my credit card to a machine in the lobby to claim it. The movie was a sequel. I hadn't seen the original but that didn't matter—it was an action thriller, full of explosions and car chases just like the explosions and chases in other movies, only more so because this one was newest. Right away I knew what would happen and also what wouldn't, so I could settle into the film like I might settle into a long bus ride through a landscape that never changes and is familiar from the first moment on. I stayed awake through the whole movie, but when it was over I felt like I'd had a restful night's sleep because it had passed through me as easily as a dream, only smoother because there were fewer surprises.

After being out late at one movie, then watching another one at home on TV that was more or less the same as the first, I slept through most of Sunday and it wasn't until evening that I remembered I had no job to show up for the next morning. Sunday nights I usually watched TV and thought about what all the people I'd invented and spoken for on the company's marketing blogs were doing over the weekend, and what they would share with the world the next day, but none of that mattered now. They weren't doing anything anymore, and they would have nothing to share and no means of sharing. I could have kept on writing their lives at home, with my own computer, but they'd always lived on the company's time, stolen time, and that made their lives worth living alongside my own.

I ironed my shirts for the week ahead, per usual, as if I would need them, and I scrubbed the floors in the kitchen and bathroom of my bland, boxy apartment—a kitchen, a bedroom, a family room all to myself. I did all the chores I could think of, even sorting the pantry full of canned goods and packaged meals, until I was finally tired enough to fall asleep without thinking for too long in bed.

I'd turned off my alarm clock, but Monday morning I awoke at the same time as always, at the time routine had trained my body to wake. I had my coffee and oatmeal then sat at the kitchen table for hours. I needed to look for a job but I knew there weren't any to find. Everyone knew that, because we'd been told and reminded by TV and by papers and by each other for months. So I thought I might take some time, a few days at least, to do something I'd always wanted to do but had never found the time for, or I might go somewhere new in that city I knew only vaguely despite living there for my whole life. But after a few hours' trying I still hadn't thought of anything I wanted to do or anywhere I wanted to go. Not one idea, not one buried desire or secret scheme came to mind, though I sat at the table until I was hungry for lunch. So I ate a sandwich instead.

During the afternoon I wondered, out of habit, what my bloggers were doing and then I remembered again they were gone. So I wondered instead what my former co-workers were doing. I didn't know their names or what their jobs were, but I knew that in the afternoon the man with the mud-flap mustache on his red face would stand at the window and pretend he was looking through files. The bird-legged woman who always wore sneakers and ankle-high socks would power walk laps around the department after eating lunch in a rush at her desk. I imagined this Monday going ahead like any other for them, perhaps so ordinary they hadn't noticed the absence of my invisible presence in the far corner where they never went. To them, I might exist no more or no less than I had a few days before.

After a few days my inner clock and calendar were so screwed up that I couldn't sleep and I didn't know when I was hungry. I stopped putting the shades up or opening the curtains, and I rarely had a sense of what time it was, day or night, except when a TV show—morning news, or late-night talk—gave the hour away.

I watched the news about how many people were losing their jobs, and I pictured them all alone in apartments with the shades down and watching the news like I was. I watched reports about companies going bankrupt and employees losing pensions, and owners disappearing with billions of dollars or giving themselves massive retirement payouts. People complained and the news anchors shared their pain and the next day was the same thing all over. There were aerial shots of job fairs at malls, where crowds of the unemployed, papers flapping in their hands, stretched across parking lots like an invading army. And there were also stories about the rich—the very rich, wealth on a scale no one else could imagine—paring back their lifestyles, at least in public, for fear of anyone knowing how rich they still were.

There were stories about the very young, the just starting out, graduating college with no hope of finding a job. They were interviewed and sounded genuinely disappointed they might not be able to work, and I thought if they only knew. Other stories showed older workers, close to retirement but not there quite yet, who knew they wouldn't be hired again because of their age. There weren't many stories about people like me, people at neither the top nor the bottom, too young to retire but long past starting out.

I thought of how my bloggers would write about that, blaming the recession on people like me, on companies like Second Nature creating too many products nobody needed and employing too many people who produced nothing but blog posts that had no real need to be written or read. Then it became a bit much so I imagined turning off a computer and making those voices go quiet again.

With so many offices closing, and no new tenants moving into their left-behind spaces, I pictured acres and acres of Second Nature greenery abandoned in cedar-chip beds and on the banks of lobby lagoons, the plastic plants as green and efficient in an empty building as they had been with people around. No water, no sunlight, no pruning, no problem. Whatever happened, whoever came or went in the offices and hallways around them, those self-sufficient plants I had rooted there would be fine.

The news said attacks by fired workers were on the rise, people returning for revenge on the companies they'd been fired from, so I tried blaming the submanager for my lost job and for my boredom. I tried to work myself up with fantasies of storming his office, guns blazing, or of filling his desk drawers with snakes and with bombs, or of a scorched-earth email and online campaign to destroy his credit, his family, his reputation, his life. All my dozens of bloggers teaming up to drive the poor bastard into ruined submission. I pictured myself breaking into his house and waiting there for him, his wife and his children hog-tied and duct-taped around me. But I didn't know if he was married, or if he had kids, and as much as I tried to convince myself all of this was his fault, I couldn't get angry at someone whose name I didn't know and who hadn't been part of my life before or after the few minutes in which I was fired. He hadn't hovered in the background of my working days, waiting for me to slip up. He wasn't an archenemy, just a middle-management toady with no more control over his own fate than I had.

I lay on the couch thinking about all the different ways from relief to violence in which a person might respond to losing a job, and I decided which of my bloggers would respond in which ways. I drafted posts in my head about their newfound freedom to pursue pottery or poetry or Zen Buddhism. Others I imagined hurt and betrayed, missing their co-workers and blaming their bosses, and one of my bloggers—a middle-aged man, single and older than he expected to be without a family or a genuine, productive direction in life—I imagined buying a gun on the way home from work, nursing his anger all weekend, but cooling down before storming the office on Monday. I imagined he was a triumph for all those HR experts who advise that terminations should happen on Friday, for exactly the reasons my blogger had shown. Not that they'd ever know how close I'd imagined he'd come.

Some of my bloggers weren't as stable or steady as others. One of them, I knew right away, would kill himself instead of hurting anyone else. But he would have a hard time working out how. I stared at the plaster swirls on the ceiling and thought of pills, and of trains, and of bombs strapped to chests. But none of that would appeal to him. He wasn't selfish, just sad. He had two rules: number one, no mess left behind, and number two, no shocking discovery of a body that might damage someone for life.

It took me all night to settle on the most polite, selfless suicide I could muster on his behalf: he would sneak into a restaurant's kitchen after closing and enter its walk-in freezer with a body bag and sleeping pills. Before taking the pills, he'd hang a note on the outside of the door asking restaurant staff not to open the freezer themselves but to call the police to do so. Then, in the freezer, he would take all the pills and zip himself into the bag. The opaque body bag would prevent anyone but trained professionals from accidentally seeing the corpse, and the freezer would keep it from decaying and creating a stench.

Satisfied with the suicide I'd scripted for my cipher, secure in knowing it would meet his needs and give him the end he most wanted, I fell asleep on the couch and snuck through the longest part of the day, one day among many, a long string of days stretching far out before me without a job or a prospect of finding one soon, and not sure I wanted a new job at all. I only knew I had more time than I knew what to do with, and there was nothing I wanted to do.

4

Those hikers I hid from have stayed. I thought they passed by yesterday afternoon, but the sounds I heard last night must have been the two of them setting up camp. I might have known, I should have realized what I was hearing as I sat in the glow of my fire, but it's been so many years since I heard the clatter of two people working together that human labors were far from my mind as I guessed at the source of those sounds. The rustling of unnatural fabrics, the whisper of sleeping bags, backpacks, and tent, were like the wind in high leaves, and the chatter of voices was lost in the murmur of the river that carries all the way up to my cave, when the wind blows the right way. So I didn't think anything of it until the half-risen sun told the truth of those sounds and showed me those hikers this morning.

Just before dawn I stepped out of my cave for the morning's first piss, that glorious relief more worth rising for with every day older I get, and the orange dome of their tent shone through the mist off the river like a mushroom cloud on the horizon. My eyes were a bit better that morning. Bright as it was I didn't notice at first, too busy stretching eyes-closed in my doorway, fingertips playing my xylophone ribs, scratching the thick brown calluses of my feet—like overshoes of my own skin, I was thinking the other day—against the rough rocks of the fire ring outside my cave, and it's a wonder they didn't wake at the creaks and the cracks of my back or the rattling of my old bones.

I can't say how old exactly, but neither too old nor too young, somewhere in between; I was forty-three or perhaps forty-four when I moved to this cave and stopped counting, but it must be much more than a decade since then. Without a calendar, without holidays marking the passage of time, and without anyone else to tell me it's passed, one day is the same as another. In this land more or less without seasons, my only clocks are the sun's daily arc and the moon's wax and wane, and the whitening of my own whiskers—and those bleached white as bones so quickly after I came here that it may well have happened all at once on the day I arrived. So if I went by my whiskers to measure time, they'd tell me I've been here much longer than I think I have, and that I'm older than I think I am.

I'm sure those hikers know what year it is, in their bubble as orange as the sunrise behind it, on the edge of the blackberry patch that's crept toward my garden for years, the brambles that fence in my food. I had to blink a few times before I could be sure that blurred orange blot wasn't a strange second sun. My eyes take longer and longer to wake every morning, even on one of their better days, and I had to creep close to find out the shape was a tent.

They seem to be quiet enough. So far they seem to be sleeping. But I don't know why they've come here or how long they might stay or if they know someone lives in this cave near their camp and that the someone is me. They must have noticed my garden beside them, even setting up camp in the dark. Surely they spotted the glow of my fire last night, though they didn't light one themselves that I saw, but my vision is much worse at night—if I'm by the fire, I can't see anything outside its glow. And to think, I eat far more carrots now than I ever did in my other life. Another bit of old wisdom disproved.

So there are these hikers, and there is their tent, and what do I do with them now? If I've learned anything at all from the river it's to let jarring events come and go, that such tiny disruptions have no more weight in the world than fallen leaves on the water. A few ripples, a barely audible splash, and the surface soon returns to order. To swim toward each intrusion, to fish out a leaf and to sling it ashore, only prolongs the disturbance.

So I made my naked way out of the cave as I do every morning, aware for once of how naked I was, aware because whether or not they were looking, there was for once someone nearby to notice what my furred, feathered, and finned but never dressed neighbors don't mind. I was aware but I wasn't bothered, because this is my garden and these are my woods and this is my own naked life. To change my routine because of these hikers, because of their tent burning bright by my bushes, would reject what I've learned from the river. To give up the gains of the many years cascading in the white whiskerfall of my beard. And breaking my usual practice hadn't worked out very well the morning before, so why invite lightning to strike me again?

After porridge for breakfast and dawn meditation on top of my cave, my feet carried me on familiar steps toward the river—even with my eyes closed, even blind, the thick, filthy soles of my feet could feel the strip of grass and packed earth worn thin in a stripe from my door to the water—and past their camp in no hurry at all, as if they weren't there, as if their tent weren't outshining the sleepy-eyed sun. I stopped as I often do for a handful of berries, so close to the zippered door of their shelter that had they emerged at that moment, they could have caught a handful of my own berries. But no face or fist appeared through the zipper and I carried on toward the water, down the hill past the hum of my hives. The drone of the bees is a portal I pass through each morning, wiping my mind clean for meditation, and once on the river I went about my routine as if those slumbering hikers weren't there. I did what I do every day, what I've done every day for every one of my days that has mattered.

But I would be lying if I denied to myself and to the Old Man that those hikers have rattled my leaves like the strong winds of that storm. They've blown down upon me like the branch I found crushing the stubby greens of my potatoes. Should I have known that storm blew an ill wind? Should I have worried and wondered that trouble was aglide on its gusts?

Who's to say one has to do with the other? Who's to know why those hikers are here any more than why the storm was?

The Old Man has asked me to meditate on their presence, and I'm not surprised he has. Not so much that he wants me to wonder why they are here—though I will—but to think about my response and what it should be. It's been a long time since any strangers passed by and none ever stayed for the night, so already they've brought me disruption. They've called up the concrete world I left behind and deposited old memories on my idle tongue, but as ever there's no one to tell. They've made me wonder for the first time in forever how long I've lived here, how much time has passed, about the world that isn't my garden—not that I'm planning to visit, not that I'll go anywhere, but apart from the seagulls whose legs are sometimes plastered with soggy scraps of unreadable news, little word comes my way from that world. And now here they are, a man and a woman, and their arrival makes me remember my own after so long spent living as if I have always been here, like I was born in this garden as what I've become. They've reminded me how all this began with losing my job: the garden, the cave, my swims in the river and years spent in silence, all stemming from that unspoken meeting with the submanager.

They've already disrupted my day before they're even awake. They've already intruded upon my routine. But I was welcomed into this garden, I was given what I needed here when I needed it, so it's no easy question what kind of host I should be. If the answer is somewhere, if it's for me to find, it's in how I came to be here myself, so that's what I'll spend today's hours on the river thinking about, adrift on my back and backward in time, led by the faithful scribe in my mind through the archives of my own story.

5

Before getting fired I'd never measured how much empty time makes a day. I'd spent years writing blogs on the company's dime, leading dozens of made-up lives with their own careers and diseases and hobbies, and all those voices I had to keep speaking carried me through each eight hours of work and through five days of the week in which enough tasks and chores piled up at home to last me the weekend. And now, with seven of seven days free? Without those extra lives to occupy mine and at home every day to keep up with the house? I'd always worked at one job or another and though I'd never enjoyed it, that's what I knew. As often as I might have imagined winning the lotto and quitting my job, now that I'd come closer than ever all that shapeless, idealized freedom had lost its appeal.

Working at Second Nature had been boring and I didn't do very much while I was there, but I knew what I was meant to be doing whether I did it or not. I'd had a title and a boxful of cards to confirm it. I'd known exactly how much time I had in each day for projects other than those I was paid for, and I could rely on not being bothered for as long as I sat at my desk. Now, with no desk to sit at and all the time in the world to myself, I was overwhelmed by my options—who could I steal time from now?

I spent days and then weeks sprawled on the couch or on the white carpet floor of my white living room, following the stuccoed swirls of the ceiling around and around with my eyes until its pale blur assembled into a daydream. The tie I'd pulled off upon coming home that last day coiled on the floor between coffee table and sofa, and I imagined it rising snakelike to dance on its tail, or trailing into the air like a long, slender ribbon or one of those prayer flags I'd seen on TV.

I stopped wearing shoes and I let my beard grow and was shocked at the white it contained. I'd never gone more than a few days without shaving, and didn't expect the pale stripe that emerged like a ski slope on a forested mountain. (And if it was a snowy stripe then, it's a whole frozen forest years later, hanging like a bib to my belly.) In the dormant screen of the TV set, with the living room lights out around me, my reflection was reduced to only that stripe and if I moved my head back and forth I was smoke passing against the night sky of the screen. My hair grew shaggy and the more time I spent on the couch and the longer I went without washing, the more pronounced and persistent my bed-head became. I looked like I'd been caught in three or four gusts of wind blowing in different directions at once.

I watched animal shows with the sound turned up loud but the brightness down low, and I pretended my couch was in a faraway jungle as some baritone narrator described my place in the world. I hadn't watched those shows very often before, and I'd never spent much time outside except walking from the front door to my car or across parking lots, and I discovered that the world of lions and zebras, of penguins and baobab trees and deadly piranhas, was more exciting than I'd ever known. I wondered if I'd missed the boat on nature, and if it was too late to do something about it.

As time passed and I went without washing, without changing out of the foul shorts and T-shirt I'd had on forever, I started to stink. Then I went beyond stinking to something new, a sharp tang I'd never imagined my own body could produce. It was almost an accomplishment, I almost felt proud, like my commitment to inertia was announcing itself through my pores.

And I thought I smelled a little bit wild, like the jungles I was listening to on TV would have smelled if broadcast technology were more advanced. If TV was real life.

I daydreamed without interruption from the ping of incoming email, and spent unbroken hours following unguided thoughts through my head. My bills were all paid by automatic withdrawal, so I had no idea how much money was going out or how much had come in as my severance pay from Second Nature. I ate when the idea of a meal crossed my mind but I never shopped for more food. Soon there were only forgotten canned goods at the back of the pantry and a refrigerator door full of condiments orphaned there over the years. One night it was creamed corn with instant gravy, the next cranberry sauce with parmesan-flavored flakes. I was driven to eat by curiosity as much as by hunger, wondering how one thing might taste with another. When I finally exhausted the two jars of bacon bits I couldn't recall ever buying, I was disappointed because they went so well with everything, and that disappointment was the first genuine, recognizable feeling I'd had in a while.

When I had been working I wished for free time and daydreamed of how I might spend it. Traveling abroad or wandering the streets of my city, learning to paint or to sail or to decorate cakes. Now, with nothing but time on my hands, I didn't know where to start and it was simpler to not start at all. I had no more interest in finding a job than I had in anything else, and the couch molded itself to my body as my mind molded itself to the comfortable weight of all that free time.

When the landlord began to leave messages, I knew my money was gone or at least that the rent had stopped being withdrawn from my bank account. The phone company called, and the electric company, too, but I never answered; I let all their warnings and threats spew into the room from my answering machine's tiny speaker. It was only a matter of time, I realized, until the lights and the TV went dark and until the landlord came knocking. I should have done something about it, but I preferred not to. I watched and I waited in part because I didn't know what exactly to do, how to respond apart from getting a job to get some more money to get the bills paid, but I also waited because I was curious what really happened to someone who stopped paying rent. Would my utilities actually be turned off, and after how long? I'd seen these kinds of things on TV but never in my own life; I took the consequences of being a deadbeat on faith, just like the existence of snowballs and blue whales and other things I'd never seen, and the surface of the moon not being green cheese, and because of that faith I'd always paid my bills and my rent and invested for my retirement like everyone else. But now that I was up against it, against eviction and severed phone service, it wasn't as scary as I'd thought it would be. After weeks on the couch doing nothing, it was even exciting to worry if the landlord's appearance would break up the routine of my days.

And he did come, I think, in the dark while I tried to remember the myriad ways in which the swirled ceiling caught light and shadows when there were light and shadows to catch. When I had first moved into my unit in the apartment complex, I was annoyed by those bland textured whorls and longed for smooth plaster, only to discover their vast complications when I gave them the time they deserved.

There was a knock at the door, and another, the scraping and clanking of keys but none sliding into the lock. I heard a guttural curse, then heavy battering both high and low, like someone punching and kicking the wood. The door rattled and the front window shook but I didn't get up. If they were coming in, they were coming; what difference would it make if I stayed on the floor or sat on the couch or opened the door to greet them? Then the noise stopped and the quiet came back. I returned to recalling my ceiling by daylight, then daylight returned and my ceiling became its old self again and I tried to remember where night's shadows had fallen across it, and eventually I fell asleep.

Days and nights I wandered the web, reading a few words on this site and a few words on that, and watching videos I forgot as soon as they ended. I found that I missed getting email—not reading emails, not the requests they made or the work they demanded, and not the jarring sound of their arrival, but the simple pleasure of a new message arriving and the promise-filled moment before it was read. The only email address I'd ever had was for work, so I made myself an account with a free online service and I signed up for mailing lists and listservs and weekly coupons and anything else I could find that promised to fill my inbox. I spent hours with the computer as warm as a cat in my lap; I watched movies and infomercials and all the nature shows I could find, and I read every email that came. I read the spam, about growing my penis and firing my boss and saving Nigerian princes; offers of drugs just approved for the market and invitations to test those that weren't; genuine college diplomas and ads for DVDs that would teach me how to quickly get rich selling get-rich-quick DVDs. I read all of it. I looked for patterns and secrets and codes. I read between the lines, I looked beneath the strategic typos and awkward word choices for signs of human intention—I tried to locate the person behind the machine that randomly assembled those texts, the personality behind the promotion. Sometimes they seemed to be written for me, when the arbitrary, half-sensical subjects referred to events in my life or came from names I recognized, and I wrote back as if we were friends. I told Nigerian princes to hang in there, their family's fortune would be safe soon, I was sure; they could trust me, I had a good feeling for them. I told lonely, horny young women their princes would come in due time, perhaps from Nigeria, and I gave them each other's email addresses to help the connections occur. I wrote quick notes and long letters, but none of my correspondents ever replied. Until one night who knows how many weeks into unemployment and how many hours away from eviction, an email arrived in the deep part of morning, an email sent out to the whole nocturnal world but aimed directly at me:

> Are you a quiet, contemplative nature enthusiast available for full-time employment? This is the opportunity you have been waiting for and thought would never arrive. We offer a competitive salary and excellent benefits, including all lodging and meals. Daydreamers and introverts encouraged to apply. May we assume you are interested?

So I replied only with "Yes," a single-word email cast into the night like a desperate bottle tossed asea from an island, with just as much hope of reply. And then I read some more spam and wrote to more princes and fell asleep as the dust-crusted blinds of my dreary apartment began to glow orange again.

6

I was woken by more banging against the front door; I didn't
know if I'd been sleeping a few minutes or hours because I was
pulled from my dreams so violently that I remained disoriented
and groggy, on my back on the couch, one arm still asleep where it
hung off the side and a crusted drool trail tightening my cheek,
dried midstream on its way toward the floor.

The landlord, I thought, had returned to evict me, his thick-
armed thugs brought along to drag me out—though where I came
up with them I don't know, because I'd never actually *met* my
landlord, the actual owner of the vast hive of apartments I lived
in, identical to other hives in other parts of the city. I'd only ever
dealt with the constantly rotating staff in the management office,
and none of them were thick-armed thugs. Mostly they were
bored college graduates waiting for a better job to turn up, though
whether they left the complex management office because they
found those better jobs or because they couldn't bear to stay any
longer, who knows.

I rolled from the couch to the floor, with the coffee table
between my body and the front windows, where I might not be
seen right away if the landlord let himself in. The banging went on
and went on, rhythmic and metered, firm but not angry. It went
on longer than I'd expect a landlord to wait before using his key or
his thugs to open the door. Then it stopped.

I waited, still flat on the floor between table and couch, then I
lifted my head to look for a shadow behind the blinds, but there

wasn't one. I waited a moment longer then stood, crept on bare feet to the door and peeped through the peephole to find not the landlord, not his thugs, but a tall, ropy chauffeur standing outside, a few steps back from the door and staring straight into the hole at my eye. I'd never seen a chauffeur before, a real one, but he fit the role so perfectly I could tell right away what he was. He looked like every professional driver I'd seen in a movie or on TV. From the gray suit, peaked cap, and suede driving gloves, I got the idea he was an ex-race-car driver and also, conveniently for his employer, a former champion boxer, the kind of driver you'd want waiting outside in case your meeting took a bad turn, if you were in the sort of business that might involve that kind of meeting. He tipped his hat and nodded toward the peephole, the slimmest smile on his lips, so what could I do but open the door? He already knew I was there.

As soon as the door opened, as soon as fresh air blew into the room, I nearly gagged on the scent of myself. I hadn't minded when there was nothing to contrast my smell with, but now in that fresh air I knew I was rank. I wasn't the wildness of the jungle so much as I was its damp rot. But the chauffeur was too professional, too good at his job, to react to the smell. And I was impressed.

"Good morning, Mr. Finch," he said. "I believe you answered an email from my employer. He would like to discuss the position, so if you'll please step into the car."

The car was a gleaming silver limousine—a Rolls Royce, maybe, but I don't know cars—so long it stretched from my door all the way to the far end of the building, past the neighboring unit. So what could I say? Whatever the job, whether or not I decided to take it, at least I'd get a ride in this car. That wouldn't ever happen again, not to a person like me. And, not quite awake after not enough sleep and not eating well for a while, maybe I was more conducive to direction than I might have been under other conditions. I've heard that can happen, with religious cults doing brainwashing and that sort of thing.

I climbed into the back of the limo, onto a wide leather seat as soft as a cloud but blacker than night, and once the chauffeur closed the door behind me I realized that none of the windows let any light in: there were lamps on the walls and the ceiling, and glowing bulbs over the bar and the electronics cabinet with its stereo and DVD player; there was light cast by cable news playing on the TV that hung from the ceiling, but I couldn't see anything outside the car. Whenever I'd seen a limousine with dark windows passing on the street or onscreen, I'd assumed the glass was only opaque from outside and that the passengers had a clear eye on the world. But this one blocked the view in both directions and maybe all the others had, too. Maybe when you're that rich you don't want to look at the world.

The leather seat was so deep I could stretch my legs straight, offering an unpleasant view of my feet—flapping in flip-flops I'd slipped on at the door—and of my pale, spindly legs poking out of the filthy shorts I still had on. Not what I would have chosen to wear for an interview, but I'd been given no chance to change. And as soon as I'd sat down the car was under way. I couldn't see any sign of our motion, but my body felt it so I knew we were moving, passing through the identical cul-de-sacs and numbered streets of my apartment complex, probably toward the entrance and exit gate that led onto the highway outside. I found a remote control waiting at hand exactly where I would want it to be and I turned up the news. It was about the economy like it always was, interspersed with bits about wars that were either good for or bad for economics depending on who you asked, depending which network you watched and which side you were on, and for a few minutes I flipped back and forth between news stations in the middle of sentences, trying to create collages out of what all the experts were saying, trying to attach a word from one pundit to a word from another so the combination of words might make sense.

Then I got bored, the way I always do when talk turns to money and markets, forces and frauds so far out of my realm that I don't care one way or the other. So I found a children's program about wild animals and I learned about the emperor penguin's protective devotion to his egg. At first I tried to include the penguin in my channel-changing collage with the economists and talking heads—nest eggs and hatchlings merged into a few funny lines—but quickly I was more engaged by the birds than the numbers, so I stopped flipping and watched the penguins uninterrupted.

Only when we stopped for a moment—at traffic lights and intersections, I guess—was I reminded that we were moving at all. The car was taking me somewhere, but if not for the TV shows ending and being replaced with new shows I had no sense of time passing or how long I'd been riding around. I couldn't see what neighborhoods we were passing through or which direction we were traveling or what the weather was outside my dark cave of conditioned (perhaps even scented?) air. In that city, my city, time didn't mean anything. In its traffic a few miles might mean hours of driving, but in another direction and away from downtown those same hours would put you out of state. People spent their days jammed like logs on a narrow gray river, waiting for the waters of a faraway thaw to run through and set them all free— driving to Second Nature each morning and home at the end of the day sometimes had taken me twenty minutes and sometimes two or three hours, so I'd planned each day on not planning at all. So for all I knew the limo had gone one or two miles despite the time passing, or we were already out of the city. Or we were circling my apartment complex as the buildup to some elaborate joke. There was no way of knowing, and there was nothing I could do about it while I was in the car. So I sat back and waited, as passive as if I was asleep and still dreaming (and for all I knew so far, I was). And I noticed now that not only were the windows all darkened, but there weren't any buttons to lower the glass.

The knock on the door, climbing into the car, all of it happened so fast that I never wondered what I was doing and what danger I might be getting into. The car was there, the chauffeur was beside it, and it didn't occur to me that I might say no, I might refuse, until the limousine was moving and I was alone in the back and it was too late to say anything. This was my first trip out of the house in a while, so I may not have quite been myself. I might even have been sleepwalking; it's happened to me in the past, not in a limo, but I have woken up in the shower or standing with my head in the fridge.

Then I felt the limousine turn more sharply than it had so far on our journey, and I heard the faint crunch of gravel beneath the wheels. Soon the limousine stopped and the door swung open, flooding my sunless chamber with light so intense and so white that my head swam and I closed my eyes.

The chauffeur stood holding the door, but from my position inside I could only see him from the neck down. "Mr. Finch," my headless driver announced, "we've arrived."

I climbed from the car almost disappointed; the broad leather seat and dark chamber had been so comfortable and the notion of a trip undefined by any predetermined—to me—destination had been relaxing in a strange way. But what met my eyes when I emerged from my automotive cocoon was worth rising for: waves of green hills rolling away toward the ocean, golden with soft early light. The view was so perfect, so sun-kissed that I wondered if it was planned, that the car should arrive at this moment, that my door should open onto this view and not the other side of the car. But who would plan something like that?

I realized at once where I was, a part of the city I'd never been to before because I'd never known anyone who lived up that high and might invite me to visit. Down below, in the valley where I'd spent all the years of my life, thick clouds of gray and brown smog drooped day after day, but now it turned out they were under a layer of softer white ones that I was seeing for the first time. The city beneath me, that ugly, boiling, exploding city, nestled, *nestled* into the folds of the hills. I'd never known my city could nestle, that it could do anything more than seethe and devour. Skyscrapers pierced the murk, but none were tall enough to emerge where the sky was actually blue. I felt like I was seeing the city—*my* city—for the first time, that I'd finally realized its shape and its size.

I'd discovered, in a flash, that hill dwellers have the advantages of scope and scale: the billionaires on these hilltops have dominated the city for as long as they've been here, and maybe it's simply because they see all of it before them at once. Even as they sit on their toilets they must have a grand view; what passes as a necessary waste of time for everyone else, a few hurried minutes in some boxy bathroom tucked at the back of a boxy apartment, becomes a quiet time for reflection from a throne with a broader view of the world. When for some people even taking a crap is empowering, it's no wonder the rest of us work for them.

"This way, Mr. Finch," said the driver, and I turned toward a house at the top of a white gravel driveway that wound up a hill. A house not remarkable so much as huge, a generic adobe monolith with terracotta roof tiles and black ironwork on the windows and doors and in other tasteful, familiar locations. It looked—so far as I know anything about houses—like a mansion is meant to, everything brand new and well-fitted and designed to impress, a house born ready for its close-up but missing something so badly I could feel it at once. It could have come from a kit and it probably did, from some architect's file of reusable plans for interchangeable houses all over the world. The whole estate, the house and the hills and even the hedges sculpted into spirals and parapets and animal shapes, made me feel like I'd shrunk and been dropped on a model train table.

I followed the driver across gleaming white stones, the teeth-chatter flap of my sandals on gravel behind the crunch of his heavy black shoes, and before we could knock on the double front doors they swung open and a butler (a butler!) asked me to come in as he bowed with a surprisingly serpentine motion that left his face looking up toward me even as his back stretched out flat. He looked remarkably, precisely like a butler should look, like a person who, if seen on the street, would shout "butler" however he dressed and whatever he might be doing. I wondered if he'd been hired because he fit the bill right from birth, or if he'd grown into it through years of butling.

The driver handed me off to the butler—I never saw the driver again—and I was led through a two-story foyer flanked by a round staircase on either side and a fountain gurgling away at its center, supplied by a waterfall that fell from the ceiling and filled the room with sparkling mist. If I hadn't arrived there by answering an email and getting into a strange limousine, if I hadn't been greeted by that view of the city, I might not have believed such a house could exist.

The butler and I wound up the glistening wooden coil of the stairway, the air full of the waterfall's quiet crashing, and upstairs I was led down a long hallway, past mirrors that showed just how ragged I was with my unwashed hair and rough beard that favored one side of my face but didn't do either side any favors. As we walked I heard how the voices of my hyperefficient plant enthusiasts would describe all of this on their blogs, some of them gushing over the decor and design of the mansion while others decried its vulgarity and decadence and overwhelming, oppressive wealth; still others would be afraid or confused or laughing at how they'd found their way into such a strange situation. I almost laughed a little myself, imagining how they might tell it.

At the end of the hallway, my butling guide knocked on then opened a door. "Mr. Crane," he called into the room, "your guest has arrived."

He was answered not by the sinister, ominous, archvillainous voice that might make sense at the end of a mysterious journey like mine, but only an ordinary man's voice like any other that said, "Send him in, Smithee," and the butler's hand on my shoulder steered me right through the door.

7

There are days when all this can become a bit lonely, when the Old Man falls quiet or the rain falls too hard or some ill-chosen berry or leaf makes me sick and I'm stuck on my pallet in unnoticed pain, wishing for someone to boil my tea or make me some soup or recognize, for God's sake, that I'm suffering. Those are the days when I picture my scribe, the hunched-over monk who writes everything down, scribbling away with a fluttery quill as he follows me through the day in his hooded brown robe. Making note of my meditations, and charting the course of my thoughts. In those slow, stupid hours of self-pity I imagine he exists for my suffering; I imagine the scrolls he produces and that someone, somewhere, awaits his account of my life.

My blogs may have been fake, they may have been forced and financed by Second Nature and only aimed, in the end, at marketing plants. But they spoke to someone. They had an audience reading their words. My stories about plastic plants and, at the same time, about children and parents and illness and health, and jobs kept and jobs lost and jobs found, may have made a difference in somebody's life. Now I only tell stories to the scribe in my head, and I imagine he writes them down and files them away, and that's better than nothing on my rare dour nights, when even a listener who isn't quite real is enough, and a fantasy about my life being recorded carries me across the brief gaps in my satisfied solitude.

Modest, isn't it, imagining my own life to be worth preserving? And conjuring someone with nothing better to do than record it? Here's me in the shadow of the blackberry bushes, squatting to squeeze something awful from my angry bowels—don't miss a grunt or a groan of my genius! And there's me in the crook of the towering tree where I once perched as my portrait was painted. Be sure to capture each of my silent musings about seed helicopters and the sweetness of syrup and the slow, sticky passage of time! Sharpen your quill; grind up blackberries with those red ferrous rocks from the river for ink—that's how I've imagined I'd do it, if I ever needed to write, but I haven't, not yet—and make sure you get every word.

I know my scribe is an invention, a crutch for my stumbling moments, though sometimes I get carried away with the fantasy of being recorded and spend days adrift in my memories. I ask him questions and imagine him finding the answers, combing through his old scrolls to recall what I ate on the day the bird's nest fell on my head, or how many potatoes I dug on the morning I found the dead fox in my field. Little things, long-ago minor moments, but they give us both something to do, so why not? And who's going to tell me to stop, who's here to rein me in but my scribe, and he only tells me what I already know—even if I've forgotten—and nothing I don't want to hear.

On my longer nights, his loyal presence helps wait out the far shore of sunrise, and I don't see the harm in that. There's no one to know it but me. Me, and the Old Man, of course. And my kind chronicler helps me keep myself straight, helps me make sense of my memories so long since I've shared them with anyone else. I've been surprised how easily time's track is lost, and how disordered my own past becomes when there's no one to remember it with. Imagining that someone recorded my past makes it easier for me to recall. I picture him at my ear, reading back old events I can't quite lay my memory on, like a librarian or a search engine. He may not be real, but he gets the job done. He helps me remember how I came to be here, and when I need to hear it he reminds me why I've stayed so long. Who else could I ask?

The Old Man remembers, but he isn't saying. The Old Man knows the back of my mind because everything drifts through his view. Like the strange new fish I've seen lately, shimmering pink beneath his blue surface, picking with puckered lips at his sandy bed for the insects and eggs piled there. "Fingerpinks," I've called them in my head, because there's no one to tell me their name and there's no one who needs it but me. I'd never seen them in the river until a few weeks ago when I was roused from my meditation with a shocking sharp nip on the cheek of my ass, so perhaps they swam up from the valley or even all the way from the ocean. Or perhaps not the ocean, if I think of it clearly, unless enough time has passed for saltwater swimmers to adapt to these fresh waters, and I don't think this river is old enough yet to have spurred evolution already. But those fish must have come here from somewhere.

Perhaps they crawled up from the mud, the same mud that soothed the oozing rash on my body this morning, all over my legs and forearms where I fell into that bush yesterday—it must have grown in the wake of our recent rainstorms, rough buds and raw briars and branches. Relying on memory to move through the world as I do, picking my way through the garden as I know it once was instead of as it is now, these things happen sometimes: something moves, something grows, something isn't where I expect it to be and I can't make out the difference seeing it only in blurs and vague shapes. But I found the mud and it calmed my clamoring blisters and scrapes. Was it there all along and I never noticed, or did that mud of all muds emerge at the moment it could do the most good? Modest me, thinking the Old Man takes a personal interest in the itch of my thin, broken skin!

Those hikers came from somewhere, too. They're tan and they're healthy, well-fed and young, and all they seem to do so far is sleep, and sometimes kneel with their eyes on the ground so intensely they must see something there that I don't. My eyes were improved a bit yesterday, and I got what counts as a good view of them outside their tent, on their knees muttering and humming together as I slipped by. Up close I could see that those two are as ragged as I was when I arrived here, but in much better shape than I ever have been, like they've been hiking and camping for months, like their bodies have been working as bodies and have never once been in an office.

Because they were kneeling I couldn't see much but their backs and their heads and the filthy, bare soles of their feet, and even that much was blurry—until I got close, until they fit within the dark frames that have formed in my eyes, they were nothing but soft shapes and colors. His beard is patchy and sticks out to one side, and his blonde hair is tangled in dreadlocks woven through with colored bands. Her hair is the same orange shade as my carrots and shines as brightly as their tent, though it still smells like a shampoo factory exploded when they're nearby.

After my swim this morning, I walked back toward my cave for a lunch of stewed carrots. I still call them carrots, but they're really not, they're a combination of carrots and potatoes, one of the more successful hybrids I've grown over time at the Old Man's instruction, in the garden Mr. Crane left me. Briefly, I tried calling them "carratoes" in my head, but I realized it didn't make any difference so I stuck with "carrots" because the word was already familiar. Who's to know that what the word means to me, in this garden, isn't the same as what it means to everyone else? I could hand one of my hybrids to the hikers, and whether I called it a carrot or a carrato or an overcoat, they still wouldn't know what it was. It might look a little familiar, but not enough for them to know it by name. There's really no need for me to call my vegetables by name at all, or to call them anything other than lunch when I serve them up to myself with a cup of birch brew.

Today's lunch was a high point after a shallow, disturbed meditation this morning. I was unable to hear what the Old Man was saying, too consumed by this intrusion into my garden and trying too hard to undo my ungenerous feelings. As I was welcomed here I should welcome them, but that's easier said than done; I don't want them to stay, I confess, and for now I have taken the tack of ignoring their presence with my body if not my mind. Until they approach me, until they ask me for something or the Old Man asks on their behalf, I'll leave them to find their own way as I did and continue to do. But in case more is expected of me, I'll work to keep my mind idle until fog clears away from the answer.

I wouldn't have approached the hikers and their campsite if I hadn't needed some carrots for lunch, and if they weren't camped between my cave and my crops. Not just close to the garden, as it turned out, but actually blocking the gap in the blackberry bushes where I enter my field. The gap I've been entering through for almost as long as I've had the garden, since the brambles were allowed to grow up around it. Back then I could see it from a long distance, and now some days I have to feel my way along the bush for the gap. Their tent filled the space like a dam on a river, and I stood outside its rustling, rippling fabric walls, frozen by the surprise. There are other gaps where I might have entered the garden, at least there were when I could still see well enough to look for them, but this was the one I'm used to, part of my routine. To find another way into the garden would have been too big a disruption, it would have been allowing the hikers too much impact on my life. I might as well have begun talking to them, if I let their tent unchart my usual path.

So I laid the palm of my hand on the curve of the tent, shocked by how smooth and slick it felt, almost an electrical shock, and I felt my way around it toward the brambles in hopes of a space to squeeze through.

And I found one, a few inches wide but large enough for my thin body—thank goodness I'm all skin and bones! As I moved around the tent, I heard the hikers whispering to one another inside it, apparently just waking up. Apparently woken by me.

"He's outside," she whispered, a sentence, a phrase, and I was trapped by those two words with one hand still splayed on the tent and one foot inside my garden. Her voice was like... how can I even describe it? I'll leave it to my faithful scribe to come up with some useful description and just say for myself that it was a shock.

"What's he doing?" the male hiker asked, the first time I'd heard him up close, and his was a voice that sounded like muscles, like strength. Like a man who knows what he's doing; a bit like Mr. Crane's voice, I suppose, though rougher. And that second voice, the man's voice, shook me out of my stupor, and I stepped all the way into the garden and slipped my hand from their house with the rustle and wheeze of its factory fabrics.

As I moved away, I heard the woman say what sounded like, "the way it was in the movie," and I could have sworn the man's answer included "Smithee." But my ears, I suppose, are no more reliable than my eyes after so many years getting untuned to speech, filling in gaps in what I know of the world with the few names and voices I've heard most recently though long ago. So the man sounded like Mr. Crane, and they mentioned someone I knew; my ears filled in empty spaces from memory, like my optimistic eyes sometimes tell me a shape up ahead is my cave but it turns out to be only a shadow.

In my vegetable patch, with the blur of their tent out of sight from most angles, I could pretend I was almost as alone as I wanted to be. My carrots, at least, were right where I'd left them, minus a few given over to rabbits and whoever else had come by.

So I pulled up a bunch, brushed them clean of dirt on some grass, and turned back toward the bright orange dam.

But this time, squeezing through the same way I'd come in, I stepped on something so sharp it penetrated the ironclad sole of my foot, an unfamiliar sensation because nothing in this garden has been jagged enough to do that in years. I walk over rocks, over sharp sticks and stingers, without feeling more than slight pressure. No more than I'd feel through a shoe. But this I felt, and it was all I could do not to shout out in pain.

I dropped my carrots and reached for my foot, but stumbled over some piece of the hikers' campsite—something hard and round, a canister, maybe, because it rolled underfoot and threw me backward into the billowing wall of their tent. The fabric swallowed me like a pebble thrown into the water, and all I could see was a great orange expanse, all ripples and shimmers and shadow and light. I panicked, and thrashed, and I was almost glad, for once, that my eyes were bad so I didn't have to see myself in that moment of shame.

The hikers, still in their tent, grunted beneath me. I may not weigh much, but I weigh enough to be a surprise when I fall through your wall. I felt them scrambling and squirming. He yelled, something guttural, not a word, and she groaned, then the two of them pushed their way out of the tent, winding me tighter in their wall as they went, and my own thrashing and wriggling probably wasn't much help.

Then they were outside, standing before me, and she told me to wait, to hold on, and he said, "Settle down, man, settle down." They grabbed my arms where they reached out of the fabric cloud and pulled me onto my feet. "It's okay," she said. "You're okay." Then he said, "There's something in your foot, let me get that," and the blur of him crouched and reached out for my throbbing foot, still stuck with whatever I'd stepped on. I twisted my body out of his grip and hers, and I almost fell down all over again but somehow I stayed on my feet to hobble away to my cave, led in my blinded confusion by muscle memory or the adrenaline of wounded pride. One of them rushed up from behind and pushed my dropped carrots into my hand, then I felt their pitying eyes on my back with every step.

I sat down on my pallet to take a look at my foot, and what I found was a strange metal pin of some kind, an inch or two long with a knob at one end like the pointers that used to be inside filmstrip projectors. I pulled it out, wincing and biting my tongue, and a blood blossom bloomed where I had been pricked, trickling into the deep cracks and crevasses of my calloused sole.

What I wanted to do was return it, by slashing right through the side of their tent. But instead I tucked whatever it was into one of my wall nooks and left it there for reflecting on later. And to remind me that I'd been provoked to such unwelcome feelings, something else on which I will need to reflect. I get frustrated, sometimes, when things don't go as I'd like. When a crop fails or I break a finger. I got worked up a few years ago when I tried to build a clay oven and it wouldn't work no matter how many times I built and rebuilt it. But I haven't—or hadn't—felt actual anger, an impulse to rage, for as long as I've been in this garden. Until those hikers provoked it.

Until I allowed myself to be provoked, if I'm honest. How fragile and frail my self-sufficiency is if I let others dictate my own feelings for me—others I don't even know. And I think that's what bothered me most in the whole awful scene with the tent: I needed their help to get up, I was stuck, and I only stumbled because I've gone blind. It was their tent, and if they hadn't come I may not have fallen right then but I would have fallen on something else in due time, and I'm sure I will fall down again before long. It's the loss of my safety, of my pure self-reliance, that is worse than losing my eyes.

Perhaps the Old Man has brought them to help me. Perhaps he's led them here, or perhaps they've just come on their own. Whatever it is, I wish he had given me warning. He might have led me to useful reflections before their arrival. But who am I to ask why he does what he does?

I kept an ear out for the hikers approaching as I boiled lunch tea on my fire, afraid their sympathy might bring them over, that the incident had broken the ice and they'd come share my kettle without being asked. And I owe them, of course, after that. I owe them at least a cup of shared tea whether they need it or not. Whether I want to give it or not.

I hope they've brought food and drink of their own. My most recent potato harvest was thin, but I have plenty of carrots and beans I might share, and the blackberries and apples grow wild. Lately the fishing hasn't been great, or I haven't been great at fishing. It's hard to tell where my hook hits the water, and if I'm wasting my time in the weeds. I throw a line and I hope for a bite, but I can't do much to improve my chances these days.

Even as I sat there, my eyes seemed to worsen. The fire a few inches before me lost the licks of its flame. It happens like that for me some days; my sight is dying like weather, I think: sometimes better or worse, more or less noticed, but always there in some form. A breeze kicked up while I sat, though, and brought fiercer crackling into my fire and dusted my legs with fine ash. Across the distance between us I heard snippets of conversation from the direction of the invisible hikers.

The man said something that ended with "if we could ask."

And the woman replied, "Would he answer?" followed by something I couldn't make out.

"He might gesture or something," he told her, and I knew they were talking about me and it made me feel strange. Nauseous, maybe, or dizzy; after not being noticed by anyone for so very long, to have been touched, and helped, and now to be spoken about was a series of staggering blows. My world didn't feel like my own any more.

"Maybe it's worth a try," she said. "Other things aren't like I expected. It's much... smaller, I guess."

"It is, isn't it?"

I don't know what they were talking about, or what they want from me. But whatever it is I'll wait for his word, I'll wait for the Old Man's direction. Maybe it will be sharing with them and maybe it won't, but so far he's said nothing and that's what I've done. My birch tea is boiling in case they come calling, in case they rise from their knees and pick up their heads and notice me over my kettle, carried back into my meditations by its sticky steam. It took months, I think, for me to find a bark that made tea worth the name. After I ran out of actual tea leaves a long time ago, the tea leaves Mr. Crane left me, I tried boiling every plant stem and stalk, each color and shape of leaf I could find, and I suffered sour stomachs and bitter taste buds before boiling birch twigs made a brew I was satisfied with. And, birches being one of the few trees I can recognize, I actually know what it is when I drink it, unlike so many of the other things that I tried.

So making tea is one of the greater achievements of my time in the garden, as every cup poured reminds me. Maybe that's why some small, proud part of me almost hopes that the hikers approach for a cup, while the rest of me hopes they will leave and take their trap of a tent along with them. I should think about that while I'm swimming, I should ask the Old Man if my ego is running away with itself and if the pride I take in my tea might be clouding my mind. I might need to give up drinking it, if it's become a distraction and if I'm getting carried off course on its steam.

8

The butler ushered me into a room longer than it was wide, lined with bookcases ceiling to floor and its far end a full wall of windows. In front of the glass an enormous desk, as big as my car, spread nearly across the room. There didn't seem to be enough space to step out from behind it, to squeeze between the desk and the shelves at each end, and I wondered if there was some secret doorway I couldn't see.

"Good morning, Mr...." said my host, seated and half-hidden behind the leviathan.

"Finch," I replied, trying to be loud enough for him to hear me at the other end of the room, but it came out as a bit of a yell and he may have started in his chair at the sound. Or perhaps he was just leaning back; at that distance, it was hard to tell.

"Mr. Finch, yes." He looked toward the doorway and said, "Thank you, Smithee."

"Sir," said the butler. He left the room and closed the door behind him.

"Come closer, Mr. Finch," my host said. "Please sit down." As I walked toward the desk for what seemed like millennia, he asked, "This room... it's intimidating, isn't it? Makes you feel small?"

"I... it's very nice."

He laughed. "The room's meant to do that. According to my architect, anyone coming in should be so overwhelmed that they concede to what I ask of them before getting their bearings enough to bargain. It's built to be the seat of my power. Are you overwhelmed, Mr. Finch?"

I hesitated, concerned this was one of those trick interview questions I'd heard about, and I arrived at the desk before finding an answer.

My host rose from his chair and extended his hand, but I could only reach it by standing on my toes and stretching across the gleaming wood surface. "Wiswall Crane. Thank you for coming."

I couldn't tell if he had an accent of some kind, perhaps European, or if he just spoke very clearly in a manner I wasn't used to. It seemed strange for him to thank me for coming when I'd had so little choice in the matter, when his driver had whisked me away half-asleep and still wearing the same filthy clothes I'd worn for weeks, but he sounded sincere. And I was in no position for making complaints, not knowing where I was, or how I'd gotten there, or—most of all—how to get anywhere else.

Mr. Crane wasn't much taller than I am, but his rigid posture made the difference seem greater. He filled space like a much larger man. He might have been in his fifties, or perhaps he was twenty years younger; it was hard to guess at his age because he gave the impression of having always been just as he was, never older, never younger, never out of his dark gray suit. His temples flared like white wings on his head and I thought of Mercury's ankles, wondering if those bright blazes were natural or artificial, strategically bleached to lend him a look of speed and distinction (which they did). Natural or not, he looked as much like a rich, powerful man as the butler had looked like a butler and the chauffeur like a chauffeur. I didn't know how Mr. Crane made his money, and I never found out, but I could tell right away that he made a whole lot. It wasn't the room, or not only the room, but the confident way he carried himself. This was a man with a good view of the world from his bathroom window.

He gestured toward a leather wing chair beside me, and I settled into it as gracefully as I could, crossing one leg over the other in what I hoped was a relaxed and confident pose, a pose capable of offsetting the trickles of sweat I felt on my face and dripping from my armpits down over my ribs. I tried to project a confidence that would draw attention away from my weathered flip-flops and filthy T-shirt and shorts and the bird's nest of hair and beard on my head. I pictured myself as a diorama caveman summoned to a meeting with the museum director, and it reminded me of my final day at Second Nature. I felt like I was about to get fired again rather than interview for what I thought was a job.

Mr. Crane spent a long time looking me over without saying a word, and consulting some papers far away from me on his desk; he looked back and forth between pages and person in a way that made clear the papers had to do with me, but what they said and where that information had come from was as mysterious as everything else about my morning so far. I didn't know if I was meant to speak, so I didn't. What could I say except "Why am I here?", and I knew he would tell me in time if he was going to tell me at all—why take the risk of being demanding? I looked over his shoulder at the huge window because it seemed like the sort of thing a relaxed person would do as he waited for an inspection of himself to finish.

Behind glass so clear the room was practically open to the outside, a long green slope rolled away from the house. In the near distance there were thick trees and low bushes speckled with flowers, and half-hidden in plants was a mound of gray rocks, like a small mountain standing alone. An impressive, expensive-looking telescope stood on a tripod in front of the window, and I noticed that it was aimed not at the sky as I would have expected but down, toward the ground and the garden. A pair of binoculars and a brass sextant and an elaborate tabletop compass all stood near the window on a low built-in shelf, and they flickered in silvery light from, I supposed, a screen concealed under the desk.

"You answered my email, Mr. Finch. So let me tell you what I'm looking for in this position. It is somewhat... " Mr. Crane paused mid-sentence, his mouth hanging open just enough to look gracefully thoughtful rather than vacant. His hands froze in a gesture that kept his index fingers and thumbs outstretched toward each other while his other fingers curled in; his hands framed an upside-down heart shape over his chest, and the dark red of his tie made it a heart full of blood.

"It is somewhat unusual," he finally said.

"Yes, sir," I replied. I'd never been one for formal titles— ma'ams and sirs and your highnesses—but something about this house, this room, had me speaking like the butler, only, I'm sure, less convincingly. Mr. Crane's voice had changed as talk turned to business, the jocularity of his greeting replaced with a flat, no-nonsense inflection, and while it wasn't as friendly, I was more comfortable with it. This was what I expected an employer to sound like, not lamenting the design of his office or asking my opinion about it, but sharpening his point before pinning me down.

"It's a demanding position. Full-time, residential. I'll be looking for a multiyear commitment. After a probationary period, naturally."

He seemed to have skipped over telling me what the job was, or else I had missed it, but it seemed too late to stop him and ask, to backtrack and confess that my mind had wandered while he was talking. So I let him go on, not that he sounded like a man who could be stopped by much. He was reassuring that way, wearing his authority right on his sleeve but in a quiet way that made me more relaxed the longer he spoke.

"There won't be much opportunity for contact with your family or friends, or... with anyone, really. But I don't imagine that will be much of a problem for a man of your constrained social circles."

"No, I... I don't think so," I said, and wondered what was in his file, the same sort of plain beige folder the submanager had opened before me at Second Nature. Did he have my accumulated history of browsing and searching?

Mr. Crane laughed, and leaned toward me. His arms didn't look long enough to reach from one side of the desk to the other, but somehow he managed to rest his hands on both ends at once. "But you'd like to know what on earth I'm talking about before you agree."

"I guess so. Yes, sir. If you don't mind."

He stood up and moved toward a bookcase, drawing a thick leather-bound volume from a shelf but not opening it. "What we need to know about a people, Mr. Finch, we know from their gardens." He turned to the window, his back toward me and the book still in his hand. "The French like everything ordered. Straight lines, trimmed hedges, paths lined with coral or stone. The French keep a businesslike garden. They know where everything is, when it will grow, what will grow in time to take its place. Everything under control." He slapped his palm against the book when he said, "control," not hard, but it made a loud, punctuating sound.

"But the Georgians, Mr. Finch, the Georgians! They enjoyed nature for its own sake and in its own state. They liked it just as it was, though of course they made improvements to keep it that way."

As he spoke, Mr. Crane pushed a button set into a brass plate on the wall, and an opaque screen slid down from the ceiling to cover the window and block out the light. I heard humming behind me, and looked up to find a data projector suspended from the ceiling. A photograph of an elaborate garden developed before me on the screen, then faded as another one took its place.

More gardens came and went before he continued. "This house," he said, "I could take it or leave it. It serves its purpose. But my garden, the grounds, are the reason I stay." He looked toward the window as if to admire his garden, but because of the screen he looked instead at a photograph of some other garden in some other place, an example (I assumed) of whatever the slides were meant to be showing me. I wasn't sure if I should be seeing differences between the slides and the gardens they offered, or if these were all examples of the same thing, whatever that was.

"Do you know, when I bought this house—not *this* house, but the one that was here before I removed it to have my own built—it only came with two acres. Two acres! Hardly enough space to look out the window. So I bought out every landowner on this ridge, dismantled their houses, and turned the land into my garden."

"I didn't know you could do that," I blurted out, before I could stop myself.

"Anything's possible if you're willing to make it happen. It wasn't cheap, I can tell you that much. The stubborn held out, people who'd grown up in their houses or lived in them most of their lives, raised children and that sort of sentimental thing. But I convinced them, of course, and here we are. They were well-paid, Mr. Finch. I don't take advantage of people."

Mr. Crane stepped in front of the screen where it covered the window, and the green of a lawn growing somewhere painted his face.

"It is quite a view," I said.

He smiled. "It should be. There were a few rooftops visible in the distance, but I had those removed. Some others I lowered by a story or two. And now," he said, and gestured toward the screen—at that moment showing a castle surrounded by hedges and fields—and I assumed at the gardens beyond. "Everything you see out there is mine. You'd never know we're so close to the center of one of the world's busiest cities."

"No," I agreed, "you really can't tell."

He pushed the button again, and the screen climbed into the ceiling. The projector fell silent behind me, and light rose from several wall sconces. I looked through the window, and it was true: I couldn't see anything beyond the edges of Mr. Crane's garden. I could make out the shimmer of water far off without a roofline or streetlight between, and I took that water to be the ocean, all the way on the other side of the city, but after all he'd just told me, how could I be sure?

He turned from the window to face me and set the book on his desk before sitting down. "You've been working in marketing, Mr. Finch. Most recently at Second Nature Modern Greenery, which I happen to own."

He looked up. "In fact, you've worked for a number of my interests in the past. Though I don't suppose you knew that. I work hard to keep my holdings... discreet. Doing business quietly is the nature of my business."

I'd been about to ask what his business was, but after he said that I held my tongue.

"I imagine you use items manufactured by my companies more often than you realize in the course of a day. Most people do." He turned in his chair to look out onto the garden. "Though I suppose you're still wondering what all this has to do with my email, and with the position you've come to discuss."

He didn't wait for me to answer before he went on.

"The Georgians, many of them, were at their best when they looked upon their gardens for reflection. To consider natural life in its purity, away from the trappings of a complicated, busy society and its politics. Its gossip." He paused, and furrowed his brow before adding, "Its money."

In the distance, through the window, a bright orange fox darted out of the bushes on one side of the garden to cross the emerald lawn and vanish into a thick stand of trees. Until then, I'd never seen a fox in real life and hadn't known there were foxes in this part of the world, at least not here in the city (if this could still be called part of the city—it might have been inside the limits, but it wasn't inside the city itself).

"It was a fad, and, yes, to an extent it was ostentation, but I think there's more to it than that. Something worth emulating."

Once again I was afraid I'd missed something important, a description of what we were talking about, what I was being interviewed for. "Yes, sir," I said.

"But they couldn't live in their gardens, of course, as much as they might have liked to. No, they had too many responsibilities, as we do today. Too much to manage. So they employed other people to do it."

"To live in their gardens?"

"Hermits, Mr. Finch. Any respectable estate had a hermit in residence on the grounds. Visible from the windows, in the background as the estate holders and their guests strolled the lawn, that sort of thing. Usually for a term of seven years, subject to evaluation, of course. How does seven years sound to you, Mr. Finch?"

How did it sound? I didn't know—it sounded perfect, and it sounded absurd, and it sounded like an elaborate practical joke in which I'd been ensnared. So I just asked, "As a hermit?"

Mr. Crane looked startled, as if I hadn't understood him as clearly as he'd expected, as if he'd been talking about one thing and I'd burst out with something entirely unrelated. For a second, if that, he looked like he'd made a mistake. But it passed.

"Yes. Exactly. A hermit. Is that something you think you could do? I understand you have a... " He looked at something behind his desk, then said, "a predilection toward distraction. To daydream and wander from the task at hand. I'm sure you've been told that's a problem. No doubt it's held you back in your life, but that's precisely what I'm looking for. That's why you appealed to me."

It sounded, for a moment, as if Mr. Crane had approached me directly rather than my replying to spam in the middle of the night out of boredom, but I didn't ask. How could I ask one question when there were so many others hanging between us and filling my head?

"Naturally," he said, "you don't need to commit to seven years right away. We'll consider the first year a trial period and reevaluate when the time comes."

I was curious, and I think he could tell, but could it be real? Mr. Crane appeared perfectly earnest, confident in a manner that precluded all doubts; I could almost believe, as he so clearly did, that there was no real choice in the matter. I wondered if all this might be a test to see how I'd react, to determine whether I was suited for some other job, the *real* job. Or an elaborate setup for something worse—I suddenly remembered that movie about rich men bringing the poor to an island for hunting.

"What would I... what would you expect me to do?"

"Not very much, really. In a way, that's the point. Mostly I'd want you to sit where I could see you from the window and think about things. Nature, the clouds, the grass growing. Commune with the trees and so forth. My people will provide your meals, so there's no need to hunt or any of that."

"And I would live in the garden."

"Not in the garden itself, no. You'll sleep in the cave." He turned and pointed through the window. "That outcropping of rocks, I've had a cave made inside it. It's perfectly dry. I'd go so far as to call it 'cozy.' I don't need to tell you it never gets very cold in this part of the world, and my architects assure me the cave's design is sufficient to keep out the rain."

He added, "I may ask you to do other things as you get settled, expand your duties as we proceed. Nothing too difficult. Some gardening, perhaps. I trust you could manage?"

"I think so," I said. "I've done some gardening before. I've had window boxes."

He was talking as if I'd been hired, but I hadn't heard anything like an offer and I didn't think I'd agreed to anything. Though it didn't feel like I had an option to disagree, either. I still couldn't shake the feeling that this whole conversation was a prelude, the test question I'd suspected extending far beyond what was normal. At any second I expected to find out what the job *really* was, and that all this was psychological screening of a very strange kind. But it felt... inevitable, somehow, as if my working for him (again, apparently) was a foregone conclusion. Maybe the room really was that convincing, or maybe the white wings at his temples made everything move so much faster than it did in the world apart from Mr. Crane.

"I expect there will be some things you'll have to get used to. We'll provide you with new garments, but nothing fancy. There's no need to be formal when you live in a cave. I get tired of looking at people in suits. And I'll have to ask you to stop shaving, and to stop cutting your hair, which I don't imagine will pose much of a problem." He smiled, then added, "I appreciate that you've already gotten a head start."

"Yes, sir."

"Bathing... there won't be very much chance for it, I'm afraid. It's important that you appear natural, like you belong where you are. It wouldn't make sense for you to be taking showers and smelling like soap and that sort of thing, but we'll work something out." His voice trailed off, and his eyes turned toward the ceiling and squinted a bit. Then he pushed a button on the edge of the desk and spoke toward it. "Memo. A hot spring for installation in the garden.

"Compensation," he said. "You won't need any money while you're under contract and living here. Nothing to spend it on in the cave, and it might be disruptive if you kept a wallet or bank card around. So what I'd like to do is open an account in your name and deposit your salary directly. We can sign the papers together so you know it's been done and you won't have to worry."

Mr. Crane lifted a page from a stack on his desk to read the sheet beneath it. "Would you be agreeable to, say... well, why don't we say five million for the first year and, as I said, we can reevaluate if things work out. And let's agree to half that amount if you leave for any non-medical reason within six months."

I choked a bit and wasn't able to answer that yes, five million dollars would be more than okay. It would also be more than I'd made in my life. How could I have said no to money like that, to being paid so much to do what sounded like nothing, to sit in a garden and think about trees? To sleep in a cave with catered meals and be made a millionaire for it? With that kind of money, I could hire my own hermit someday. I thought about all the animals in the nature shows I'd been watching at night, the snow leopards and tigers and bears, and wondered if they knew they could be so well paid for their work.

"Good," Mr. Crane said, moving on with our conversation before I had spoken. "Good. There is one more thing. I'd like you to stop talking."

I hadn't realized I'd been excessively chatty, but I apologized for it then hoped those very words wouldn't break the camel's back and cost me the job.

He looked across the desk at me, puzzled, then laughed. "No, no, not now. No, I mean while you're working. While you're under contract. I'd like you to take a vow of silence, so to speak. The Georgian hermits committed to living silently as part of their contract, and I think it's important to the endeavor. Frankly, you'll be living in the garden alone, so there won't be anyone for you to talk to most of the time. And I understand that you aren't the most loquacious fellow to begin with, Mr. Finch."

The conversation, the contract, how much he knew about me... it was all so far beyond me by now that I'd given up on saying anything else, but Mr. Crane didn't seem to be fazed.

"Finch," he said to himself. "Finch... yes, that's fine. A good name for a hermit. No need for a change." He flicked through some papers in a folder on his desk, then laid several sheets out before me. "My people have written up the contract. It's fairly standard, you'll find. Why don't you go ahead and look that over."

He slid the papers toward me, along with a pen, and I made a show of looking at them and nodding sometimes, making noises of acknowledgment and understanding, but most of it was nonsense to me.

Mr. Crane stood from his desk with both palms pressed to its top. "I'd like you to start immediately, of course. To keep word of our project from getting out—you'll see in section 7.G that there's a standard nondisclosure agreement included in this, but I don't suppose that will be much of an issue once you're at work and aren't speaking. You won't meet many people to tell about what you're doing, once you're in the garden."

I flipped to section 7.G as I expected he wanted me to, and said, "Oh, yes. I see."

"Now, I don't believe there's any business you'll need to tend to before you undertake the position. I've taken the liberty of settling your rent, your utilities, and so forth. No loose ends, after all. We wouldn't want to overlook something that might distract you from the task at hand."

"No," I said, and something broke like a dam inside me, and my reservations, my nerves and resistance, all washed away and I gave in to riding this wave of confusion to where it would go— to trusting the raft of Mr. Crane's offer and trusting the current of his currency to have my best interests in mind. Maybe, I thought, I was meant to be here, to do this. Perhaps my life had been leading me to it; losing my job at the right time, answering his email for no particular reason—all to deliver me here.

"As to your apartment, my people are boxing it up as we speak. We can store what you'd like to keep in my house here, of course. No problem. Just let me know what you'd like them to bring, and what can be disposed of."

I pictured my stark apartment with its barren pantry and clothes on the floor, the phone I couldn't use any longer and the old newspapers and magazines I hadn't thrown out. And the landlord arriving to padlock the place. My computer full of the bookmarked detritus of hours and hours of aimless browsing, and the ink worn from the buttons on my TV remote by night after night of fidgety, insomniac fingertips. If all this worked out, the next time I needed a remote control or a phone, I'd have enough money for new ones. If nothing else, I'd have a few years to figure out what I wanted to do with the rest of my life. I'd be in my fifties by the end of the contract—not so old, after all—and with enough money to live without having to work. I'd already wasted more than seven years at Second Nature. What were a few more in a position as easy as this one sounded like it would be?

I thought about my desktop fountain, and almost asked to have it collected, but then I pictured it in the foyer beside Mr. Crane's own fountain. I said, "There's nothing I need."

The contract had red stick-on flags beside every space where I needed to sign, and I went through it quickly, scribbling my name until it was done.

"Wonderful," Mr. Crane said. "Smithee will show you where you'll be working. A pleasure, Mr. Finch." He shook my hand over the desk, and though I was leaning far toward him, Mr. Crane didn't seem to be reaching at all. "I look forward to your work."

I hadn't noticed his arrival, but by some silent magic Smithee was at my shoulder, ready to lead me out into the yard.

9

I followed Smithee down through the house and out the back door to a veranda. The long green lawn sloped away before me, and the cave that would be my home was just visible through the thicket of bushes and trees. A white rabbit was mounting a brown one a few yards away in the grass until the butler clapped his hands and they scampered off. "Sir," he said, and it wasn't "Sir, whenever you're ready" so much as "Sir, can we get on with this," so I walked down a short flight of steps and crossed the morning-wet lawn toward the outcrop of stones I'd seen from Mr. Crane's window.

Off to my right, in the direction of the faraway ocean, a circle of pavement sparkled with dew and with what may have been tiny fragments of glass mixed into the surface. At first I didn't know what it was, maybe a foundation for another building to come, but as I moved through the grass and my angle changed I realized it was a helicopter landing pad, right there in Mr. Crane's yard. I'd seen mansions with their own landing pads in movies, of course, but I'd never imagined people actually had them.

As I slowed to look at the landing pad, Smithee kept moving quickly, charging along at his efficient but effortless professional pace. I rushed to catch up but slipped on the wet grass of the hill and ended up sliding past him on one foot, waving my arms to stay upright, and one flip-flop slipped from my toes to tumble away in the grass. I might have cried out but I didn't fall down. As I chased down my sandal, Smithee said again, "Sir," but he might as well have told me that I was the most pathetic creature he'd ever seen, and that he'd rather smack me in the head with my sandal than wait for me to retrieve it.

He was able to pack a whole lot of meaning into his "Sir," but I suppose that was part of his job—to respond to all the situations of the household with a limited, unobtrusive professional vocabulary. Maybe, I wondered, that's what the verb "to butle" actually meant, and if not that's what it should mean.

I walked with more care the rest of the way, sure to keep up with Smithee so I might avoid his sharp eye and tongue.

The cave, when we reached it, was fifteen feet or so deep by about ten feet wide and better lit than I had expected, though my eyes took a moment to adjust when I stepped from the sun of the garden into my shadowed new home. The walls were carved with niches and nooks of all sizes, some stocked with candles and others hosting pinecones and feathers and the types of objects a hermit might choose (or be told) to collect in his home. The cave made me think of amusement park rides with their mountains made of fake stone, each rock painted to convince passengers of miniature railways and roller coasters as they speed by. But this cave, my cave, had been built from real stone, carefully chosen and painstakingly quarried and carried up into the hills to Mr. Crane's yard, where it was blasted and chiseled and carved with water cannons to simulate years of erosion and weather. Smithee told me all that as we approached it, in a bored monologue that sounded rehearsed.

A low wooden pallet stood at the far end of the chamber, not quite against the wall and layered with straw. Two dark gray blankets—one thick, one thin—lay folded upon it. They weren't a uniform gray but were speckled, almost the same as the walls of the cave, and beside the blankets lay a dark tunic made from the same rough material. I lifted it from the bed and it unfolded to hang to my knees, and a length of frayed rope—my new belt—fell out of the folds. Shaking the fabric even that much stirred a strong, stomach-churning scent of lanolin, and the cloth—if I can call it that, as scratchy and raw as it was—coated my fingers with oil from whatever sheep had been shorn for my sake.

"If that will be all, sir," said Smithee. "Your present attire will be collected when a meal is delivered. Mr. Crane reminds you that silence should be undertaken immediately, so now is the time to say what you will."

He looked so bored with the possibility of my last public words, so disinterested in me altogether, that instead of something profound or considered I said just, "Okay."

In reply Smithee said only, "Sir," of course. Then he walked away toward the house on silent, gliding steps that gave him, in his dark suit, the look of a movie vampire. At the bottom of the hill, though, where he would have been hidden from the view of the windows, Smithee stopped. He pulled a flat black notebook from the inner pocket of his jacket and followed that with a pen. He wrote something down, then flipped back a couple of pages before writing something else. Then he tucked away his tools, smoothed the front of his jacket with the palms of his hands, and carried on up the hill to the house. I hadn't been able to tell while walking behind him, but watching him from a sideways distance I noticed that however steep the slope of the hill his body stayed perfectly straight; his feet must have met the ground at an angle, but the rest of him never leaned. Not that it meant anything, but I'd never seen anyone walk like that before.

I stripped off my clothes and stood nude in the air of the cave, pale and tender and pink, aware of each pore and pimple and each pound of flesh in a way I never had been. A cool breeze blew in and I broke out in goose bumps, every hair standing straight up off my body. The sudden cold on the parts I'd kept covered made my whole body shiver, the way it happens when opening your fly at a urinal in a cold bathroom. It looked warmer outside, so I left the cave for the grass with the tunic and belt in my hands. Sunlight fell on my cock and balls for the first time perhaps ever, and I stood with my hands on my hips, thrusting myself slightly forward into the warmth.

Then I looked up the slope of the lawn toward the house, toward Mr. Crane's window on the third floor, and saw the round glint of his telescope lens with the silhouette of a person behind it. And, below his window, a blonde woman sat in a patio chair looking in my direction.

I ducked into my cave to pull the tunic over my head and knot the rope belt around my waist. For the first several seconds there was only the smell, that lanolin smell, closing my throat and watering my eyes, but then I moved some part of my body in some tiny way and the itch was explosive. Prickling like millions of dagger-sharp fibers were sticking and stabbing my cotton- and nylon-spoiled skin, and I burst into bright hives all over. My body had been bound and trussed all my life, covered by clothes I had rarely noticed were there. I pulled them on in the morning and took them off again at night to wear other clothes made from the same fabrics, but pulling on that tunic was the first time in my life I could feel every inch, every thread of a garment where it crossed my body, and it burned. I attacked myself with my fingernails, and rubbed my back and ribs against the rough walls of the cave, and the itch began to feel a bit better if only because the bloody welts I raised with my scratching were so painful themselves that they drew attention away from the other discomfort. Until the fibers of the tunic scratched those raw wounds, and everything hurt even more.

And like that my days in the garden began to go by.

The smell of the tunic and blankets faded as the stink of my own unwashed body usurped the last trace of the sheep I blamed for my suffering, whose coat was the source of my own. And while the itch became less pronounced and more irritating than incendiary, my body stayed swollen and red—as it would for a while—and I took every chance I could steal to rub my back and my sides against a rock or a tree, or to reach with a stick and scratch until I was bleeding and raw.

Meals were delivered, and I ate without knowing whose hands had brought them. Trays appeared in the wall niche by my bed while I was outside or before I woke up; I tried a few times to watch their arrival but somehow they always snuck by.

My first night in the garden I couldn't sleep, kept awake by the rustling and snuffling of animals and worried by the wide-open mouth of my cave. The noises weren't unfamiliar; they were the same sounds I'd heard in hundreds of nature programs. It seemed like they should be less scary, these sounds, because they were part of the background, the atmosphere, not isolated and enhanced by microphones. They should have seemed less real to me, I thought, less present than the snarls and sniffs I'd heard loud and clear on TV, without the wind or the rain or any night noises to muffle them. But these noises were scary, and close: I saw the pointed-snout shadow of a fox creep into the mouth of my cave and watch me pretend to be sleeping before strolling off unperturbed by my presence. A skunk wandered right up to my bed, black and white body rolling side to side like a furry round rowboat as he walked all around in my cave. He (maybe she, I don't know) raised his tail not two feet from my head—and I knew from TV what that meant, so I held as much breath as I could— but the skunk was only stretching. He leaned forward on his front legs like a cat or a dog, wheezed out a yawn, and was off into the garden again. All that in one night, my first in the cave, and with so much going on I didn't have time to realize until morning that I'd passed a whole sleepless night like all of those I'd passed in my apartment, but I'd done it without fantasies or long, derailed trains of thought and hours of empty TV. I'd passed a whole night by watching the world as it came to my door.

The next morning and every one after I found footprints of all shapes and sizes laced together across the ground outside my cave, and I followed them as far as I could, trying to reconstruct the nocturnal routes of my neighbors. There were hawks (or falcons, maybe, or eagles; I don't know the difference) in the daylight, swooping and diving to snatch prey off the ground, and at night I listened to the interrogations of owls. I heard once on TV that owls call the name of the person who will be next to die, but Mr. Crane's owls only ever called, "Who?" the way owls are meant to, and it made me feel welcome instead of afraid, as if they were inquiring about the new guy in the garden.

Wandering the garden by daylight, I discovered flowers and trees I'd once described as inferior for Second Nature: genuine palm trees and rubber plants, and magnolia blossoms that were brilliant and bright for a couple of days before browning and rotting with the most awful stink. The real plants were impressive, but I still thought there was room in the world for hyperefficient magnolias, and for bushes that don't harbor thousands of bugs in their branches, waiting for some city slicker to lean in toward their blossoms before unleashing stinging and biting and skin-scratching hordes all over his face and his body. There were lots of other plants, too, but if I'd never written about them for the company I didn't know what they were. My knowledge of flowers and trees was limited to the ones I'd been paid to malign.

I tied long chains of dandelions to wind around tree trunks and rocks for no other reason than I was there and so were they. I smelled flowers and tasted berries and watched rabbits go at each other in fast, fluffy orgies, then scatter when foxes came close. I classified birds by shape, size, and color and gave them all names because I knew what so few of them actually were, and in time I could recognize a few nesting pairs and pick out some individuals from one another, the ones with misshapen wings or strange-colored spots on their bodies.

There were no sirens or crashes or drunken neighbors trying to pound their way into the wrong apartment at the end of their night on the town. There weren't any airplanes or trains far away in the dark. At first I heard only the space left behind by those noises, and the world seemed half-empty. One afternoon while up in a tree and watching the clouds—a grizzly bear eating a sandwich, and a steamship passing over the moon—I almost fell off my branch because the cell phone I'd left behind was ringing above me. But a few seconds later a gray bird hopped out of some leaves into sight, skipping his way onto a limb close to mine, where he delivered a pitch-perfect rendition of my old ringtone, one of the country's most common.

Most of the time I did nothing. I could say that I contemplated—that's what I was being paid for—but even that sounds too active, too focused on solving a problem. I wasn't focused on anything but watching the world as it happened.

Not quite nothing, actually, because I sneezed. A lot. I was allergic to everything in the garden: the pollen, the leaves, the grass, possibly even the air. My eyes watered, my nose ran, my inner ears and the back of my throat itched so badly that I came close to trying to reach a long, skinny stick inside my head to scratch. If I accidentally killed myself, I thought, at least I'd stop being allergic.

I didn't miss all the distractions I'd left behind in the valley, the TV and computer and couch. Not until it rained so heavily one of those early nights that the noise kept me up, and kept the local creatures safe and dry in their dens, leaving me with long hours to fill but nothing to watch. I tried to remember the theme songs from as many TV shows as possible, and sing them all in my head. I recalled old commercials and PSAs about not telling lies, about helping your neighbors and the benefits of one chewing gum over another, and I marveled at how completely I could recreate each of those in my mind: the dialogue, the music, shot-by-shot frames

of each ad. In my apartment, on a long night like that, I would
have watched reruns and movies I'd never consider wasting time
on in daylight, but in the cave I lit a candle instead and danced
shadow puppets around on the wall.

I still wondered at least a few times each day about the voices
I had abandoned, my bloggers and message board ciphers.
I imagined them getting on without me, living their lives but
having no one to tell about them and no outlet for sharing their
moments—not so unlike me, alone in the garden, encountering
foxes and owls and skunks and keeping it all to myself. Apart from
my meals appearing out of thin air, I hadn't seen a sign of anyone
since moving in: not Mr. Crane, not Smithee, not the woman I'd
spotted sunning herself. I imagined the bloggers' audience
waiting, refreshing websites impatiently in hopes of new content,
or sending emails and making comments but not getting answers.
Some nights, before I learned to sleep in the garden, I lay
watching the small screen of sky framed by the mouth of my cave,
and pretended it was a computer and I was typing the stars, that
they were the text of my abandoned voices, and I drafted blog
posts and updates in my head until they spun me to sleep,
imagining all the ways they might describe the days I was having,
but always falling asleep before finding the words.

It would have been close to idyllic if not for the allergies and the
hives. Every time my thighs rubbed together or brushed my balls
it was hell, and I walked bowlegged like a bad movie cowboy. But
overall it was much easier to accept my new life, to settle into it,
than I had guessed it would be. Giving up speech wasn't so hard,
not without someone to talk to, and I could still hear all the voices
of TV and movies and the web in my head, so I could have
conversations anytime I wanted to. I could scroll through the
archives of each of those bloggers, recalling the stories they'd told
a year or two years or five years before, and that was like having
someone to talk to. Everything in the garden was comfortable

quickly—except for my clothes—as if it had all been designed just for me, sized for my body, and an awful lot of it had. So when I imagined how my bloggers might write about all I was doing, how they might tell it, I couldn't get far because who wants to hear a story of happiness achieved by dumb luck, without struggles in the way of the journey, without obstacles greater than an itchy rash on some joker's balls?

10

After the incident with the hikers, after I stumbled and tumbled into their campsite, I sat up late by my fire as it burned down to embers and darkness crept into the space left behind. Then a bobbing, blurry bulb of orange flared up and danced in the dark—a flashlight inside their tent, I suppose, and the first electricity I've seen in so long. Seeing that bright glow so counter to the way of the world, against the cycle of daylight and night, filled me with a sadness I didn't expect. I thought of email and movies and television, blenders and car radios and the evil empire of alarm clocks and phones. The light didn't last, just long enough to rummage in a backpack for something or arrange sleeping bags before bed—a few seconds, a blip of illumination—but the shock to my eyes was almost painful after all these years in which I've had only the sun, moon, and stars and my own tiny fire to light up the world. A second sun suddenly risen right here in my garden, and though it burnt out quickly I couldn't pretend it hadn't been there. If it had been any more than a glowing bright blur, if I'd seen it clearly, it might have burned my old eyes right out. That's a thin silver lining for my fading sight.

It burned longer, though, in the back of my mind, where its heat and its light kept me awake long into the morning, listening to the skitter and scuffle of creatures outside and the harsh rustle of nylon and fleece. Murmured words and muffled laughter carried from their campsite into the amplifying cone of my cave, echoing loudly like they were right beside me or camped on the foot of my bed.

This morning they were up soon after I was, and I watched from the roof of my cave as their featureless shapes emerged from the tent's orange bubble as the sun rose behind it. First him, unfolding through the low door like a spring suddenly released from under a weight. Then she unwound herself in a way that made me remember some time-lapse images of a sunflower growing too fast I saw once—source material for Second Nature, but by now I can't recall what I was meant to be learning—and the two of them stretched side by side but leaning in opposite directions so together they formed a tall, skinny chalice with the half-risen sun in its cup.

I say now that they looked like a chalice, but it was really a big letter Y I thought of at the time, their bodies hazy and indistinct, tan with blotches of color I took to be clothes. I've filled in the details in the telling, seeing more in my mind than I saw at the time. Everything looks like other things to me now, shapes without details and without distinction, and it's easy to mistake one thing for another and to see things I don't really see. I might say it makes me visionary, or that my mind's secrets are projected through my weak eyes, but mostly I think it's memory filling in blanks the way it always has done but finding so many more empty spaces these days. Like my mind tells me I watched her T-shirt rise up as she stretched, lifting away from the tiny shorts she'd slept in and flashing a tan, muscled stomach. I didn't see any of that, I couldn't have across such a distance even if it was there to be seen in the beige haze of her moving body, but I let imagination run wild on the shapes of her shirt and her stomach.

In yesterday's fall on top of their tent, when they helped me up, I felt the first touches of human flesh on my own in so many years, and how strange that in all the confusion and chaos I didn't make much of the feeling—I know it was there, I know I was touched, but I missed paying attention with everything else going on. I might have liked to hold on to that sensation, to spend some time thinking about it. It might be a more pleasant subject than the difficult meditations I'll need to make about everything else that occurred, my angry reaction and routine disrupted.

I went for a swim with my flute while they boiled some food on a tiny camp stove. Its burner roared like a jet taking off when they lit it, then settled into a sinister hiss; no wonder they've had no fire so far, with a futuristic contraption like that close at hand. And I'll take this as a good sign they can't stay any longer than their bottled fuel and packed food hold out. Their dependence on those devices, on those supplies, will send them away when their stores are depleted, I hope.

When I returned from the river, after a few hours' reflection on the strange sights and sounds of last night, after working through long, shapeless tunes on my flute as I floated, they had hung dripping laundry on the blackberries. Their bright fleece jackets and thick hiking pants crawled on the bushes—not real fleece, not sheep, but fleece as if shorn from some synthetic creature with tight, purple wool—and I thought of a plane crash and lost luggage exploded all over. Perhaps because the roaring of their stove had already called to mind planes. When I came close I saw branches bent down and breaking beneath the weight of their washing, and unripened berries had spilled to the ground, before getting a chance to be grown or to darken from green to pink and to purple and to stain my fingers and lips and the droppings of this garden's birds.

One of their T-shirts—his, I suspect—had large enough print for me to squint close and read it, to see that it said, "END THE WAR," but it didn't say which war and it didn't say where, or else it said so in letters too tiny for me to make out. The last time I saw fine print was the day I signed Mr. Crane's contract, and my eyes are too weak for it now. Maybe it's the same war that was going on when I came here, or maybe some other, but I have no interest in knowing—there's no place for that here. There is violence, of course, between animals, but it's the violence of eating and being eaten instead, the violence of staying alive. The animals, the birds and the foxes and bees, go about their violent business when they need to, and they leave me alone. I only mind the never-ending battles between hills of ants if I happen to step in their scrum; the ants only attack when I'm clumsy enough to intrude with a careless misstep. They don't bring the fight to my cave. Even the bees leave me alone for the most part these days, unless I'm harvesting honey. A war in that far-off other world doesn't so much as nibble at my calloused feet, and that T-shirt—its words so large and so loud they would not be ignored—was an unwelcome intrusion.

Seeing their belongings all over the bushes, their campsite overtaking my home—and, I admit, there was some residue of painful shame and resentment left over from yesterday's incident—that earlier anger came back, that unfamiliar frustration and fury. The hikers themselves, for the moment, were out of earshot, and before I could stay my hand it was tearing their clothes from the bushes, throwing them onto the ground, kicking their campsite and its rubble of strange shapes and mysterious objects. I threw a tantrum, for lack of some better word. I grabbed up their shirts and their socks and their presumptuous, invading underpants from the poor berry bushes, ready to throw them all into my fire, to pounce on their tent and stomp on their sleeping bags and bundle up their whole campsite to cast into the river to be washed away. My berries! My bushes! My whole quiet world!

My arms filled with the wrack and ruin of their belongings, and my bundle grew larger and larger as I swept up their things. Strange fabrics and sharp corners and hard surfaces scraped and brushed on my surprised skin. I raged in my head, my thoughts a low, angry mutter that never reached my numb tongue. Then I tripped over something, perhaps the same round shape that tripped me up yesterday when I fell into their tent, and the entire load slipped from my arms and took my flute with it to bounce off and be buried somewhere in all of that junk.

And all of my anger fell away with it; my fists and teeth slowly unclenched as I felt the rage drain from my body and out through my feet to the soil where it could dissipate across the whole garden, spread thin until it posed no threat and all that energy could be put to use. Shame crept into its place, shame at the damage I'd done and my cruel disrespect, shame at my own stupid lack of self-control. All the autonomy I'd learned in this garden, all of that independence, what was it worth if I let other people dictate my most private feelings? How self-sufficient was that?

I crawled through their campsite on hands and knees, looking for my lost flute and trying to arrange things the way they had been, trying to move blurry shapes back to where they belonged. I spread their clothes on the bushes, though perhaps not the same clothes that had been there before, and I tried to arrange their other equipment more evenly over the ground instead of piled in the angry clump I'd constructed. But when I was done, when I'd done my blind best, there was still no sign of my flute, only a sharp tang of detergent stinging my nose from crawling so close to their clothing.

I deserved it, I knew that. I'd earned the loss of my long-faithful flute through arrogant rage and selfish desires to smash up the camp. I'd wanted to tear down their home—albeit a transient one, a tent—and now I'd lost something in it. Disappointed as I was, I couldn't call that unfair, so I stood up and I picked my way out of their campsite and returned to the task of getting my meal. Fluteless, but with a new note blown through me by the Old Man's firm breath. If he had wanted me to evict them, if he had wanted me to respond to their presence at all, he would have told me what I should do. I should have done what I'd done for as long as always, as if those hikers weren't here. Harvesting carrots and digging potatoes, scraping bark from birch trees and picking rose hips and, on a good day, snatching fish from the river.

I spend so much more of my time finding food than I did when this garden was new, and when I was new to this garden. Hunger wasn't a problem while Mr. Crane and his house were still here and my meals arrived as if by magic. Nothing fancy, porridge in the morning and a bucket of stew and a hard loaf of bread to split between my other meals, but those meals kept me fed and they came every day. Simple and solid as my cave and my ratty old blankets.

As simple and solid as me, too, I would like to think, but these unwelcome and angry emotions have thrown me off course. To have been so provoked and pulled so far out of myself—there's no question what I'll spend the rest of today and who knows how long thinking about as I float and I harvest and weed. These hikers are colonizing more of my energy and time than I'd like to admit, and much more of my meditations, but it's me who is letting them do it and it's me who must make it stop and must go about life in this garden as my life is supposed to be lived.

After all that, my attack on the campsite and the loss of my flute, my own shameful loss of control, I was too sick to my stomach to eat lunch at all, so rather than head for my cave and my kettle as I'd intended, I walked toward the beehives to sit on the hill that rises behind them. At moments like that, when my mind is a muddle and focus is hard to find, the droning hum of the hives helps me center by blocking out every sound—something that has become harder and harder now that my hearing is doing double work to make up for my eyes.

On the way to the hives, following the dark wall of the blackberry brambles until I reached the rock where I needed to turn, I heard the hikers approaching from the other direction.

I heard them thrashing their way through the brambles, still stomping in heavy boots, and as they came near I heard her ask, "Should we introduce ourselves? How does it work?"

"I don't know," he told her. "What do you think? It didn't really get into that, did it?"

"No," she said, and I missed the rest of their conversation because I rushed to turn away and out of their path, toward the bees and their blanket of buzzing—childish, but I had no interest in being nearby and in sight when they arrived at the mess of their camp.

11

After my arrival, time in the garden quickly became more about memory than measure, and my days went as shapeless and soft at the edges as my whole world is now. A few weeks into the job, my breakfast basket brought a note instructing me to perform tai chi outside my cave every morning. So for a few days I pretended I knew what I was doing, going through the motions of knowing the motions, until another note arrived requesting sunrise meditations on top of my cave instead.

I hadn't climbed up there yet, I hadn't discovered the surprisingly comfortable seat carved from stone, but that morning I found the footholds and scaled the wall of my home in the dim predawn minutes and was settled and ready to watch before the sun showed its face. I've kept that routine ever since, with a few exceptions when Mr. Crane had me briefly try something different. But always, before very long, he sent me back to my rooftop reflections.

As thin orange light filled the garden, I saw that the leaves and grass were still wet with night and I watched brown birds hop to the ends of branches to shimmy their feathers dry. A beehive tuned up nearby but out of sight, up somewhere in a tree, and someone close to my cave—A fox? A skunk? Maybe me?—released a slow, whispering fart, or else the wind blew in a way I wasn't expecting. Leaves drifted down from the trees and landed around me on that rock, and stayed where they settled until another wind rose and lifted them off. Insects landed—flies, beetles in various sizes and colors, a butterfly as purple as grape juice—and sat cleaning their wings and rubbing their legs and going about their own morning business as I went about mine. Most of my encounters with bugs until then had been smashing and scraping them out of the house or watching them splatter against my windshield while I was rushing to work on the few stretches of road where it was possible to go fast enough for a bug to be splattered. Cars, I realized from atop my cave, were too fast even when they weren't moving. Too fast for me to have noticed before all of these slower things, leaves and beetles and mornings unfolding at their own pace and with their own rhythms. All this had been happening every day of my life, while I'd been moving too fast and with too sluggish a mind to take note. While I'd been too busy shitting and showering and shaving myself, trundling myself off to work in a mental fog that lent itself to traffic-jam driving but not to being alive. I sipped the tea I'd carried up to the cave top in my wooden mug, and through its thin steam I watched that brown bird on the branch fluffing and smoothing its feathers with quick darts of its beak.

If not for my morning marathon of sneezing and wheezing from pollen and particles flown into my cave and into my nose and my throat overnight, and from the blankets I'd spent the night under and the tunic I was still wearing, that first sunrise on my cave top might have been perfect. And even with all that discomfort it was still pretty good. I drifted off into my head, not thinking about anything so much as trying hard to think about nothing; I was getting better at meditation but I wasn't there yet, I wasn't where I am now. Where I am on a good day, at least, when I'm adrift on the water and in my head alike, when I'm nowhere at all for long hours at a time.

That first morning atop the cave, my quiet reflections were interrupted by someone whistling, the first human sound I'd heard since my arrival in Mr. Crane's garden, and I turned away from the sunrise toward the house and the hill. A woman was walking in my direction on legs so long there's no way to describe them without stupid clichés. She wore cutoffs so short that a tongue of white pocket hung down each leg, and her hair was as yellow as waxed lemon rind. Like a magazine page on the move, her breasts were barely draped in twin triangles hardly large enough to suggest a bikini. I hadn't seen a woman in a long time, and what a first woman to see. She carried a gray metal bucket, and it bounced against her thigh with each step.

As she drew close, the mist rose around her like a special effect, giving the moment a sense of slow motion or of a TV show's opening credits (an impression that made more sense once I realized who she was). I wasn't sure if I should climb down to meet her or pretend she wasn't there. I hadn't been instructed on how to respond when visitors appeared at my cave, and I hadn't had any yet. Smithee, the last person I'd seen when he showed me the cave, was an employee like me, but this—I assumed—was Mr. Crane's wife, not one of his workers, and I wasn't sure if I worked for her, too, or should go about the task her husband had set me like she wasn't there.

I decided to stay on my perch and stay in contemplation, keep watching the world with utmost concentration, because that's what I was being paid for. Maybe she'd report my commitment back to her husband. I tried to keep my eyes on the sunrise and the wakening flora and fauna, but it was hard to ignore her approach. Her feet were bare, crosshatched by wet grass from her walk down the hill, and her toenails and fingernails were all painted the same shade of orange as her bikini and dangling surfboard-shaped earrings.

Oh, I'm glad I could still see in those days, and more glad that memory hasn't gone with my eyes. Thanks to my scribe, I can flip back through the days of my life in this garden and recall more than I could on my own.

She stood by the mouth of my cave on the broad, flat stone that serves as a threshold, and she brushed some of the grass from her feet but let most of it be. Then she climbed the side of the cave, easily, like she'd done it before, and sat down beside me. Her feet left wet shadows on the gray stone.

I tried to ignore her, to go about the business of my meditations like I was alone. I tried to do my job without interruption. On the branch of a tree I'd decided was cottonwood only because its flowers were white and puffy, a black bird spread his wings, revealing red shoulders, then flapped hard and rose in a spray of fine mist.

"So you're my husband's new hobby," she said. "His hermit."

She was facing me, but I didn't turn away from the garden. She leaned closer, warming my leg with her own, and as her heat spread over my body, I was glad for once to have the uncomfortable tunic covering my lap.

"I'm his old hobby, his wife."

Mr. Crane had mentioned his wife was an actress, or maybe Smithee had said it, and now I realized which one: her name escaped me, but she'd been on a cop show a few years before, as the buxom young officer always wearing bikinis and maid's uniforms to go undercover. That's why she'd looked so familiar coming down the hill from the house; it was an outfit like one she'd worn in the opening credits, pushing her way through saloon doors in the midst of a brawl, bringing the whole wild bar to a freeze.

My rash escalated its itching, and it was all I could do not to scratch at my balls or throw my tunic open to catch some cool air. Mr. Crane's rule about bathing was beginning to chafe. I didn't mind smelling, but the itch was driving me mad. But with Mrs. Crane beside me I tried to bear it, though I think the strain showed on my face, because she gave me a strange sort of look.

"Finch, isn't it? I think that's what he said." She paused; it was my turn to speak, but when I didn't she said, "It's awkward talking to someone who doesn't talk back. I don't think I'll enjoy having another man like that around." She waited as if I might answer, then leaned so close I could feel her lips moving. "Listen, I don't know what my husband hopes to accomplish by having you here. But I know why you're here. I'm sure he's paying you well."

She looked toward the house and, I assumed, toward the window of her husband's office. I didn't turn, so I couldn't tell whether he was watching; by that point in my tenure, after worrying about it for a few days, I'd pretty much forgotten I was being observed except when the telescope's lens caught the sun and flared way up on the hill.

A few yards from us, two bright male blue jays lit into each other, squawking and screeching and thumping their chests, batting each other's head and body with swinging wings, and wet as the grass was they tossed up so much water while tumbling around that it looked like one of those cartoon fights, a dust cloud of disjointed limbs. Then one bird flew off in a huff as the victor berated him from the ground.

"He isn't here, you know. My husband. He's gone to China for some meeting or to buy another company or to do whatever he does. He's gone out into the world to make himself richer. You aren't being watched. You don't need to perform."

I hadn't thought of my job as "performing," and I might have said so, but even without her husband at home I didn't want to start speaking. I was enjoying my silence; everyone I might come into contact with in Mr. Crane's garden (though she was the first) would already know that I couldn't speak, so there was no pressure to say anything. I wouldn't be rude to ignore them, I would simply be doing my job and doing it well for perhaps the first time in my life. And, I thought, Mrs. Crane tempting me to open my mouth could be a test from her husband.

"Oh, hell," she said, "this is boring. I thought you'd at least be more fun. Come on. We're going to pick berries. You hold the bucket."

She climbed down from our perch, but I hesitated and hadn't moved yet when she reached the ground. "Oh, come on," she called over her shoulder, already walking away—and that walk! "I'm not going to bite."

I looked toward the house, then back to her.

"Okay, you work for my husband. Fine. But I live here, too. So you also work for me, right? Now get down here and hold my bucket before it's too hot out here."

If Mr. Crane asked, I thought I might do better explaining why I'd done what she told me rather than why I hadn't. Should he care, should I have to explain myself to him at all. So I climbed down and hoisted her pail, the perfect tin pail, exactly the one you'd expect to find in a picture of people out picking berries in an outdoor clothes catalog. Hand-carved wooden handle darkened by years of berry-stained palms, dented in just the right places, no doubt from being dropped by excited berry enthusiasts running up and down rolling hills, or else thumped precisely by technicians in a pail factory.

I'd been to the blackberry patch already during my early weeks on the estate. It wasn't far from my cave. But I hadn't done any picking because, to be honest, I wasn't sure I was allowed. My meals came from the house, so I thought the blackberry brambles and blueberry bushes and apple trees and all of that might be decoration, like Second Nature plants were. I was meant to be decoration, so why not the plants and the animals, too?

But Mrs. Crane was intent on picking blackberries and just as intent on my holding her pail, so I followed her out of the glade that surrounds my cave and over the roll of the hill that put the house out of sight. Every step in the tunic was like sliding sandpaper between my legs. I felt my skin redden and blister, and it hurts to think of it even now, years after shedding my tunic for good.

She dropped berries into her pail by the handful, moving fast from one bush to another but choosing fruit carefully, not scraping every branch bare. She ate some, staining her lips, and juice trailed down her tanned neck and onto her chest, and the whole scene started to feel like a letter to a skin magazine: *I never thought it would happen to me, but there I was picking blackberries...* When the pail was more than half-full, she stopped picking and sat in a circle of sunlit grass on a downward slope near the bushes.

"Sit," she said, patting the ground, so I sat close enough not to seem unfriendly but not too close, in case Mr. Crane emerged from the bushes like Dr. Livingstone watching his tribe. In case I'd been offered the temptation of his wife's company (if she really was his wife and not hired for the day) to make sure I could be trusted around her and with the job I'd been given to do.

It was a nice spot, and I could tell that later in the day, when the sun grew too warm, the bushes would be well-positioned to offer some shade. I was looking into those bushes, imagining how their shadows would slide across the ground as day passed, when I spotted the first of the cameras. It stood on a thin stalk a foot or so into the brambles of a blackberry bush, its tiny lens no bigger than one of the berries, no bigger than someone's eye, and as I watched it swiveled a bit to one side, away from me and toward Mrs. Crane.

Mrs. Crane spun on the seat of her shorts and stretched her legs in the grass, and laid her blonde head in my lap. She arched her back and her body went taut against mine, her arms reaching up so one brushed my face, and I was concerned—why wouldn't I be?—that something might stir without being asked in my loins; a beautiful woman I'd watched on TV, and not for the quality of the show she was on, and here she was in my lap and in a bikini and wearing shorts too short for the name. I focused my mind and all of my nerves on the itch of my rash in hopes of avoiding any other sensations.

Now that I knew I was being watched by more than the telescope in the window, now that I'd spotted the camera, I knew I had to control myself. I knew it was a test after all, a test of my commitment, of my restraint, of my ability to be trusted in another man's garden. Maybe she already knew that the camera was there, maybe she was in on the test, and if I alerted her to it that would be failure for me. Or maybe she didn't know and if I told her somehow—a gesture, a directing gaze—the camera would notice, and that would be failure, too. So I needed to hold myself and my body in check. I needed to be professional about it all.

"It's nice to have someone to talk to," she said, looking up with eyes as blue as they'd been on the screen.

She rolled onto her side across my thigh, looking away toward the water far off in the distance, and her hair smelled like coconut and laundry dried in the sun, and I imagined my rash was on fire and frozen all at the same time because that seemed like the most unpleasant sensation I could possibly feel and therefore the most distracting. I tried not to look at the camera, in hopes it hadn't spotted my spotting of it, in hopes I could pass off as natural my professional, trustworthy behavior.

"This is my favorite part of the garden," she said. "The view from right here. It would be nice if the ocean was closer, but it's fine as it is. Quiet. Even if do I miss living on the beach. You could probably see my old house from here, if my husband hadn't torn it down. Had his men do it, I mean. He doesn't do much himself." She shifted her weight more heavily onto my thigh and said, "He doesn't need to."

She rolled onto her back in my lap, her stomach arched and smooth and her breasts... God help me, it was all I could do just holding my tongue.

"Is that what you like?" she asked. "The quiet? Is that why you're here?" She paused, still leaving space in our conversation for me to answer. "I thought it was so strange, to hire a hermit. But I think I understand. I understand why you'd do it, I mean. I don't get what's in it for him, but there must be something. There always is."

She sat up, and I breathed a silent sigh of relief.

"I think I could be a hermit. He didn't ask me, but I think I could do it." She laughed. "Maybe I'll live in your cave with you. We'd have some fun."

My heart and stomach swapped spots when I heard that, and in case she'd noticed I smiled at an angle I hoped she would be able to see but would stay out of sight of the lens in the bush.

"Let's get more berries," she said, and stood up. "My pail's almost full."

I gave Mrs. Crane a second to turn her back and start walking before lifting myself from the ground, then followed with the bucket held in front of me for the sake of discretion.

12

One morning soon after my berry-picking excursion with Mrs. Crane, a whistle carved from light wood appeared with my breakfast. I blew through its open ends until my cheeks and head hurt without making any sound more melodic than my own spit and sputter. Then I realized it was a flute, not a whistle, and tried blowing across a hole in its top. It hurt my head less that way, but the result was no closer to music. Still, I couldn't imagine I was meant to master an instrument on my first try, so I decided to make it part of my morning routine. I carried the flute to the top of the cave with my tea, and after watching the sunrise spent an hour or so puffing away, huffing and hacking and—I thought— showing the promise of progress. When I was wobbling and wheezing and thought I might fall from the cave, and dark worms wiggled at the edges of my eyes, I set the flute aside and climbed down to get on with the day.

The next morning the flute was gone. I searched the cave, but there weren't many places a flute might be hiding, in my wall nooks and niches or wrapped in my blankets, and it wasn't in any of those. It was just gone. I'd only had it a day but was already looking forward to learning the flute, though perhaps I hadn't shown enough promise in my first attempt to meet Mr. Crane's expectations.

As the days and weeks passed my breakfast tray brought with it all sorts of objects and tasks and requests. I went apple and berry picking when I was told to by either one of the Cranes, and I sat in trees all day every day for a couple of weeks. Some of Mr. Crane's requests I enjoyed and others I didn't, but it was hard to get too excited about any of his passing interests when I knew they weren't likely to last. And, in the case of the hot spring he'd mentioned, when those ideas never materialized. Most of his requests were as fleeting as the websites I used to surf through at work to pass time, or the spam I responded to in the long hours of night (though responding to spam had turned out all right at least once, and once was enough to have altered my life).

When the beehives first appeared downhill from the blackberry brambles, a row of five bright white boxes, I didn't know what they were. It was early and the swarms were asleep, but as the sun warmed them those boxes buzzed and I swear they shook side to side as the thousands upon thousands upon millions of bees shook out wings numb with sleep the way my leg is some mornings, cocked funny beneath my own weight.

I don't suppose Mr. Crane could have known that I was allergic to bees. Or that I just plain never liked them. And I had no way to tell him, not without losing my job one way or the other: break my contracted silence, or refuse to do what he asked.

Overnight the hives had been installed by unseen delivery forces, and a note the next morning asked me to gather honey. No further instructions, no diagrams for assistance or gloves and mask, no fire hose or bazooka. Only five hives of bees growling like tiny pit bulls as they awaited my unprotected approach, and as able as dogs to smell fear. Maybe smell allergies, too—who knows what lurks in the cruel apian heart?

A cipher of mine at Second Nature had once written to a beekeepers' journal, proposing that plastic plants could be dusted with synthetic and hybrid pollens to attract a decorative hive. These pollens were also a mild tranquilizer, able to keep the bees under control in ways wild plants and unpredictable pollens made impossible. I'd learned about bees for that letter, to make it convincing, and I remembered that bees communicate using dance: a scout returns to the hive, the other bees gather, and he (she?) pivots and wiggles and pirouettes toward the site of some succulent flower. Or, I imagined, toward an exposed and stingable patch of available flesh.

Where were those pacifying pollens when I needed them? The louder the buzzing in the boxes became, the surer I was I could see their sides shake, rattling racks of honeycomb as more and more bees danced for the pure, violent joy of stinging poor me as soon as I came close enough.

Dramatic, I know, to assume those bees knew I was near and that they cared. But so much of fear is inflation, an assumption our own terrors matter to others. To think that of all a neighborhood's houses, the escaped psychotic killer will choose our own, or the bear find our tent; that our own plane will be the one in a million to crash.

But in this case I was right; for once it was all about me. As I sat on the hillside beneath the brambles, overlooking the hives with the sunrise behind them, it almost could have been beautiful if I hadn't been wondering how I might get at the honey. And all of a sudden the warmth in those boxes reached some critical point and so did the furious joy of the bees, because they erupted in five long, dark ribbons up into the air and—I swear it—turned in midstream at sharp angles and all 799 trillion of them rocketed in my direction.

So I ran away. What else could I do?

But I was running uphill and in a panic, and I tripped after one or two steps. Bees, it turns out, are much faster than anything else in the world and are especially faster than me. I was still wearing my tunic in those early days, but even that didn't offer much cover: the bees stung my arms and my legs and my back, they were in my hair and stinging my scalp, and one industrious bee managed to plant his stinger between the two smallest toes of my left foot. Try to imagine a less pleasant spot to be stung. Then rest assured I was stung twice there, too.

I'm pretty sure I saw Smithee watching from up on the hill, in the shadow of some broad bushes, but I could be wrong about that. I was paying more attention to the bees on my trail than to anything else. If he was there, he didn't step in to help me, but I couldn't blame him for that. I wouldn't wade into a river of bees to help someone I hardly knew, either. He probably thought I was a goner. I know I did.

I have no doubt they would have stung me to death, only some of the bees alerted their cruel colleagues to the flowers on the blackberry brambles. How Mr. Crane's gardeners managed their berry bushes to always be both in bloom and in fruit I don't know, and somehow they did it without being seen. But I'm glad they did, because as fast as they had been upon me the bees were off to the bushes, swarming the branches and blossoms the way they'd swarmed me.

And that's when I fainted, right there in the grass. I woke up facedown and sneezing and wheezing and swollen and sore all over my body, jerked back to the world by the *whump whump* of a helicopter descending onto the pad by the house, and by the rush of skittering, twittering birds escaping the sound of the craft. It was a long black helicopter with no markings on it and with a slender, bent tail that looked like the biggest of the billions of tiny stingers I spent the rest of the day scraping out of my skin.

I tried, while I scraped and scratched, to imagine my bloggers all telling the story: who would be sympathetic, who would be cruel, who would have stepped in to help had they spotted a frantic man swarmed by those billions of bees. I tried, but I didn't get anywhere. In the past, I had imagined the interface I used for writing blog entries, picturing the words as I would have typed them, then those same words posted onto each site, and I imagined reading the words on a screen. But that day, while ridding myself of the dead bodies of bees that had stung me and stuck, still hanging out of my skin, on that day I couldn't concentrate on my bloggers. I couldn't make them speak, or type, any longer, and when I tried to flip back through their archives, scrolling my mind through all their back pages, I couldn't recall those words either. I had lost all those voices at last, drowned out by the droning of bees.

The silver lining of my near-death encounter was that rather than such a massive, sudden concentration of venom killing me, it somehow cured my allergies instead—not just to bees but to everything. All the sneezing and wheezing and coughing I'd done, all the pollens and seed puffs and dust that had driven me crazy in those early weeks, didn't bother me at all after that. And I have only those damn bees to thank. I even took to harvesting honey, as I'd been instructed to do, once I developed my technique of waiting for a day with strong breezes on which I build a fire downwind from the hives, a technique I'm still using with only minor refinements. Once the smoke calms them I slide out the combs and take just enough honey to fill my pot made from a hollowed-out stone (I didn't hollow the stone, I found it that way in the trees by my cave, but it works perfectly). I never take more than I'll add to my tea over a couple months' time, and I try not to bother the bees any more than I must, and they haven't stung me again. Maybe they all got their fill of my flesh the first time, or maybe they're making their plans. I don't trust that many animals working together.

Once my allergies faded, there was only the itch of a tunic that may as well have been a hair shirt, and the rash it left on my body. I still spent a long part of each morning scratching, and the itch still woke me sometimes at night. I'd taken to tumbling and rolling on the dewy lawn when I woke, while I waited for my tea water to boil. That was my shower, though without any soap or shampoo, and sometimes it soothed me more than anything could and other times, other days, it didn't soothe me at all. Plant after plant, leaf after leaf, I crushed every green, purple, and even red stem, stalk, and shoot to smear juices and pulps on my erupteous skin (Did I make that word up? I haven't seen a dictionary in a long time, and my imaginary scribe shrugged his imaginary shoulders when I asked him if he knew. "Erupteous," then.) but none of them did me much good.

I'd never had trouble with itching and rashes before I came to the cave. And I was too embarrassed to tell anyone, because how would I tell without speech? I might have lifted my tunic and waggled my wang until somebody noticed, and hoped they'd deliver me cream instead of a slap or a kick, but who's to say? And who would I show? Since moving into his cave, I hadn't seen more of Mr. Crane than his notes, and so far as I knew he was halfway around the world and passing his notes via Smithee or some other employee I hadn't met. Though his helicopter landing suggested that he had come home at least once, if it had been him on board.

I'd seen Mrs. Crane a few times since our first encounter, enlisting me for more berry picking, and sometimes she came and sat beside me on the cave top and talked. One afternoon she'd asked me to spread sunscreen across her back and the backs of her legs as she laid in the sun, and had I been in my right mind I might have thought to smear some of that lotion onto myself, but who could think straight while trying to keep himself calm in the face of all that: the face, and the rest of her, too? With his hands on a woman like that? And my problem wasn't sunburn but rash, after all; maybe her sunscreen had aloe mixed in, but I didn't look away from her body to read the bottle.

But a day or two after I was attacked by the bees, a welcome rain rolled through the garden, breaking a thick haze of heat that had hung on our hillside for days. I stripped off my tunic and had a tumble, wiggling and writhing on grassy green ground until I was wet if not clean and smelled a bit better to my own calloused nose. I did my front first, and wasn't it nice to feel slippery wet grass on my rash-scabby body (I don't know grass species, but this kind had soft blades; I made sure first, because who needs grass cuts in any old place, let alone his tenderest places?) instead of rough fabric. Then I flopped over and with my eyes shut dug both shoulders into the mud and stuck my balls in the air and into the sun, arching my back like a leprous yogi. The mud was cool and the sunlight was hot and between both of those, oh, wasn't that what I'd been needing?

Then somebody coughed and I flopped onto my belly like a fish in a pail, my whole body red as the bird who comes to share my breakfast some mornings, the one with the feathery white peak on his head.

Mr. Crane stood a few feet away in a white-striped gray suit, hands in his trouser pockets and dark glasses hiding his eyes. "Finch," he said as if he hadn't just seen me humping the air or whatever he thought I was doing, as though we'd happened to meet on the street.

I grabbed for my tunic but it was out of reach on the grass where I'd left it before wriggling away in my reverie, so I had to scrabble and crab on my hands and my knees before I could pull it back onto my body. Which probably ended up being less dignified than staying nude would have been. Then I stood at attention or something like it and waited for what he would say.

Mr. Crane stepped past me and kept going, moving away from the house and from me, before he said without looking back, "Walk with me, Finch. I have something to tell you."

Well, I thought, that was that. I'd had a good run in his yard, not as long as I would've liked, but here I was baby-bird naked and wiggling around, and I would fire myself if I came upon that. He'd hired me to be his garden hermit, not a garden-variety pervert.

But I hurried after him all the same, and caught up to walk two or three steps behind him through the bushes and trees.

He led me away from my glade and my cave, down the slope of the hill toward the blackberry brambles, and I thought maybe I had gone too far with his wife, smearing her creams, holding her pails, listening to what she told me instead of ignoring her as she passed by my cave. That he was taking me back to the scene of my crime.

But it wasn't about his wife, or the bushes, or even about me spotting his camera and pretending I didn't know it was there. At least, he didn't mention any of those as we walked right past the tangly brambles where the camera was hidden and down toward the thick band of trees at the base of the hill.

I hadn't spent much time in that part of the garden, especially not since the bees had arrived, though those trees stood only a few minutes' walk from my cave. Most of my walks ended at the top of the hill where the berry patch was. This time, though, we stopped inside the tree line.

I stood behind Mr. Crane as he said, "I was in China recently, Finch. Toured a dam as big as anything you might imagine. A few of my companies did some work on it, so I had to make an appearance for the local officials. You know how these things are. And there I was up on top of the thing, high over the tiny villages on the banks and hundreds of rickety boats and barges and homemade rafts down below, listening to a couple of engineers fight with an economist about how the thing should be built, about unsafe materials and cost-benefit, and that's when I realized what we should do."

He stopped, and the skin around the edges of his dark sunglasses tightened as if he was squinting at something or had in fact closed his eyes, but behind those black lenses, who knows. So I waited, picking grass blades with my toes and lifting twigs, and I plucked a big, bushy spider from my big, bushy beard; after all that time it had become quite a thing, a pale corona around my whole head, thick enough to hold a decent-sized stick or even a small stone, if I wove it in right, and all kinds of other things I had tested it with.

It was so long before Mr. Crane spoke again that I forgot we were talking and was busy scratching myself as if I was alone by the time he went on.

"The river, Finch. The river's the thing. All the life on that water, my God! Those fishermen, their boats, the same families of fishermen catching the same families of fish with the same nets and boats since so long before either one of us was born. Think of it!"

I thought of it because he'd told me to, and thinking of what he told me to was my job. I imagined what the things he'd described might look like based on the little I knew about China, most of it from TV and pictures on the walls of take-out restaurants in the city below his estate. But more than I thought about China I thought that all this preamble seemed a funny way to build up to firing me, so I gained hope something else was afoot.

"Magnificent. They'll have all kinds of new opportunities now, with the dam and the freighters and large-scale fishing coming into the region. Lots of tourism—*lots* of tourism. All kinds of modern convenience, up and down that river." He adjusted his sunglasses. "There's been protest about all the towns being removed for the rising water, of course. There always is. That can't be helped. But one of the engineers said—I really liked this—he said that time is a river, too, and that it's rising over those towns the way it is meant to, so the future can flow in where the past has hung on for too long."

I didn't know what I might say in response to that, so I was glad I didn't need to respond. I stood beside Mr. Crane, unsure where his eyes were behind his lenses, and I tried to look thoughtful in case he was looking at me instead of the trees.

"We should have a river, too, Finch." He reached out an arm and swept it before us from one side of the view to the other, palm down. "Here," he said, "flowing along the base of the hill and down into the valley."

I thought he was just telling me it would be nice to have a river on his property, but then he said, "My people will start tomorrow, early. You may hear them, but I've instructed them to be discreet and to leave you alone. It shouldn't take long. Your work shouldn't be too badly disrupted. There's already an underground lake to tap into. Simple enough. When it's done I'd like to see you in it, of course. Swimming. Floating. Maybe we'll stock some fish for you to catch. Are you much of an angler?"

I shrugged and meant it to say, *I've done some fishing, but I'm no expert, and that was a long time ago,* but I'm not sure Mr. Crane noticed before he kept talking.

"Fishing," he said. "I'll enjoy that."

Then he turned away from me, back toward the hill and back toward the big house that stood hidden over its rise, and he walked away without another glance or word spoken to me. I hurried after him, assuming I was meant to, but he seemed so engrossed in talking to himself about rivers and fishing that I doubt he knew I was still there. So as we passed close to my cave, I went home and watched him head away up the hill, hands clasped behind his back and head bent like a monk or a minister in meditation.

13

Something I've learned about seagulls: they make seven distinct sounds by adjusting the length of a throat or an angle of beak, by expanding their lungs and their chest. I spent today watching gulls gull until I had their whole range worked out. I've been at it for years, taking a crack whenever a gull shows up in the garden. But it's often a long time between visits, and sometimes I forget what I learned before the next gull arrives and allows me to continue observing; sometimes I get so excited about what I'm doing that my poor scribe can't keep up. So I've always had to start over with every gull, until today, until three chatty gulls spent their day with me, squawking and sputtering and providing the concert I needed to finally work out their range. And I silently thanked them for letting me sit close enough—closer and closer through the years of my watching, as my eyes have grown weaker and weaker—to see the shapes of what they were doing. Bird-watching was easier for me when I could still see the birds and not just a red blur or brown spot, a cluster of gray smudges gliding against a gray sky.

In my excitement I needed to let someone know what I'd learned. I wanted to find those hikers and drag them down to the bank where the seagulls were talking so they, too, would learn what I had.

I ran up from the river, past the hum of the hives and along the long wall of blackberry brambles. Overgrown, untended for years by Mr. Crane's invisible landscaping crew, now those bushes tumble downhill all the way to the river. They've driven out flowers and choked out young trees and doubled and tripled in every direction. And they climb past my cave and my crops, all the way up the hill to where the house used to be, and that's where the brambles and berries are thickest. There was nothing else there once the walls were torn down and the helicopter's pavement torn up, not even grass for competition, and the brambles rambled uphill like a backwards avalanche in slow motion, until the long slope I walked down my first day, the slope Mr. and Mrs. Crane walked down to reach me—though never together—became the almost intraversible blackberry maze it is now.

I've managed between my shovel and hoe to cut back the bushes closer to home, but I gave up on the hillside a long time ago; it was never part of my part of the garden, so I didn't lose anything when the bushes took it over. And down below, between my cave and crops and the banks of the river, the berries make a map I can follow by keeping their tangles to one side as I walk. They're a line leading me through the parts of the world I still use.

So I was off up the slope to seek out the hikers, almost to the top I could tell because the hill flattened under my feet, when suddenly my feet tangled in branches and I pitched down into a pile of limbs and leaves, tumbled and twisted and scratched all over my skin. And my right knee, the one already scarred from dragging it over a left behind freezer coil under the river—another of Mr. Crane's abandoned ideas—twisted and popped and sent lightning bolts of pain up my leg sharply enough to churn my stomach and make me groan. Not a word, not a break in my silence, but sound, so much more than I'd made in such a long time. Perhaps since the last time I'd hurt myself badly, which was probably cutting that very same knee underwater.

Cuts and scrapes are an ongoing hazard of living nude, and it has only grown worse since my sight began going. I've broken fingers while stacking stones—my left pinky hasn't been straight for years—and one of my toes is as round as a bulb and throbs on the rare rainy day ever since I dropped a log on it long ago. But the pain in my knee was beyond the pale of those everyday aches. My eyes teared up and my stomach knotted like a towel about to be torn, and I retched on the ground beside me.

That tree limb hadn't been there before. I know this hill, I know this garden. It's my visual memory of familiar spaces that lets me still move through the world, and when something moves but is not moved by me, it knocks my whole world askew. I could already feel my knee swelling, and my whole body throbbed along with it. I was bleeding and sticky with scrapes and small stabs from sharp sticks, a hot ball of fire behind my kneecap, but as I lay there entangled, waiting for my stomach to settle enough to extract myself from the branch, waiting to test my weight on that knee, I came to my senses.

I couldn't tell the hikers about those birds and their sounds, I realized, because it wouldn't make sense. I might have dragged them to the gulls, convinced them to watch and to listen to all seven sounds, but they wouldn't know of my long attempts to learn the range of each creature who comes to this garden—the high and low hums of a beehive, the rolled *r* of a hummingbird's wings, the shriek of a rabbit in those awful seconds when a fox is upon it.

I could have dragged them down to the river, I could have pointed to the gulls vocalizing, but what would that have meant to the hikers who haven't been listening for years? They'll have to work out the world for themselves if it is going to make any sense, and I hope they won't be here long enough to do that. Handing it to them decoded wouldn't mean anything, and it might disrupt the Old Man's plan for them by substituting my own flawed and selfish designs. What do I know about what they need, and about what he wants them to know?

Maybe that branch was blown down by the wind, though I didn't hear much of it blowing last night, and I'm almost certain that limb wasn't lying there when I passed by on my way to the river. Or maybe the hikers dragged it out for some reason, but why would they leave a limb in my trail? However it was actually moved there doesn't much matter, because I know that branch was the Old Man's own doing: it stopped me from sharing more than I should about seagulls and secrets that aren't mine to give.

Falling on that fallen limb made me bite my tongue by scratching up the rest of my body. If they need to know about seagulls, they'll work it out on their own, and the Old Man—not me—will know when it's time. And I'll describe what I've learned to the scribe in my head, in hopes it won't be forgotten. He's good about that, he does his best to keep me from repeating my errors day after day after year, and it's not my scribe's fault when I make the same stupid missteps on slippery, wobbling stones in the river and cast a line into the same empty spots every time I go fish. It's not his fault when I make mistakes I've been making since the river arrived.

After I'd spent some time tangled up in those branches, my stomach calmed down and my knee seemed to plateau at a level of hot, shrieking pain from which it couldn't get worse, so I snapped twigs off around my body and slid my legs gently out of the snarl. I found one strong, straight branch and managed to snap it off against the ground by leaning my full weight upon it, and used it to hoist myself up off the ground. Then I leaned upon it instead of leaning upon my hurt leg. And like that I limped back to my cave, throbbing and bleeding and blind, betrayed by the branches of my own garden and wondering how I would hurt myself next, because it was only a matter of time and of my eyes getting worse, ever worse.

14

The day after Mr. Crane walked me down to the trees, the morning after I wasn't fired and instead heard him wonder aloud about fishing and streams, I climbed as always up onto my cave to wait for the sun. Now that I knew he was home, that he might be watching, I planned to make sure my contemplations were clear and convincing; I wanted him to look out the window at me and know right away how hard I was working. But no sooner had the sun risen than a rumble came through the trees, thunderous sounds from just out of sight past the brambling berries and down the hill where we'd talked about rivers. I heard engines and axes and the voices of men in between those other loud sounds, so I scrambled down from my seat and, holding my cup, I walked through the wet grass to the top of the hill. And those trees were nearly all gone! Bulldozers and diggers and some bright orange truck with an iron overbite and another with a long chainsaw nose were felling trunks left and right while other trucks dragged the downed logs away to wherever.

And where trees had been, where they no longer were, the long necks and shovels of diggers—I'm sure there are other words for the trucks I was watching, but those particular words aren't any of mine—dug a trench through the forest of stumps, deeper and deeper, as wide as that patch of forest had been. Whether they saw me or not, all those men in hard hats and big boots and bright orange vests with reflective silver rectangles on them, they ignored me up above with my breakfast and beard and the great bush of my hair standing up from my head and swaying side to side in the wind—I could see my own shadow—like smoke from a factory roof. Or like steam from the tea I stood sipping as I watched the appearance of what I very soon knew was a river, a river where no river had been the morning before.

What I'd first taken for wishful thinking, for Mr. Crane's wistfulness about rivers when he'd waved his hand out before the two of us in those trees, had erupted into his garden like all the forces of nature assembled at once, bent on the bidding of his desire. He was able to alter the landscape itself—and why did that surprise me, given the garden in which I already lived?—to bring it in line with what he thought it should be. It had never occurred to me that such a thing might be possible, to such a degree, beyond planting trees and landscaping a yard, beyond pruning hedges, but Mr. Crane was building a river, shaping its path and controlling its flow.

I saw Smithee there, too, watching the waterway under construction. He stood in the trees near the trench where the water now flows, writing things down in his notebook and taking pictures of the work in progress with a slim silver camera he pulled from his jacket pocket. What else did he have in there, I wondered? What other tools did Mr. Crane equip his butler with for the tasks of the garden and the estate? His gray suit jacket was starting to seem like a superhero's utility belt.

Then, after a few noisy weeks or maybe a month of rumbling disruption—a time during which I avoided the scene, sticking close to my cave and other parts of the garden—one morning all the diggers were gone and the river had been filled with sparkling blue water. If I had pictured a river, the most perfect example I could imagine, that's the way this river looked its first day: glistening and gleaming in all the right ways and rolling along as if its current had flowed through those trees for all time. It wasn't the Nile or the Amazon, it wasn't so broad that I couldn't cross it or so fast that I couldn't swim. But it was a river that could never be mistaken for anything else.

And that was the first time I watched Mr. Crane work or, to be fair, watched him set other people to work. I'd been set to work by him myself for a few months already by then—based on counting moons, though I may have missed one or two—but I wasn't as impressed by myself as I was by the river. He didn't make me from scratch. He found me as I already was, but the river was his vision writ large on the ground.

The river was so perfect that at first I couldn't convince myself to swim in it. Mr. Crane had told me to before it was made, but flowing before me it seemed too good for my filthy, rash-ridden, foul-smelling form. So for days I sat on its banks from morning to night, after watching the sun rise and until it went down. The bulldozers had piled up perfect banks, too, so I was able to sit with a long view of the water off to both sides, but not too far across the other side of the river, where another high bank kept my gaze low.

I knew rivers had names once they'd been discovered, but I wasn't sure what to call it, and the name hardly mattered considering I wouldn't speak it aloud. Still, I thought about naming it during those first few days on its bank. At first I thought its name should be Mr. Crane's because he'd put it there, and other rivers had been named for less, for people who simply stumbled upon them and weren't even the first to do that. But Crane River didn't seem right. Calling it that reminded me too much of the house and the gates and the fact that the garden where I was meant to forget all the rest of the world was really just someone's backyard. It might be hard for me to meditate well on a river named after a man, not a man I'd read of in history books but a man I actually knew. I indulged myself briefly and considered calling it the River Finch, but that was selfish and silly, and even at the time I don't think I meant it for real.

Of course it revealed itself it to me later, once I was alone in this garden, and now it's hard to imagine pinning someone else's name on something so vast and untethered as the Old Man. But at the time, after thinking about it, I decided there wasn't a need for a name, not from me. Not because I knew yet that a mere name can't encompass a river, but because Mr. Crane had made the river and it was his right to name it if he wanted to.

A few mornings after the river first flowed, I sat on the bank watching sleek black diving birds dart into the water and come up with fish. What kind of bird I don't know. They're sleek and they're black and they fish here most mornings; "divers," I call them, because it's as useful as any word. The fish are just fish pretty much like all others, and they were shipped in and stocked by Mr. Crane while I slept.

I'd become used to how much happened around me without my knowing, even right under my nose. Mr. Crane's garden was like that.

So I sat on the new riverbank watching birds watching fish from the branches, listening to the lapping of water. Then all of a sudden a great booming voice rent the air. It was loud. *LOUD.* So loud the air thickened and the leaves rippled and dark streams of scared birds poured into the sky and...

I may be making a bit much of it. But it was a big, booming voice, coming from speakers I couldn't see somewhere up in the trees, and living in as much quiet as I did, any voice more than a whisper seemed loud to me.

"Finch," the voice said. "Can you hear me, Finch?" As if anything could have *not* heard.

For a second I thought it was God, but of course it was Mr. Crane—the garden was his and so was the river, and so were the loudspeakers over my head.

"I'd like you to swim in the river today," boomed out of bushes and trees.

It was jarring to receive private instructions in such a loud, public way, but I don't suppose anyone else was in earshot except Mr. Crane and his wife and others working for them as I was.

"Swim for a few hours at least. Or perhaps float, instead of swimming. Yes, just float, please, and think about whatever you'd like to."

His words were followed by a few seconds of crackle and hum before the speakers fell quiet again, as quiet as if they weren't hanging overhead in the branches at all and, unable to see them myself, unable to find them even after I'd shimmied and skinned my way up a narrow white birch like an islander after his coconut, the speakers may as well not have been there at all. Except that I knew they were, and so did the birds and the foxes and even the river, whether or not any of them knew what to call the loud noises they'd heard.

But I followed my orders, and why wouldn't I? Why not spend the day floating in a perfect blue river, when I'd been given the chance?

I drifted first on my back, sliding along at the base of the hill in the shadow of piled-earth banks, bouncing from one to the other then paddling back to where I'd begun against a current that looked, somehow, so much swifter than it actually was. If I tossed a stick or a leaf or a raft of bark in the water it sped off right away, but when I settled myself onto the surface it took a long time to start moving and ages to float to the end of the river where it crawled underground and ran away to wherever it ran (who knows where brand-new rivers flow?). And it was as easy to swim against the current as it was to swim with, like the flow was with me even when I could see that it wasn't. It didn't behave like I thought rivers did, but I'd never swum in a river that I'd watched made in a place where no river had been, and they must have ways of being a river that are all their own.

Floating became my routine. I woke in the morning, had porridge and tea, and sat on my cave top until the sun rose and the mist burned away. I watched birds for a while, beaks dipping in and out of their plumage to pick nits and unruffle ruffles, then it was down to the river for me. There's a smooth, sandy spot where the bank slopes into the water, and in the days when I still wore my tunic, that's where I left it behind. It was great to be nude, to be out of that fabric so scratchy and warm, and the water was always just frigid enough to give me a shock but not so cold I couldn't settle into it as I stroked away from the bank and out into the current.

A large tree had fallen from the far bank almost as soon as the river was carved through the estate and began flowing; I say it fell, but to be honest I don't remember it standing, so I'm not sure quite where it fell from. But wherever it came from that tree stretched—and still stretches—out into the stream, making a safe, steady harbor on the days I didn't feel much like drifting or swimming or paying attention to where my body was. I'd paddle across, perhaps pause in the middle to tumble ass-up and dive for the deep, sandy bottom before swimming on toward the tree and resting the soles of my feet against its smooth trunk, like I was standing up into the current, water sliding along both sides of my body while I was held fast with sunlight warming my skin. Some parts of my body had never spent time in the sun, and in those first days on the river they blistered and burned, but even those parts were happy enough to be floating and swimming and sunlit and out of that torturous tunic.

I'd been asked to spend my time thinking but not told about what, so I tried to decide what Mr. Crane might like me to think about on the river but that didn't go anywhere. I wondered sometimes about him, what he did for a living, where all this money for digging rivers and building caves had come from: something to do with construction in China, travels to the Far

East and to Europe and who knows where else. It wasn't my business what Mr. Crane did—I worked for him, not the other way round—yet because he'd been the one to tell me to think about something, the man himself seemed as good a topic as anything else, at least to get myself started. But I didn't know enough about Mr. Crane to consider him for more than a moment, and I found that thinking of money, of Mr. Crane's money and how it was made, distracted me from the contemplations he was paying me for. So I didn't think about him very often.

It takes more effort than people realize to let your thoughts drift, really drift. It's not as simple as starting to think, to daydream, because there need to be both space and time for a daydream to become what it's going to be. With no interruptions, no external pressures, I let my mind lead me wherever it would and the river was a perfect inducement.

I thought about all the birds overhead, whether flying or sitting on branches, and I watched which species were jerks to the others. Blue jays, which I could recognize, seemed among the worst, driving smaller birds off of branches and away from pinecones and bunches of berries. I thought about the itches still itching my tenderest bits and the scabs and sores I'd put there by scratching, though the cold but not too cold water was soothing and sweet on those spots.

Sometimes I hung in the current, suspended, dragging my toes on the sand at the bottom like ten tiny anchors, holding my body upright at an angle with my chin on the lip of the river and my eyes closed and mind calm while hours slipped by without any motion or effort or thoughts passing through. There were sounds and I heard them, and my nose noticed smells and my skin felt cold and warmth and wind passing, of course, all of that, but it was nothing to do with me, any of it. I was just there, in the water, floating, submerged, and the world could do as it liked because

I was right where I needed to be. There was nothing I had to accomplish except what I'd already done by being there, nothing expected of me beyond being placid, being Mr. Crane's garden hermit, and nothing I was meant to change from one day to the next or the next unless he asked me to change it. I might spend the year, two years, seven years, floating on the same river in the same pose every day. My body might change, my beard and my hair would grow longer—and already they rippled around me, fanned on the river like a tangled logjam—but those changes would happen with or without any mind paid to them. I was becoming as gentle on the river, on the world, as the dragonfly who stood on the riverine island of my exposed nose with delicate dragonfly feet, unfurling its wisp of a tongue for sips of water so small that their absence would never be noticed.

I made sense in the river and the river made its own sense in me. How else can I say it but that?

15

Once the river became part of my practice and part of my day, Mr. Crane had other ideas. The river remained, and I kept swimming, but he made additions to the garden one after another. There were peacocks who didn't last long, screeching and squawking in harsh voices at odds with their beauty, and I was glad to see them go a few days after they came (though I can't say whether they wandered off on their own or were rounded up and removed by unseen wranglers).

A tree house was built, a square platform, really, and I was asked to move my sunrise meditations from the roof of my cave to the tree. I made the shift though I didn't enjoy it: the angle from the tree to the horizon was wrong, and the branches were too thick with green leaves and blocked the best part of the view. Then another note asked me to do tai chi moves in the tree instead of just sit. I'd tried tai chi soon after settling into the garden, with no idea how it was done, and I'd been glad when I was asked to end the charade. Now I was back to faking tai chi but this time a good twenty feet in the air, on a platform without any railings or sides, and surrounded by branches that swayed in the wind and were thick enough to sweep me right over the edge.

So my treetop tai chi, such as it was, wouldn't have been too impressive if anyone had been able to see it behind all those leaves so high in the air. I was satisfied with not falling off, never mind faking the moves in a convincing way, and was relieved when the platform was removed overnight and I went back to watching the sunrise from my cave as I had been doing before.

Every so often a new animal wandered into my cave, sometimes at night, leaving only strange tracks, and sometimes in daylight so I saw who it was. I met porcupines, ferrets, and foxes in several colors, and deer and rabbits too many to count. I didn't know if they'd come to the garden by nature, wandering in from the surrounding mountains or up from the city below, or if they'd been introduced like the peacocks. It didn't much matter to me; they were there, so was I, and I liked watching them go about their foxish or owlish or rabbitish work. In reality, I discovered, animals didn't do as much as they did on TV—I had to wait days, sometimes, to see as much activity as I'd seen in five minutes of a good nature show—but they were still pretty exciting. They smelled worse in real life, but I was in no position to hold that against somebody else.

I met several skunks including the one who'd wandered into the cave my first night in the garden, the first I'd ever encountered who wasn't a cartoon. They were good neighbors, for the most part, and the one time I got sprayed it was my own fault: I tripped over a fat, waddling skunk in the dark, not looking where I was going. If somebody stepped on my back, I might even spray them myself. The smell was horrible, of course, but worse was the burning in my ears and throat, and after a long, painful night of wheezing and retching a large kettle of tomato juice appeared in my cave with a note that said what it was for (I wouldn't have known otherwise). I scrubbed and I scoured myself and it made me smell better but didn't do much for my tunic, its tangled, tough threads holding onto the scent for as long as I wore it thereafter. Not all the time, not every second, but when a wind blew the right way or a day became hot, sharp tangs of skunk

wafted up from my clothes and made my eyes water all over again
and burned the back of my throat. Another reason I'm glad to be
rid of that garment.

But I couldn't blame the skunks for being themselves. And
watching them waddle, watching them snort and root in the
ground, more than made up for the stink they had only once laid
upon me. And, to be fair, I never saw one of those skunks spray
again. They struck the pose sometimes, when I got too close; they
raised tail and shook bum and went through the motions of
spraying, but they never cast anything out. They always looked as
surprised as I was that they weren't spraying, but I guess we grew
used to each other. Once I knew they weren't going to spray, I
could walk right up to pet them, and could scratch behind their
twitching ears. Sometimes they were too vigorous returning the
favor and tore into my wrists with their claws, but I think skunks
mostly get a bad rap.

And the skunks and foxes were small potatoes—or small
animals who later learned to eat my potatoes—compared to who
arrived next. I woke one morning like I would any other, turned
to my nook where breakfast sat steaming, and unrolled the note
curled beside it. "A lion has been released into the garden," it read.
"It has been trained to befriend you."

A lion! In the garden. *My* garden, with me and my beat-
skipping heart.

And it had been trained to befriend me. What did that mean?
How did a lion make friends and, more importantly, I thought,
why would it *want* to with me? The only training I could imagine
was rewards of meat when a lion was friendly, one fleshy treat
after another as it learned to behave, and that method seemed
plausible enough in my head except for one flaw: I happened to
be made of meat, tender meat, without very much clothing to get
in the way. A lion could almost be excused if it mistook me for a
snack, for an oddly shaped training morsel.

Had I known of some other method, had I known *something* about how lions are trained, I might not have been so afraid that I crawled back under my blankets, pulled them up to my nose—missing sunrise for the first time since I'd come to the garden—and waited for the lion to walk in and eat me.

But the lion didn't show up, and later that day, itching to swim, itching from too long spent under my blankets, I decided to emerge and face my fears like a man, or at least like a mouse (which I remembered lions were supposed to be scared of, so letting my inner mouse out might for once serve me well).

On hesitant toes I crept to the mouth of the cave, to scan the garden for lions before I committed to going outside. But I stuck my face into the sunlight and there he was, sitting beside my fire ring like he'd been waiting all morning for me to wake up. The lion turned his massive head toward me, and with his broad brown face and rippling corona of mane, he looked an awful lot like the sun. A big, brown, furry sun right outside the mouth of my cave.

I jumped back inside but didn't land well, turning my ankle and collapsing onto the cold ground. The lion rose from his haunches, shook his head so a cloud of fur erupted around him like a blown dandelion, then took three steps forward straight into my home. My heart raced, and I kicked backward across the ground until my shoulders were against the pallet and I had nowhere else to go.

And the lion took three more steps before hanging his muzzle right in front of mine, so close I could feel his hot breath drying out my nostrils and eyes, and he yawned. Right in my face, a long, creaking yawn, then he laid down on the floor at my side and he went to sleep. At least, I think he was sleeping. His eyes were closed and he wasn't eating me, that much I can say for certain.

I was glad to survive, but as lions go I was pretty let down. I thought he would be ferocious, I thought he'd be loud, roaring and rumbling and chasing me with his teeth bared for fun before tearing me down and chewing me up. I thought he would act like the lions I'd seen on TV, but he didn't, not really. I hadn't looked forward to being eaten, but I had been excited for seeing a lion. But this one acted more like one of my former neighbors' cat—I never knew which neighbor, not that it mattered—who used to sleep on the *Welcome* mat in front of my door and make me step over to get home after work.

I had a better chance of eating this lion than he had of eating me. Still, it was exciting to sit so close to an animal I'd never expected to meet, to see how much longer his body was than I'd imagined, stretched out across the floor of my cave, and to see his long tongue loll out the side of his mouth and drip a pool onto the stone. I'd learned that lions aren't vicious and wild, but models of patience and peace. He could teach me something about meditation, this lion, I thought, so I left him sleeping on the floor by my bed, on top of the woolly blankets I'd flung to the floor getting up, and I went down to the river to float and to think of how I might be as quiet and calm as a lion.

He was gone from the cave when I walked back for lunch, though it still smelled of his hot body and breath—not an unpleasant smell, either; it made the cave cozy and warm and made me wonder if anyone sold scented candles with the aroma of lion (not that I needed candles, because I had the real thing in my garden).

And I decided that evening, while sitting over tea by my fire, that I would call the lion "Jerome." It seemed like a nice, gentle name for a nice, gentle lion. I didn't expect to speak it aloud, but it gave me something to call him in my meditation, and it was easier to aspire to emulate something if I knew its name.

And in this case its name—his name—was Jerome.

I didn't see him again for a couple of days, and that time I was down by the water washing some rust- and blood-colored stones I had found. I thought they'd look nice along the edge of a niche in my cave. Crouched over the river, dunking my stones, I didn't notice Jerome approaching until his reflection fell over mine on the water. I stood, and started to turn so I could scratch his head or give him a pat, but before I could reach out he leapt toward me, claws extended, teeth bared, and a rumble tumbling out of his mouth like an earthquake rising up through the ground.

I don't know how I survived and wasn't eaten, but somehow I did. Somehow I fell backward into the water at just the right second or fraction of one for his claws to swipe the air where I'd been but no longer was. And somehow the current—that mysterious current—pushed me away before Jerome landed with a wet thump on the spot where I'd crouched in the sand. I swam, I paddled, I panicked as hard as I could to the log at midriver where I liked to float and I climbed up onto it before turning toward shore. I didn't know if lions could swim, or if Jerome would, but he seemed to have lost interest in me and was viciously attacking his own reflection, slashing and biting the water, pouncing and rolling with only himself in his grip, and casting a cloud of sand, dust, and spray up into the air.

And then, quick as quick, his whole body froze, his ears perked up straight, and his head cocked toward a sound he'd heard but I hadn't. Then he not so much roared as growled deep inside, without his mouth even moving, and ran away into the trees.

Heart pounding, whole body shaking, I stayed on the log with my knees pulled up to my chest. I sat until I was too hungry to sit any longer, by which time the sun was already low, then I quietly, carefully swam back to shore and crept as softly as I could, with as much mousiness as I could muster, up to my cave for some food and in hopes Jerome wouldn't be waiting for me in my bed.

I knew wolves did that sort of thing, but I wasn't sure about lions.

He wasn't there, though. He wasn't anywhere. Instead I found a note on the floor of my cave where it must have fallen unnoticed from my breakfast tray. It told me—not in time!—that Jerome's "pacification" had been adjusted after problems the previous day, and that I might notice differences in his behavior.

And I supposed that I had, as the note promised. There was another note the next day, telling me—as if I didn't know—that there had been some problems with the adjustment, and that they would be sorted out. But I didn't see Jerome that day to test his new dosage (I assumed his pacification was drugs) or for a while after that. Perhaps he'd been taken into the house for his treatment, until he could act more like a lion should act, however that might turn out to be. Or perhaps his correctly dosed medication had made him curl up in some quiet part of the garden for a long nap. Either way, I felt like I'd helped him a little, like the extra dosage had been a thorn in his paw and I'd been the one to pull it out, and I hoped he'd remember that favor the next time we met.

16

This part of the world isn't known for its seasons, but one afternoon not long after Jerome's arrival, as I walked back to my cave from the river, there was as much a suggestion of autumn as I'd ever seen. It was nothing as grand or as grounding as leaves going orange or falling from trees into piles, or frosted pumpkins marching through yellow-grassed fields, none of what catalogs sell as the autumnal mystique of New England. But the air changed that day. It was a little bit sharper drawn into my lungs, a coarse touch in the back of my throat. Maybe those hills were so high even the climate was different, with those down below accepting a world without seasons, one endless summer in which some days were slightly cooler than others and never knowing that up in the hills seasons came and went in ways unimagined. Maybe, like sunsets, the seasons were buried under pollution. The only leaves I'd ever seen change in the valley had been those on rare tree-lined stretches of highway, where exhaust fumes painted brown stripes every fall.

The air in the garden was crisp, and the apples in Mr. Crane's orchard to the east of my glade were red and ripe and pulling their branches so close to the ground that whether I was meant to or not I reached up and plucked one to taste. The apple was dull, even drab, without the shine I'd come to expect, and it took me a moment to realize this was the first apple my mouth ever met without the mask of wax and chemicals, the first apple I'd eaten that was only and wholly an apple. That apple started my apple-eating life over, and I silently thanked Johnny Appleseed for his scattershot planting, for founding a nation on forbidden fruit.

Second Nature had experimented with an indoor orchard once; it was expensive, but the price included a service in which Orch-ease crop technicians (Orch-ease was a word I'd invented myself, though I'd never intended for it to be used; it was a daydreaming doodle seen by the wrong eyes) would come to the client's chosen location throughout the seasons to hang plastic leaves and then blossoms, returning to replace them with plastic apples in advancing stages of color, then to pick the whole yield and haul them to storage along with the leaves until the next year's cycle of seasons began.

Orch-ease hadn't taken off, and no wonder. Who wants to stare at apples all day knowing they can't be eaten, or to be reminded that the apples they *are* eating, the waxy, too-shiny supermarket produce they've purchased, is as far from the real thing as those plastic imposters? And Orch-ease had been costly, requiring all those site visits, so while only a man like Mr. Crane could afford a fake orchard, he could also afford the real thing.

As I walked home from the river, crunching my apple, I spotted a crew of men in orange vests and hard hats. They may have been the same crew that installed the river, or not, but they stood near my cave beside something that looked like a cement mixer with a long black hose running from it. As I drew closer I heard the whir and whine of motors and blowers inside the truck, and as I watched the men hoisted that hose and sprayed wet, sticky snow all over the top and sides of my cave, all over the ground by my door, and made a small pile—a drift, I suppose—in its mouth.

They were close to my cave, too close for me to pass unnoticed, not that they'd be surprised someone lived there. They must have noticed my pallet and possessions and home. I hid behind snow-blanketed blackberry bushes to watch them at work and to wait until I could slip past. My feet were freezing, and my fingers were too; I wasn't dressed for winter in my short, sleeveless tunic.

The snowblower shuddered and shook while it spewed white foam into the air in thick streams that broke up and drifted back to the ground in soft flakes, softer and whiter than seemed possible from the horrible sound of that machine's engine and its stink of burned oil and gas.

When the snow finally stopped blowing and the snowblower sputtered to a rattling stop, rattling almost as loud as my own cold bones, the workers wound up their hose and levered levers on the sides of the truck. I hoped the snow would prevent that truck's tracks from taking too hard, and that I wouldn't be left with a reminder of its intrusion for long.

The men lit cigarettes and stood smoking outside my home, talking and laughing. I couldn't hear most of what they were saying, but it was something about Mr. Crane, something about how he'd demanded they not disrupt his estate, work out of sight, and where—as one worker put it—"that rich shit" could stick it. Then the other took off his hard hat and rubbed his bald head, and said something about Mr. Crane being in the newspaper that morning. He didn't explain about what, he didn't have to, because the other worker said yes, he'd seen it, too, and they both laughed.

The bald man holding his hat said more, but I caught just "only paper in town he doesn't own." Then they flicked their spent cigarettes into my fire ring (at least I could thank them for that), climbed into the truck, and were gone to other parts of the garden from which I could still hear the rumbling of men and machines. At last I could return on numb feet to my cave.

I'd never seen snow before, not in real life, and I was amazed it could come from machines. With the men working elsewhere, I took that chance to lay in the snow by my doorway, tumbling and rolling and slipping about, trying to make an angel the way I'd seen children do on TV, but I didn't get it quite right: my snow angel looked more like the pedestrian figure on crosswalk signs.

I was bothered by the men blowing snow on my world, not by the snow but by the presence of the people who'd made it. I was always thrown off when Mr. Crane's projects involved a disruption, a presence apart from my own. I liked that my meals came anonymously, I liked that I never saw who was maintaining the blackberry bushes and trees. So to see a whole crew of workers in orange vests, to hear the rumble and roar of snow machines and truck engines—or to have seen the crew making the river with bulldozers and diggers and dynamite—it always took a few days to recover, to put the intrusion out of my mind and for the garden to feel like my garden again.

Though for the moment, it wasn't my garden. Not the way I usually knew it. The snow wasn't any colder, really, than the river in the morning, but it was cold in a new way: the waters of the river are always moving, so the cold is like a cloud passing over. The chill of that snow hung on my body like some backwards blanket, but for all that was cozy in its cold way. I thought I could give myself up to that kind of cold, drift to sleep and forget to wake up, though maybe I thought so because it was numbing my nerves and my brain and everything else while I tried to create my first angel. Even my rash, which had flared on the short walk from river to home as my fiery thighs brushed together, had been cooled in the snow. There had been a bit of a sting and a shock in my balls as wet snow splashed up my tunic, but after those first startling seconds everything down there went quiet and calm, and I felt wonderfully still both in body and mind.

I thought of a painting I'd seen, or a photograph, maybe—or was it a scene from a movie?—of an old man in a dark coat and hat standing alone in a snow-covered field, hands in his pockets, the sky above him the same deep shade of white as the ground, and framed by a few skeletal trees filled with crows. I remembered wondering, as I'd looked at that image, whether birds hibernate in their trees. In the snow-covered garden, lying on the cold, thickened ground, I imagined myself in the man's place, out standing in my field like a shadow cast on the white world.

But my fingers turned blue and my toes went numb—no wonder people wear socks and gloves in colder climates—so I went into the cave to warm up. I lit a bit of a fire in the smaller ring of stones I'd laid just inside the cave after getting rained on while cooking outside a few times. It was early for dinner, though the bucket containing my stew was already in its nook, leftover from lunch, with a ragged, hand-torn hunk of bread at its side. I set my feet against the outside of the stone ring, and as the rocks became warm a tingle went through my toes and soles, then that tingle grew painful, and I realized I'd let my body grow colder and more numb than I'd thought and now had burnt my bare feet. I've wondered, since then, how close I came to getting real frostbite from that fake snow, and losing some of my toes.

It was cold that night in my cave. Whether it was meant to happen that way or not, whether the truck and its crew spent those hours of darkness right outside my door with their fans and their hoses and vests, all night long while I tried to sleep puffs and spurts of snow blew into my face and under my blankets and wedged tiny ice cubes between my toes (they'd melted away when I reached down to pluck them out, though the skin was still cold where they'd been).

The next morning I crawled from my pallet with stiff joints and sore bones and, I was sure (though apparently wrong), a touch of frostbite on my burn-blistered feet. I'd had enough of winter already. I set my small fire, ate my porridge, and boiled my tea, but when I tried to climb to the cave top I couldn't get purchase on the ice-coated walls, and spilled hot tea all over myself. It was too cold to sit on the ground and too cold to tumble in snow, and there wasn't any dew-dripping grass to roll in, so I ate my breakfast indoors for the first time since arriving in Mr. Crane's garden. I tried to have my morning meditation in the cave, too, but couldn't get anywhere with it because there was nothing to watch but my own flickering shadow cast by the small fire onto the gray wall, no birds and no foxes and no clouds on the ceiling, no swaying green trees or flowing blue river to catch my attention and lead it away.

The second time I emerged from my cave that day, the snowblowing crew had returned and was piling more snow on spots that had grown bare as the sun warmed them up, and making tall drifts even taller where shadows kept the ground cool. Near the mouth of my cave, buried halfway underground, I found a vent I was sure hadn't been there the morning before, blowing icy, cold air into my home, which explained why I'd struggled to sleep. There was even a camouflaged speaker beside it with a loop of howling winds and what I took to be clattering icicles, playing again and again like a call from the deep heart of winter.

I walked to the river, hoping the movement might warm me up, and on the way I noticed more speakers and vents at the bases of trees and in what I'd previously taken for rocks, so it was cold everywhere in my garden and the howling of wind could not be escaped.

I should have expected it after all that, but I was surprised to find the river stilled by a thick skin of ice, the first frozen water I'd ever seen that wasn't in a kitchen or rink. The ice held the orange shadows of workers toiling downstream, doing something at the edge of the water with long pipes that ran under the ice. In its way—in any way, really—the frozen river was beautiful; though the ice itself wasn't moving, I could still see the current flow underneath, rippling and churning as it always did, and I felt warmer already just watching the river refuse to give in to the winter thickening its water. I realized, thanks to the river and its wise example, I needed to keep my own waters flowing whatever the surface became. It was cold, I was disoriented, but I had a purpose that had to be met: I was meant to swim in the river, and whatever men in whatever vests were there and whatever sounds swelled from speakers suspended in iced-over trees, I was going to swim because that's what I did every day.

From the riverbank I spotted Jerome poking his way along the shore, sniffing and snorting and swishing his tail, scratching one lean yellow side against a tree bent by the snow. Mr. Crane's workers eyed him nervously from the edge of the ice, though they were a good distance downstream. They must have been told he was harmless, they must have been told he was trained, but he was still a lion if not such a leonine one. I couldn't blame them for worrying, because against all that snow, in that blank world of white, their safety vests made them stand out like peppers on ice cream and perhaps like snacks for a lion.

Jerome started across the frozen river but only made it a couple of steps before all four of his paws slipped in different directions and he fell to his belly, spinning like animals do in cartoons when walking on ice. He tried to get up a couple of times with no more success, then he gave a sad groan—the opposite of a roar, if there is one—and retreated to the bank, then wandered out of my view up the hill toward the house.

I found a large gray rock, silver-specked and the size of my head with one pointed end, and I scuttled over the ice on hands and knees, pushing the stone ahead of me until I'd reached the deep center. At first I tapped gently, trying to chip at the ice, but it was thicker than I'd imagined (much later I discovered the reason for this was freezer coils installed in the river itself, something I'd missed while watching it under construction). So I swung the rock harder, with both hands and from over my head, but that knocked me off balance each time I brought my arms down and pushed me around on the ice. Those blows made a tight web of fine cracks, but I still couldn't get to the water. I tried standing up and dropping my rock, first from knee height and then from my chest, and at last from overhead, which worked out too well because the surface of the river suddenly splintered and split, and the rock and I plunged through together into the arctic waters below.

My body was shocked and instantly stiff, and I tried to scramble back out of the hole but had already drifted away and was under the still-solid ice sheet downstream. I panicked, pounding at the ice with my fists and my feet, kicking and punching and clawing in vain. My lungs became tighter, my head swam and swirled, then all of a sudden—how can I explain this? how might it make sense?—all of a sudden I felt all over calm, comforted the way I've felt in my bed when swaddled in blankets and sheets, and the Old Man put me at ease. I hadn't come to call him that yet, that name wasn't mine yet to know, but I felt his presence in the garden for the first time that day—something I realized much later, looking back on that day. I knew just by knowing that I was fine, that I would be fine, and the river wasn't going to harm me. I knew all was well and that all would be well. I had honored my side of our silent bargain by coming to swim even when waters were frozen over, swallowed up by Mr. Crane's winter, so the Old Man honored his side of things, too.

I floated underwater as I had floated so often above. I drifted beneath the ice, which was so clear in places that I could look up to the incongruous blue sky above—the reach of Mr. Crane's winter was only so far; it couldn't reach into the air—and I felt warmer than I had a right to, warmer than it made sense for my body to be. I'm not saying I breathed underwater, I'm only saying that I didn't drown. There was always a pocket of air trapped under the ice right where I needed a pocket to be. And when I knew it had been long enough for my day's swim to count, I turned and carried myself against the current back to the hole I'd made in the ice, where I lifted myself without any problems and made my way to the shore.

It was colder in the air than it had been below, and my sopping, thick tunic was no help at all nor were my bare feet, so I all but sprinted uphill to my home, beating my arms and hands against my chest and my sides, taking high, comic steps to make the blood flow through my legs as hard as it could and to prevent myself tripping in snow, slipping and sliding with every step. And when I got into my cave I stripped off my garment—already frozen and stiff—and wrapped up in my blankets and started a fire and warmed my feet on the stones as I'd done the evening before, too cold to feel the pain they should have been in.

The next morning winter was over, as quickly as it had come; the snow truck was gone and the wind had stopped howling and the cold was no longer piped into my cave—even the vents had been hidden or moved. The river had thawed and it flowed as fast and as free as it ever had, and I floated all day on its surface while clouds floated on their own deep blue sea overhead. Everything was back to the way it belonged, but none of it was quite the same now that the Old Man had revealed himself to me.

When I accepted Mr. Crane's offer, when I came to this garden, I thought I'd have a few years with an interesting job in which I might figure out what I was going to do afterward and would end up with the money to do it. But after that morning spent under the ice, after the river's own voice spoke to me—so to speak—I knew there was nothing else after this, nothing else for me outside. I was finally doing what I was meant to, I had found my place, and I might have missed that if not for the ice.

Rather than the end of my seven-year term releasing me into the rest of my life, making me rich and ready to take on the world, it loomed now like an exile I knew was approaching. I would be cast from the garden, a pauper with millions of dollars. And already the moon had been full ten or eleven or even twelve times since my arrival, so my term of employment was creeping away toward that no longer distant deadline.

But thinking like that made my garden no longer feel mine; it broke the illusion Mr. Crane and I had built up together and it made my day hard to get on with. There were still a few years to go on my contract, and hadn't I only just learned from the river to trust? To go under the ice with full faith? So I shook my head clear and got on with what needed doing, which was more or less nothing at all and everything that there could be. I got on with what I'd been hired to do.

17

This morning they followed me down to the river. It was unnerving to have them so close. It was one thing to walk by their tent, to overhear zippers and buckles and the bodily noises of morning, but another to have them walking behind me, their steps obviously shuffling and slowed to keep pace with my hobbling as I picked my way down the path on my stick, favoring my swollen knee and also sore where that rough stick rubbed my ribs and armpit raw. But it looks like I'll have to keep using it for some time, the way my knee isn't healing, so I'll be calloused there soon enough. Like everything that gets introduced—the river, a lion, some snow—that stick will become part of my practice, and if they stay long enough I suppose those hikers will, too.

It's hard to forget I'm in pain, that my encroaching blindness is making this life of mine less possible by the day, when there's someone—two someones!—close by to remind me. When I paused on my three-legged walk to the river, they paused, too, and I heard them rooting around in blackberry bushes and feigning interest in trees along the path as if I wouldn't know they were only stopping for me. And that made me try to walk faster, to thump along with my stick at a dangerous pace, and inevitably I twisted my knee again and almost fell before reaching the river. But I didn't, I stayed on my feet, and got into the water where my wounds could soak.

I felt the weight of their eyes as they watched from the bank, as if waiting for what I would do, as if I would do more than float, more than think, more than ache and try to ignore it. Their expectations—the ones I assigned them—were heavy hands holding me underwater. I paddled for the deepest part of the river, out to the midpoint between its two shores, to a distance across which their gaze might burn with less heat, and I pretended as well as I could they weren't watching. I did what I do every day: I floated and sometimes fluttered a kick or a stroke to keep away from the shore. I moved no more than I needed to, I kept my body as calm as the water and hoped my mind would reach that calm, too. And though it usually does, it couldn't with those two blurry bodies up high on the bank and the eyes I couldn't see looking but all the same knew were upon me.

The two of them were standing so close together that their hazy shapes merged into one, a jumble of tan skin and bright colors of clothing, standing out against the trees and the sky behind them. Mostly because they moved faster than anything in the background—it was their motion that gave them away. Otherwise it would have been easy enough to pretend they weren't there; that's one thing about losing my vision: I can always erase what I don't want to see and can rely instead on old memories of what I saw when I last had a clear look. I can still see the banks of the river with no one upon them, and if those hikers hadn't drawn in my eye with their movements I might have been able to overwrite them up on the bank with an older image of what it looked like. But they stood between those memories and me.

I could have stood to imagine that he wasn't there but she was, flaming red hair and bare feet, slipping out of her shorts on the sand. Crossing her arms to grip the bottom of her orange tank top and, arching her back, stomach drawn in, peeling it over her head and pale, rose-tipped breasts emerging like twin sunrises from under the fabric and...

Forgive me my excess; it's been a long time. I don't know how long exactly, but long enough that I'd never imagined seeing a woman's body again, and given the unexpected chance, my eyes and my mind were too weak to take her all in, even to fill in the gaps between what I could see and what I wanted to. I'd never imagined seeing another man's body, either, apart from my own, but there would have been no joy in watching that young, muscled reminder of all I am not. That's another small mercy of this blurred veil—I can avoid looking closely at what I don't want to see.

I listened to the soft splash, and the whisper of stones and sand underwater as the hikers stepped into the river. They didn't shiver or shriek at its cold, and they kept their distance, paddling close to the bank. So I stretched on my back as I do every morning and set adrift with my eyes on the clouds, spotting an alligator chased by a rabbit, a cash register doling out quarters. Clouds are about all I'm left with these days, because the more blurred they become the more shapes I can turn them into. The whole world has been remade of clouds, in a way, and all day my eyes follow the drifting shapes of objects that aren't really there and I imagine what they might be.

It leads me to wonder about the things I must be forgetting. About all the things I don't have a clear enough picture of to ever recall them again, and the things I haven't described to my scribe well enough that he'll be able to remind me at some future point when I ask. In my mind's eye, I can still look at Mr. Crane's house on the hill, and the view of the ocean far off past the hills, though the house is long gone and I haven't been able to see as far as the ocean for a very long time. But everything before my arrival here in the garden, all the things I put behind me thinking I'd never need them again, those I feel slipping away.

Not that I need them, not that they matter any more now than they did when I could still see. But it reminds me, this creeping shadow across my memories, how little I really remember and how little of me even my faithful scribe knows. And it makes me wonder—perhaps even worry—how much else will be lost with my sight when it finally goes dark after all.

I have to give those hikers credit: once they settled into the water, once they let themselves drift, they were able to keep themselves quiet. Not silent, not still as the river is still, but quiet enough to make sense. Enough to seem like they knew what they were doing. Once or twice, for a moment, I almost forgot they were there. I almost reached a depth of concentration I haven't achieved since they've been here.

I listened as they looked for a position in which they could float. I heard bodies turning one way and another, sliding from place to place on the water, then finally they moved to a spot upstream from my own. I could tell by the change in the water, as they swam away with their ripples. I could tell by the way their failed whispers echoed to me on the water, as they clutched at each other for balance and laughed. The spot they moved to is one I avoid, where a left behind freezer coil hides under the water, overlooked by Mr. Crane's workers when they removed his machines. Years ago it sliced my knee open as I swam above it, and gave me a jagged red scar.

They'd have to be careful, I knew. They'd have to watch where they swung their legs and feet underwater and be vigilant if they dove, to avoid the sharp edges concealed now by grasses and vines after resting there so many years.

I waited, expecting to hear one or both of the hikers cry out when their flesh found metal, but not because I hoped they'd be hurt. I imagined their wonder after the cut, the questions they might ask each other about what that strange object was and why it hid under the water—a mystery for them but just part of the garden for me, a story I know but don't know how to tell. Not to them, anyway, not aloud.

So we swam, the hikers and I, but my meditations were shallow and stalled because I was tense with anticipation of the sounds of their pain. Sounds that never came; they never found that freezer coil, or else they weren't hurt badly enough to complain or cry out. Perhaps the Old Man saved that mystery for them to find on some other day.

When I felt the sun on the far side of my face, the afternoon side, I rolled onto my stomach and headed for shore. The hikers noticed and followed me in, waiting a few yards behind, I think, before coming out of the water. Back onshore my stick wasn't quite where I'd left it, and I felt around on the sand with desperate hands, trying to hold my sore knee off the ground, but it was hard to crawl and to search at the same time while crabbing on only one leg.

Then there were footsteps, his legs on the edge of my sight, and the stick slid right into my hand. Not a word spoken, not a sound made, and the hikers retreated in silence while I climbed to my foot and my branch and hobbled away toward my cave, the top of the stick digging into my side and armpit with each step. I went no faster than I had walked to the river, but this time they didn't follow. Not closely enough to be noticed.

18

I never knew how to behave when I found one of Mr. Crane's cameras concealed in the garden. Should I act as if it wasn't there, like I hadn't noticed, go on with my goings-on unaffected to preserve the illusion of being alone and unwatched? So many of the cameras were disguised as parts of the landscape, on stalks slim as stems and rising up through the center of a burst of real flowers with only shining lenses to give them away, and only then when they reflected the sun and drew me over to search in the brush. Or they were the kind of dome camera you might find on a ceiling, forming the base of a beehive in branches high over the river, or a large glassy knot on the trunk of a tree. Once what I thought was a turtle paddled past on the water as I meditated in the lee of my usual log, and as it swam by I could have sworn its eyes were cameras and I heard the whir of tiny motors as they swiveled my way, but I never encountered that turtle again.

The stranger cameras, the ones I was most puzzled by, were more obvious. Much more. They were black plastic boxes bolted to trees or badly concealed beneath bushes, standing on thin metal mounts an inch or two high, allowing them only a short range of swivel. I couldn't understand why Mr. Crane had gone to such lengths to preserve the illusion, so carefully concealing most of his tools, only to give it away with these other clumsy devices. The more obvious cameras annoyed me, not that I could complain. I learned over time to pretend that the cameras disguised as flower stems were real flowers, and if I passed the same flowers and camera every day it was possible for me not to notice unless I looked for it. But those other cameras, the clunky black boxes—once I knew where they were it was over. There was no denying, no ignoring and no going on as things were, because they sucked my eyes in like a black hole sucks in light whenever I passed through their view. I knew they were there, and often when my meandering brought me near one of those awkward lenses I changed direction, set a new course to the river or berry bushes or wherever I had been headed to avoid the disruption of those too vivid distractions.

Had I been able, I would have asked Mr. Crane about those warts on the face of his garden. Why the difference, why so little effort where so much was made otherwise? But I went on with my business of not doing business, my mornings spent on the river and my afternoons under the trees and my evenings spent sitting outside, then sleeping inside my cave. I went on as if none of those cameras were there, and I was as convincing as I could be even when one of those boxes threw off a whole day's meditation; how could I concentrate on not concentrating, how could I let things just happen, when I knew I was being observed and couldn't pretend otherwise?

I tried to float past those cameras as gently as I tried to float on the river, with my mind emptied the way I'd read could be done and thought I should be doing, but each time I told my mind to be empty, images of emptiness flooded in: cardboard boxes, abandoned houses, thousands of left behind cars jamming both sides of the freeway after some unspecified but horrific disaster. Cameras hanging from the trees with no one to watch what they filmed. I knew there was a trick to it, a means of erasure and of accomplishing blankness without letting my mind know what I was doing, but what that trick was I had not yet figured out.

Strange to think how hard it was, and how smoothly it comes to me now—I wouldn't say it's like riding a bike, but more like breathing: it happens before I remember I even know how.

One afternoon, deep in frustration from failing to quiet the hum of my mind, and surprisingly tired from the effort of staying still (but if exercise is, as they say, ninety-nine percent mental, why be surprised when thinking hard takes a toll on the body?), I rolled over onto my stomach to paddle along with the current and swim to the end of the river where the water disappears underground. As my eyes scanned the bank where I'd left my tunic—checking the whereabouts of my belongings was a habit I hadn't yet managed to lose, even with no one to take them but fleet-fingered foxes and crows—I was surprised to see Mrs. Crane sitting beside my pile of filthy, dark fabric. She wore a tight white tank top, and a bright blue and green skirt like tourists wear in pictures promoting South Pacific vacations. She noticed me looking and smiled, then waved across the water.

I wasn't sure if I should respond to her presence the way I would have had her husband showed up on the bank. As on our first berry-picking excursion, and all our other encounters, I wondered if I should treat her as an employer or colleague or part of the garden. Her position wasn't as clear as my own, or her husband's, or the birds' who nested nearby. Should I go on with my floating like she wasn't there, the work I was being paid for, or should I abandon my already broken reflections and swim to shore, acknowledge her arrival as ordinary politeness required? I knew there were a couple of cameras nearby, one lens concealed in the knot of a tree on the bank and another, a clumsier one, bolted to a branch just beneath it. Why two cameras on the same tree, I didn't know.

With my tunic left behind on the bank and Mrs. Crane sitting beside it, I couldn't emerge from the water; I couldn't even float on my back without showing her more than she no doubt wanted to see. But how long had she been there? How much had she already seen? And wasn't I meant to go about my hermitic business of swimming and thinking and shedding my clothes as if my employer weren't watching at all? That's what he was paying me for. So if Mrs. Crane wanted to watch me swim naked, maybe that was her right as mistress of the estate. At moments like that I almost wished for a rulebook of some kind, a guide to working in the Cranes' garden like the manual I'd been given once at Second Nature.

Looking at Mrs. Crane while trying to look like I wasn't looking, stealing quick glances at the curves of her tank top and the bright pink dots of her toes peeking out under her skirt on the sand, I leaned farther into the water. Trying to ignore her with my mind and my voice was one thing, but other parts of my body weren't so eager to follow commands, and their awareness of her, their zeal for her presence, wouldn't be so easy to hide if I floated nude on my back as I'd been doing for most of the day. A wrinkly, waterlogged boner rising out of the water would hardly befit the solemn life of the mind I was meant to maintain.

"Isn't it awful," she called from the bank, "to be under his thumb?"

I might have spoken up to correct her, to explain that I wasn't under her husband's thumb so much as living in the wide open palm of his generous hand, but instead I floated silently on the skin of the river as if still deep in meditation. Though by then my higher mind was long gone and my lower one was doing its damnedest to make me stare at her, all curves and secrets up there on the bank.

Perhaps she took my lack of response as lack of hearing, but she couldn't have expected an answer from me; maybe she thought I might look in her direction when I heard her speak. Whatever the reason, Mrs. Crane stood up from the ground and, inexplicably in light of what followed, brushed the sand from her clothes. I looked, I suppose, because her sudden motion attracted my eye. Then she untied her skirt so it fell at her feet, and she revealed... she *unleashed* the tiniest pair of red panties—that word, it's a terrible word, but what other is there: especially when these particular panties were so much what that word has in mind. They were exactly the underwear one might imagine a woman who looked like Mrs. Crane to be wearing beneath her clothes; exactly, in fact, what I *had* imagined her to be wearing when I watched her on TV. Then with crossed arms she rolled the tank top up her stomach and over her head just as I'd seen her do on the screen, except this time there was no cutaway to a reverse angle of her back, or to the following scene: there were her breasts, her too-perfect, tan lineless breasts I won't even try to describe.

I could not, for the life of me, peel my eyes off until she'd waded in up to her chin and was paddling in my direction. I looked as contemplative, as earnestly engrossed in a world beyond this world as I possibly could, but as the ripples of her approaching body fanned across my own submerged limbs I was as physically, corporeally present as I ever had been in my life. I was, for once, entirely right where I was, no daydream, no drifting, a body tied down to the ground. Or to the water, such as it was.

I had braced myself against the downed log with the soles of my feet as I often did, and Mrs. Crane swam alongside and took my hand. "So I won't float away," she said, then rolled onto her back so the crimson shimmer of her underwear rose up from the water, and so did the soft, round shapes of her breasts, nipples as pink as her painted nails—perhaps it's wrong of me to be saying so, and to have noticed such things, and, most of all, to have let my scribe mark it all down so I might recall it much later like this, but what on earth was I to do? A moment like that one is hard not to cling to, especially when so much of what I've seen in my life is fading to black in my head.

It was hard to hold her hand while afloat on my stomach, so as much as I knew it might shame me or worse, knowing my untethered body was bound to betray me and perhaps cost me a job, I rolled onto my back beside her. I floated and focused on the water around me. I concentrated on the drift of the clouds but one of them, like some great practical joke, slid into and out of and into another like...

So I tried instead to imagine the desert of pebbles shifting below on the bed of the river, stirred up by our swimming, blown by invisible, watery winds too soft or too shallow for me to feel. In my mind I counted those millions of grains, slowly, with great concentration. I tried to block from my senses the too-perfect body beside me, the nearness of that body to mine, and the harder I tried to ignore it the more fully her body filled my mind like few things ever had. Despite myself I pictured Mrs. Crane floating closer, drifting against me in the flow of the river, and... and above me those clouds were still going at it.

Her fingers tightened around my hand and she asked, "Why do you stay? Is it only the money?" She leaned her head back into the water, balancing her body by pulling hard on my arm, then her face rose from the river and her hair streamed back like a TV ad for some exotic resort where beautiful women are always emerging from bright blue water. "It's the money that keeps me here," she said. "As much as I hate to admit it. I've gotten used to his wealth. I've gotten used to all this like I've gotten used to being ignored."

I said nothing, and neither did she for a while, but then, "We aren't people to him, you know. We aren't ourselves. We're actors, we're objects. Tiny plastic figures he can move about as he pleases, over here, over there, wherever he wants. Whatever game he's playing that day. He doesn't care who you are." As she spoke her fingers wrapped tighter and tighter until my hand started to ache, so I adjusted my fingers in her grip which she took, I suppose, to be an offer of comfort and sympathy because she shifted her hold into a softer, more intimate one—one that seemed meant not so much to keep her from floating away as to keep herself close against me.

"I know you understand, Finch. I knew you would. We're the same, you and I."

I tried to feel each tiny pinprick of contact and friction as a long-stemmed leaf bounced its way along my body on its way down the river. Between the points of the leaf and the stem's tip, I counted seventy-two individual impacts before it slipped past my toes and away.

"We're just types," she said. "The hermit. The wife. We're bodies that happen to fit the slots he wants filled. That's all. You know that, don't you? You must."

She rolled toward me a bit in the water, the water lapping back and forth between our bodies as she shifted, its current and force increasing as it squeezed through that narrow canal, and her movement pulled our joined hands underwater enough for my own body to roll against hers, her breasts flattening against my chest, my still erect penis (despite my best efforts) colliding with the smooth, wet fabric of her underwear, and for not even a second, for the merest sliver of time, I almost took Mrs. Crane in my arms, this woman I'd longed for and lusted after in late-night reruns. I nearly wrapped myself around her and...

But no, I resisted. I summoned what was left of my composure, and even if I perhaps panicked a little while paddling backward to reopen the space between our bodies without letting go of her hand, I managed somehow not to yelp (I nearly did, I so nearly did).

"I'm more than that," Mrs. Crane said, and though it seemed like she had more to say, nothing else came and we floated side by side in silence, both of us (I think) with our eyes closed, holding hands, and I was even able to drift back into my meditations, though I wasn't as fully immersed as I'd been earlier, still too aware of the tiniest movement of her fingers on mine, as gentle and varied as the points of the leaf that had passed.

Later, as the blue sky went dark and the air cooled for evening, Mrs. Crane announced she needed to get back to the house, released my hand, and paddled toward the bank where we'd each left our clothes. I let her dress before swimming over myself, and though she stood on the bank a moment or two, looking in my direction as if she was waiting, I let her walk away toward the manor before I emerged dripping and shriveled to reclaim my tunic and return to the cave where I knew dinner waited for me, fresh and hot from Mr. Crane's kitchen.

As I wended my way, the world was somehow both asleep and abuzz with the energy of evening coming into all corners, the energy of waking and stretching and setting out for the night. Then I saw a shape, a man-sized shadow or perhaps an animal in the last of the light, but something slipped silently through the garden ahead of me. I almost followed, I almost hurried for the first time since the bees had attacked, which must have been months, but whatever was moving had moved out of sight. So I walked on at my untroubled pace, as if I hadn't spotted the swift, dark suggestion of something.

19

I haven't counted the days, but by now those hikers must have been here a week. I come out of my cave every morning wondering if their tent will be gone, folded and ferried away while I slept, but it's still in my garden as orange and bright as before. Each morning its zippers fall open, and they emerge like chrysalides from a dewy cocoon, as hazy as the real things would be while gauzed in the goo of rebirth. One then the other they push through the flaps of their pitched vestibule, glistening in lingering mist. The sun must warm their quarters until they awake with no choice but to depart the hothouse it becomes. Now that departure is part of my morning routine: I climb my cave, I watch the sunrise, and I wait for the hikers to show their blurred shapes.

I suppose I'm not really watching the sunrise these days, so much as I'm remembering those I watched in the past. Every morning is fogged in for me, arriving as blurred bands of color—first blue and purple, then red, and finally orange. It's pretty enough in its way, but in the old days I enjoyed the occasional morning of mist because it showed me something new, it refreshed the world, and the next clear dawn I watched meant that much more because of the change. But now there is no change coming, no change for the better, at least. How long will it be until I only know the sun's risen because I feel its warmth on my face? How long until every sunrise, each morning after the other, is insufferably the same? Without those variations of light and shade, my mornings in this garden might become as mundane as they were when I worked for a living.

When Mr. Crane was still here, was he in the habit of waking up early to watch me come out of my cave, as I watch the hikers emerging? Maybe I was part of his own morning ritual, as they have become part of mine. Perhaps when I performed my inept tai chi or sat in my tree house, it was Mr. Crane seeking fresh sights like I marvel at their many changes of clothes—different colors and shapes every morning, it seems. When my own drab, gray tunic wore out long ago I gave up wearing clothes altogether, and now an entire catalog has come to me like a modeling show. And if their clothes can be new every morning, what else? There might be unfamiliar flowers or unknown birds turning up but unseen all the time.

For all I know, these two aren't the same hikers I saw yesterday. Perhaps there's a new pair each morning, a rotating troupe of performers who all look the same to my eyes.

This morning I heard them stumbling through brush on the edge of my glade, and I could tell they were plucking mushrooms from under bushes and from around the shade-spreading trunks of broad trees. The mushrooms they must have gathered, the ones in that part of the garden, are toxic but not badly so; those poor culinary free spirits will have upset stomachs, they'll vomit and squat with diarrhea for the next day or two, but they'll survive and be no worse for wear. They'll ingest the poison and their bodies will purge it and they'll have learned something about mushrooms and forest foodstuffs in the process, something I once learned myself the same way.

I could have run down the hill toward their hunting grounds, waving my arms and hopping about to prevent their poor dining decision, but why? For all I know they were gathering poisons on purpose. For all I know they have good reasons, and my intrusion would have spoiled some scheme I'm not privy to. And if I did intrude, if I did try to stop them, those hikers might have ignored my mute warnings, resented my intrusion as I resent theirs, and gone on gathering fungi for reasons untold of their own.

If the mushrooms were deadly, if they were dangerous beyond mere discomfort, I might have been more inclined to step in. But I know they'll survive so I let them be, and once they get past being sick they'll know more about the world than they did when they woke up this morning.

I sat on my cave and listened in on their progress. They plowed through the brush, moving toward and away from my perch, louder and softer and sometimes calling out to each other with joy at the discovery of a larger than average prize—how could I have denied them that triumph, the only joy they'll get from that harvest? And when they'd decided they'd gathered enough, I suppose, they went back to their tent for a minute or two before walking away toward the river.

I climbed down to head for the water myself, a bit later than usual because I'd been listening to the hikers out hunting, but not too far off my routine. At the mouth of my cave, I reached for my stick where I'd leaned it at night when I limped off to bed, but what I found was something else: still the same stick, for most of its length, but the sharp, stabbing top was now crossed by a short length of smooth wood, and wrapped with strips of soft orange fleece. I set it under my arm and took tentative steps, and instead of the uncomfortable, unaltered walking stick I'd been using, a stick that had forced me to adapt my hobbling to suit its shape, this perfect crutch bore my weight as if that's all it existed to do. It instantly lessened the pain in my leg and let me limp without jarring my knee as I hobbled downhill to the river.

It was an unexpected gesture, to say the least. The birds and the foxes provide entertainment, but it's not something they give to me so much as something I steal. Likewise the bees and their honey. But to actually be given something, a gift, hasn't happened since I was given the gift of this garden.

Picking my way toward the water, I wondered about those hikers and why they're here. For the first time I asked myself who they might be apart from "the hikers" without any names, those blurry shapes in my befogged garden. What are *their* stories? I asked my scribe, and I asked the Old Man, but neither had word one to tell me.

20

I was floating eyes-closed on the river, playing the flute that had reappeared in my breakfast basket a few weeks or months after being taken away. No explanation, no specific request, but the flute came back to me so I went back to playing. Feet propped on my faithful tree, I bobbed on the water, drifting to this side and to that but always anchored against the current. And I blew and I blew on that flute until I made noises that sounded like notes, noises I could repeat on purpose, at will, rather than shrill random squeaks. Even that meager, marred music was more than I'd expected to make, so it felt like success.

I won't say I was getting good, but I managed to pick out a few basic tunes like "Happy Birthday" and "Mary Had A Little Lamb." I'd begun working my way through "The Raggle Taggle Gypsy," which was coming along slowly but surely. So I fluted and floated through the afternoon, and the river stirred me about on its surface as the wind stirred the water itself. Then I felt Mr. Crane's presence nearby. He didn't speak or make any sound that I heard, but something told me he was there on the bank, so I looked up and saw him, dark suit and arms crossed over a ruby red tie as he watched me float on the river he'd made. Perhaps his shadow had fallen across the water and on my eyelids, or perhaps something else had let me know he was there, but as soon as I knew he was watching and waiting I swam in toward shore, holding my flute overhead and out of the water. My tunic was on the sand behind him, and it seemed rude to charge nude from the water, to rush past him and put it on and only then be prepared for conversation, so I stayed in the water up to my chest near the shore. To an observer, had there been one, we would have looked like a man consulting a mystical fish the way it happens in children's stories.

He had the long green stem of a dandelion in hand, and I waited for him to start speaking—I assumed he was going to speak; why else would he be there? It had to be something important to come down in person instead of sending a note or using his speakers. I watched the stem weave through his fingers, wrapping around and around until there was no more of the plant left in play, and as he squeezed his knuckles together, glistening white dandelion milk oozed out one end of the stalk and hung suspended and shining over the sand. I waited for it to drop, but it didn't while in my sight.

"In my line of work, Finch, there are surprises. No . . . let's not call them surprises, surprises sound like something you aren't ready for. Let's say there are... opportunities. Opportunities you weren't expecting, like the one that delivered you here, to me."

He paused, so I nodded. It seemed like what I should do.

"Success is about waking each morning and inspecting the world, knowing what's changed overnight and how you can best take advantage. Adaptability, Finch. A political feud becomes an armed conflict, a bombed neighborhood needs rebuilding. All those things you see on the news but it's too late by then. If it's on TV, I guarantee you that everyone important already knows and has made their move, and opportunity has passed you by."

I would have liked to get back to my swimming and flute, back on my back in the water with my eyes closed and the sun on their lids, wiping my mind clear of the sorts of things Mr. Crane was talking about and, sure, all other sorts of things, too. I'd seen and heard so little of him, my employer—only a few visits since I'd arrived, far fewer than I'd expected from someone who paid me so much—that sometimes I forgot he was up in the house, and

I forgot for long stretches of time that he owned the garden and that my home was in someone's garden at all. But I tried to look interested, I tried to look concerned, I tried to look like an eager employee in a very important meeting, which I suppose our riverside conversation was despite my being naked and underwater while it took place. If clothes make the man, I don't want to wonder what that made me.

"It's not only noticing changes before someone else. No, it's putting those changes in motion, making them your own as fully as if they'd been your ideas from the start. Capitalization, Finch. Capitalization."

He spread his fingers, and the crushed stem split in several places along the span of his hand.

"They won't always be the right moves. They won't all pay off. Of course not. But it's the move that matters, Finch—the bold gesture, the confident stroke. Men at my level understand that. We take that for granted. But if other people don't realize what matters most, if someone who's never moved at the fast pace I've set can't see the point in what I'm doing, is it my job to explain it to them?"

He paused, the way his wife always did, leaving room for me to not speak.

"No! No! Why would they, the myopic bastards? If they had any vision they'd be making the world keep up with them instead of slowing it down. They would offer a vision of what things might be instead of clinging to ignorant notions of what the world never was."

With the last word he hurled what remained of the dandelion onto the sand, but though the force in his arm's motion was evident, the light flower dropped as slowly as if it were floating on a calm pool of water. Quietly, as if to himself now, he said, "It's only creative destruction. It's only what makes the world run."

He looked down at the stem, then said, "Oh, and Finch, you should know steps were taken to redress the disrespect shown to your work here by the winterization contractors. It won't happen again." He slid his hands into his pockets and kicked at the dirt with a leather shoe the color of dried blood. "It's always unfortunate to work with those... those less professional than ourselves, isn't it, Finch? It's always a test of our patience and of our resolve."

Then he crossed his arms over his chest and paced back and forth on the bank, parallel to the flow of the water, muttering under his breath while I knelt on the bed. Still talking to himself as much as to me, perhaps even more to himself, he said something about hunting mushrooms, about how it looks to someone who hasn't done it himself: the patience, the creativity, some other necessary qualities I couldn't quite hear as he walked back and forth, in and out of earshot. He didn't actually tell me to do anything, but I'd long ago spotted the mushrooms sprung up overnight, every night, all over the garden each morning. So I took his mumbled remarks as an instruction for what I should do with my time. And I couldn't be sure, I didn't quite hear, but I think he thanked me for our conversation.

Then he turned away from the water and headed uphill toward the glade and my cave and his own house beyond, leaving me to float away from the riverbank back into the deep run of water, back to my flute and back to my back, and the rest of the afternoon passed without interruption save for a bird taking a crap on my head from a branch overhanging the water (and it wasn't the first time for that, and there was no one to notice the shit on my head, so no reason to do something about it; the river would wash it away).

Early the next morning, I set out mushroom hunting. I lay on the ground where a cluster of orange-spotted white mushrooms huddled by the trunk of a tree, and I watched them for an hour or two, maybe longer, trying to imagine the way they might think. They didn't move much, but I'm fairly sure I saw one of them grow; I saw it grow, or else I watched a mushroom move that wasn't really a mushroom at all— if beehives and bird nests could be cameras and speakers, why not a microphone disguised as a mushroom? A few months earlier I might not have noticed a mushroom growing, but I'd become attuned to a slow-moving world. I'd definitely never noticed any growth in the wide range of mushrooms produced by Second Nature, companion pieces for bushes and trees and fake fallen logs and often just the right touch for a convincing lobby display.

I watched, and I waited, and I discovered that a growing mushroom likes to be dwarfed by something taller beside it, likes to live in that something's long shadow. These particular mushrooms, the whitish ones with orange spots, depended on the tall, solid tree they'd grown against (I think it was a maple, because it dropped helicopters, and its leaves looked like the logo on bottles of pancake syrup) for its protection and shade and, I assumed, nutrients and water supply. Sometimes they were also half-covered by grasses and moss, close to concealed and easily missed by an eye not looking for them.

So I learned a lot about mushrooms and their shy lives. I learned that they're quick to cower and quick to hide, that they're willing to keep quiet and small so long as they're left to grow—not too tall! not so big!—in relative peace. They prefer dull, drab colors, colors that won't grab attention, and the ones with bright tops, orange domes and red-speckled saucers, I guessed were more often than not only setting a trap to keep danger away from their less eye-catching kin. Those, I thought, were the mushrooms most likely to be poisonous—the ones that grabbed all the attention.

Thinking like a mushroom came quickly to me, and it worked. In the first place I looked, brushing aside a soft curtain of moss and weeds, I found three perfect mushrooms crouched in the shadow of a large rock. They were so close they were practically—but not quite—touching each other, and as soon as I leaned close and disturbed the air around them my nostrils filled with the sweet scent of secrets, of wine cellars and old canning jars and the thrilling surprise of turning a stone to find a bustling community of potato bugs and millipedes thriving beneath. The excitement of life where it wasn't expected. Gently I plowed a small circular furrow around each mushroom's base with my index finger, then snapped their stems off as far below ground as I could. I don't know why, that just seemed like the best way to pick them. It seemed important to keep them intact as much as I could, at least until they were eaten.

My first chosen mushrooms were the color of clouds, not cotton-white clouds but creamier ones, clouds when there's going to be or has been a storm and the sky isn't gray but it isn't blue, either. That kind of cloud. That kind of mushroom.

I found another set of three almost immediately, then a few more, and before the sun had crested the peak of the sky my wooden soup bowl was piled with a whole morning's harvest, and I decided those were enough. What would I do with more mushrooms, me alone in my cave? I could only eat so much in a day, and I already planned to pick more the next day or the next— I had the knack, and neither the mushrooms or I would go anywhere. So I strolled slowly back through the trees with the tiled roof of Mr. Crane's house visible through the leaves, and lit by the sun in a rusty red glare.

That evening, when my soup came, a knife arrived with it, and I knew it was for slicing my mushrooms; someone had noticed my project that day. I shaved them into my pot over a small, slow-burning fire, and as they roasted the rich smell filled my cave and my stomach growled. The food Mr. Crane's kitchen provided was delicious enough, and always hearty, but it was exciting to prepare food I'd gathered myself—unlike the meals I'd made long ago in my apartment, this wasn't just something to fill up my body and keep it upright, an experiment in ingredient mixing, but food and aromas I'd actually earned through my own hard work and through Mr. Crane's, too—he'd built the garden, he'd sown shadowy spots where mushrooms might grow, so my harvest was also his. I nearly walked up to the house to ask him to join me, but no, that didn't seem right.

At best I could have silently held out a mushroom, roasted and darkened and steaming, and we could have eaten together. But if Mr. Crane wanted mushrooms, mushrooms picked from his own backyard, I knew he could have—and had he already?—gone and gathered his own.

And it was a good thing I resisted that impulse to share, as things turned out, because only a short time after eating—not quite half a log had been burnt in the fire—my stomach knotted and cramped and my legs went rubbery and I collapsed on the floor of my cave. My belly churned and moaned and twisted, tighter and tighter like a wet paper towel that refuses to break in strong hands, and seven times I felt myself ready to retch and crawled to the mouth of my dwelling, only to have nothing come up. Until later, when it came up and showed no signs of stopping.

I lay for what I later estimated to be three whole days on my pallet, three long, painful days without pause, moving only to drag my wretched bowels and bile a few yards from the cave. As always my meals appeared in the wall nook, and at one point I swam up through the murk of my sickness to surface in the dark of my cave, and I saw Smithee sliding a tray of food into my niche. At last the mystery was solved, but I was too mired in misery to care. My eyes were hardly open, and he must not have noticed that I was awake, because I watched as he wrote in his notebook and poked through the pinecones and stones and oddly shaped leaves I'd collected, all stashed in one nook or another; it looked like he was making a list. Then he pulled out a camera from his wonderful pocket, not the same camera he'd had by the river but a video camera smaller than I'd ever seen, and he swept it around the walls and the floor of my cave and even over me deep in my blanket nest, all the while mumbling to himself (and, I suppose, to the camera's microphone) so softly I couldn't hear what he was saying.

I didn't think much about what I saw at the time—I couldn't think about anything, except how awful I felt—but later I assumed Smithee was taking notes for Mr. Crane, maybe for changes to come in my cave. Whatever he was doing there, if he wasn't in fact a mushroom-induced hallucination, he didn't stay long and I soon sank back into the swamp of my feverish dreams.

Some time later I was awoken again, by the thundering arrival of Mr. Crane's helicopter, and crawled outside the cave to be sick one more time. Then I crawled back to bed, where I tried to be as still and as small as a mushroom myself, in hopes the sickness would pass like I'd passed so many mushrooms before finally stopping to look, before trying to think like they thought.

I think Jerome wandered in, too, at some point, but I saw all sorts of creatures in the hot, festering jungle of my feverish mind, so maybe it was him and maybe it wasn't, but whoever it was laid his hot, heavy head on my leg and made me feel a little bit better. Or at least I dreamt I felt better, which in that sorry state was more or less the same thing.

On what I think was the third afternoon, I woke from dreaming I was a spy—but not a good one—and rolled over to find Mr. Crane standing inside the cave, hands together behind his back. He wasn't quite looking my way, more off to the side, but he was talking as if I'd been listening and as if he'd already been talking for a long while. Almost like it was still the same conversation we'd had by the river, the last time I'd seen him.

"A man has to dictate his landscape, Finch." Mr. Crane said. "He has to know who's doing what where and when and how and, most of all, why. What is that, over there, far away and out of sight of most people, going to mean for me here? No, nothing can ever be out of his sight. Nothing! Perspective must be maintained, his view onto the world must be kept under control at all times—what use is a visionary without projection? Hm? What good indeed."

I sat up and nodded to show him the interest I didn't quite have—it wasn't that I didn't care, but I had no idea what he was talking about, and I still felt so wretched—but right then he stopped talking. To my shock and surprise, Mr. Crane sat down on the edge of my pallet beside me, right on top of my filthy, ragged blankets with his creased and pressed and clean pants. I hoped that the fleas I'd been battling lately had taken the day off and gone on an outing somewhere, perhaps revolted by my mushroom-tainted blood and in search of redder pastures. The last thing I wanted to do was infest my employer with parasites.

"I do things, Finch. I get things done. I make decisions and they affect millions of people. Dams. Bridges. Whole infrastructures. The roads people drive on to visit their mothers and the pipes they draw clean water from. These things aren't cheap, Finch. They aren't free. It takes vision and planning and, yes, it takes money to get these things done. And that money has to come from somewhere. Maybe it comes from somewhere that isn't as... *convenient* as running water and indoor plumbing, so they don't put me on magazine covers, and I'm never the man of the year. Fine. I can live with all that. I have what I need, more than I need. But this."

And he stopped, right there, in the middle of whatever point he was making, and we sat there, the two of us silent for a long time. I tried to suppress my gurgling stomach and did a fair job aside from a few long, squeaky groans and one loud, thunderous, wet-sounding fart that Mr. Crane ignored with impressive, professional tact. But he had known about the mushrooms, after all, so might not have been as surprised as I was.

"I try, Finch. I anticipate, I predict—I pay other people to predict, lots of people, lots of money, to tell me what's going to happen and who's going to make it happen, which is usually far more important. I need to know who I can trust, who I can't, who's going to come after me or who I need to go after. You understand what I'm saying."

Had I done something, I wondered? Was Mr. Crane referring to me, to some betrayal I hadn't intended? I'd been practicing the flute like I thought he'd wanted me to, I'd been swimming and thinking and I'd eaten the mushrooms, as horribly as that had turned out. Was he mad because I was sick? Was I being blamed for poorly performed—but well-intended!—mushroom hunting? What a way to be fired, I thought to myself, even for someone adept as I was at losing jobs.

"Landscapes, Finch. It's all landscapes. Views, perspectives, call them what you like, but that's what matters. Seeing as much as you can and seeing it the way you want it seen and, more than that, having the ability to make other people, all people, see things as you see them, too."

It no longer sounded like Mr. Crane was talking about me, then he stopped talking and I may have drifted into a fever daydream. But eventually he stood, slipped his hands in his pockets and walked away from my bed, the usual buoyancy back in his step. As his details darkened into a blank silhouette against the sunlight at the mouth of my cave, he said again—I think to himself— "Landscapes." Then he stepped out of my narrow home and out of sight, leaving me alone with my own twisted and angry organs.

Alone, and—I discovered once I'd recovered and crawled from my bed the next morning—without my flute, which had once more been taken away. Its back and forth trips were becoming annoying.

21

Soon after my failed attempt at mushroom hunting, I returned from a swim to discover a long, rustic box of light wood propped against the inner wall of my cave. Its brass hinges were tarnished but still functional, as was the clasp. In fact, the tarnish looked like it almost belonged, like it was part of the metal rather than its decay. Inside the box were a dozen or so tubes of paint and several brushes in various sizes, all smeared and stained, as if they'd been used. There were also a folding easel, a bundle of canvasses, and various tools and devices I assumed were required for painting without knowing how. All my life I'd had a hard time even drawing a circle, and now—apparently—Mr. Crane wanted me to paint for him. I hoped he was more interested in watching me work than enjoying the works I produced. And I couldn't be sure, but based on the conversation we'd had, I thought I could safely assume landscapes were what he wanted. At least it wasn't circles I was meant to be painting.

I rifled through the paints and the brushes and knives, hoping for some sort of guidebook or instruction manual or even the simplest pictogram of how to set up the easel. But there was nothing in the box of that kind. The more closely I looked at all of the paint tubes and everything else, the more worn they appeared. The corners of the wooden case were battered and scuffed, though still solid enough to be trusted. The brushes had straight, even bristles, but the glossy finish was worn off their shafts in exactly the spot—I discovered—where my own hand best fit. Even the palette, when I put my thumb through it and made my hand comfortable, had a thumb-shaped smudge on its surface where my own thumb naturally fell and would later leave a fresh layer of smudge, once it had paint on its tip. It was all like I'd been using this paint set for years, except that I hadn't. I'd say it sparked déjà vu but it didn't, it sparked the opposite feeling: the sense I *should* recall doing something that I hadn't done. As if the palette and brushes and box should feel déjà vu about me and ask if I had painted with them in the past.

After eating lunch, filled with false courage and confidence by my immediate if artificial familiarity with the tools, I tucked the box under my arm and set out to see what I might paint. My first thought was to carry the paints to the roof of my home and paint the view. But try as I might to scramble up the stone wall, as many times as I'd done it before and have done it since, I couldn't work out how to climb with that long, awkward box making one arm unavailable. So I gave up. Besides, I reasoned, the view wasn't as interesting at this time of day, and painting the sunrise from memory seemed more difficult—all of those colors, plus the unusual light. Surely I should begin with something simpler, something monochromatic and small and even static.

A leaf, perhaps; a single green leaf.

I thought I might paint Jerome, but I might also spend the whole day looking for him instead, checking his favorite nap spots, and never get to do any painting.

Or I could paint one of those mushrooms. I hadn't done so well at eating them, but perhaps Mr. Crane's desire for mushroom hunting would be appeased by a picture for him instead of more poison for me.

So out I went after mushrooms again, thinking as they thought (or as I thought they thought), crouching near tree trunks and bushes with my cheek to the ground as I eyed-out for moist, shadowed spots. It didn't take long to find a cluster of three good-sized gray buttons in the shadow of a half-rotten tree trunk that something had bored full of holes.

I opened my paint box and tried to set up the easel, only to find that it wasn't as simple as it appeared. An easel, I thought—unfold the legs and tighten some nuts and bolts and off you go, painting. But it wasn't like that, at least not for me: each time I straightened one leg of the easel, the other side collapsed to the ground. I felt like an old comedian in one of those silent films, the ones who struggle to paint houses or catch pies off an assembly line and all that. I was beginning to think my easel was rigged, that it was not meant to be used but only to frustrate its would-be user. I wondered if that was the point, what Mr. Crane was really after, and if he was watching my struggles and laughing before the silvery flicker of his monitor the way he might laugh at one of those old slapstick shows.

Maybe, I thought, I could prop my canvas against something else, avoiding the problem of the easel altogether. It seemed like a reasonable idea, so I looked around for some rocks or logs I could use, but it soon occurred to me that Mr. Crane had provided the easel along with the paints and the rest of the kit, and I was probably meant to use it. I was being paid to use the tools he'd provided, that's what he wanted and he was the boss, so I needed to figure out how to make it stand up instead of pretending it wasn't there.

And eventually, though not gracefully, I did get the easel together. The trick, it turned out, was to wrap my hands around the jointed knees where the upper and lower sections of each leg were bolted together. I could hold two legs at a time while using my mouth to tighten the butterfly nut on the third, and once I'd figured that out it was pretty quick to get the contraption assembled. Getting paints onto the pallet was simpler—I just squeezed the tubes—but it was hard to know how much of each color I needed for painting a mushroom and even harder deciding which colors to use. There were tiny bands of color around each metal paint tube to indicate what was inside, but after holding them all up against the mushrooms one or two at a time I was disappointed to learn that the color I wanted—an ashy, brownish gray—was missing, so I'd have to mix it myself.

I tried mixing brown and white, but that came out muddier and darker than what I wanted. I couldn't get it with black and white, either, or black and brown, which I tried just in case. One after another I squeezed my paints onto the palette and swirled them with one another, and though I made lots of colors, some of them ugly and some of them not, I couldn't find the right shade for the mushrooms. Frustrated, I knelt beside the fallen log and pressed my eye right up close to the fungus, trying to pick out all the shadows and shades in its cap, and then there it was, clear as day like a voice had spoken it into my head: yellow! The mushroom was gray and brown, but it was also yellow. All the other colors of the cap were layered on a pale glow. After that realization, it was like my palette mixed the color itself, so perfectly mushroom-hued was it, and I was ready to paint.

Except that I wasn't sure how to begin. Should I make a background first, the log and the grass and the sky? Or should I ignore all of that and set the mushroom alone onto a white canvas? Doing it that way seemed easiest, and this was my first time painting, so easy seemed the best way to go. I tried to sketch the shape of the mushroom with my paintbrush, as lightly and simply as I could, but I ended up with more of a blob. I tried to fix that and now had a blob and a smudge. Then it was a blob, a smudge, and the painted prints of three of my knuckles, so I gave up on sketching the mushroom and tried to paint it without any outline to follow.

I looked from canvas to fungus and then from fungus to canvas, back and forth, trying to capture its shape; I held my thumb out before me the way I'd seen painters do on TV, gazing around its smudged tip to the mushroom behind, but something didn't seem right. The mushroom I'd chosen, the tallest in its trio by the log, had a big black spot on the left side of its cap that I hadn't noticed before. It wasn't a perfect example of mushrooms, and if I'd been picking them for food I wouldn't have trusted it, assuming the spot to be rotten or poisonous or both (and perhaps a similar spot had been my earlier downfall).

What to do? If Mr. Crane wanted me to paint his garden, I was sure he wanted it looking its best. He wouldn't want a picture of a spotty, rotten mushroom to hang on his wall. I could just pretend the spot wasn't there, paint the mushroom I wanted it to be, but that seemed wrong, too: I was sure Mr. Crane didn't want me to lie, to pretend his garden was something it wasn't. Someone as concerned with getting things right as he was no doubt wanted an accurate picture. I had no choice but to start over and paint a new mushroom.

Frustrated, already fed up with painting, I chose one of the smaller mushrooms beside the black-spotted one, and started painting again. But I'd only made a few strokes with the brush when I noticed that the gills of the second mushroom were hanging loose in an unattractive, unappetizing manner. I wouldn't want to look at a painting of that, and I don't know the first thing about art, so there was no way, I assumed, Mr. Crane would want to see it with his refined eye.

So I gave up on those mushrooms and set out to find others more deserving of paint. But hard as I tried, I spent the day moving from one stand of mushrooms to another, repulsed by bad spots or awkward shapes or funny colors. Sometimes I noticed before I started to paint, and a few times I began with my brush before realizing the flaws of my subject, but I never got very far into a painting before being forced to give up and move on. I started over so many times that my canvas looked like a puddle of mud or a big water stain on a ceiling, but I didn't want to use a new canvas and waste the first one; when I found the right mushroom I could just cover up those mistakes.

But it wouldn't be that first day, because the sky was already darkening, and I was hungry and ready to rest. An entire day lost to imperfect mushrooms and an afternoon without swimming; I felt dried out, and anxious in a way I hadn't felt in a very long time. So I collapsed my easel (much easier than setting it up), packed my paints, washed my brushes by the banks of the river—lingering a few minutes to wade to my knees, the best I could do—then carried everything back to my cave where a pot of soup and a loaf of bread waited for me in their niche.

As I'd taken to doing, I ate my dinner outside the cave by a very small fire—enough light for me to see what I was doing, to see what I needed to see of myself, but not so bright I couldn't see past my small circle of light. I'd made that mistake in my first months, building fires so large they blocked out the world, and a large fire burned so long that I never reached the best part of the night, after the logs have all burned to ash and embers don't outshine the eyes emerging around me in the brush. That's when I know where I am, where I live, that I have neighbors and I'm part of something much more than myself. That's when I remember the world, and if I build too much of a fire I forget; I'd already missed out on some swimming that day, and missing my afterglow hours as well was out of the question.

Jerome strolled over—it still didn't seem right, for a lion to "stroll," but there's no other way to describe the casual, carefree way he meandered, like he'd forgotten he was the king of the jungle or maybe was so secure in his crown that it never once crossed his mind he might need to defend it. He strolled over to where I sat and curled up on the edge of the light, where the glimmer of flames slid over his yellow body and made his fur look like it was in motion. He was facing the mouth of my cave and wasn't far from it, so when he fell asleep and started to snore—and he always did—the sound echoed in and out of my home in a passable performance of thunder.

After the last log collapsed into molten coals, when my last cup of tea for the night was all gone, I heard a noise somewhere out in the garden but not far away. An animal, I thought, perhaps one of the foxes who sometimes come to my cave after dark or an owl swooping down for a meal. But when I heard other noises, metallic scrapes and the clicking and clacking of tools, I knew it wasn't a fox or an owl or any of my other neighbors. The noises weren't loud enough to wake up my ferocious, snoring companion, so I crept away from the forecourt of my cave to track down the source, walking slowly and trying not to scratch through my tunic, the itching of which seemed to get harsher the slower I moved— hardly ideal for my profession of living at a very slow pace.

I crept through the glade toward the blackberry patch, then heard more noises, louder now, and corrected my course toward the river where they seemed to be loudest. At the top of the hill, looking down on the glistening water, I stopped. I lay flat in the grass and I watched. Someone was down there—a tall silhouette, smooth-headed and featureless as a ski mask, reached into the branches of a slim tree and manipulated one of the boxier, more obvious cameras. I watched, still and silent, and it was only a matter of minutes before the silhouette slid his tools into a pouch at his waist and snuck away into the garden; I heard the soft splash of his steps into the river, then his (or her?) unwelcome swim strokes while sliding away.

I stayed where I was, too shocked to move. Was this how Mr. Crane adjusted his garden? Was this how he managed my world? It didn't seem right, it was too obvious and too clumsy, and why would an employee of Mr. Crane's need to sneak away through the water? Why not head up to the house?

This was the first person I'd seen apart from the Cranes and Smithee in a very long time—since the workers who had sprayed my garden with winter; perhaps this man or woman in black was one of them, returned to perform other tasks?—and the sighting left me feeling sick.

I rolled over onto my back in the grass to think about it, to wait for my stomach to settle, but silvery clouds were sliding over a thin slice of moon and putting on too good a show for me to withhold my attention, and when it was over—when the clouds were too thick for the moon to show through—I was tired and made my way back to my cave and to bed, where sleep was fitful all night.

22

They're feeling those mushrooms this morning, clambering in and out of their tent in a tangle every few minutes, stumbling over each other in a rush to contain themselves until they've reached open ground. Or my unfortunate potato patch, which seems to have been designated a vomitorium for the moment—and that may be just desserts for my not warning them about the mushrooms; perhaps I was meant to, perhaps it was an opportunity for discovery by me, not by them, arranged by the Old Man as a test I've now failed.

I'll have to think about that.

I heard them even before I left my cave this morning, before sunrise when they're usually quiet—quiet in the way of the world, which is snoring and belching and rustling around in their sleep, so not really quiet at all. They weren't quiet today, they were churning and hurling and moaning aloud to each other. Their runs back and forth from the tent to the bushes made a racket like bulldozers plowing the garden, and I was torn loose from the last strands of sleep to the melodious tones of their retching and splashing and the explosive charge of their bowels.

And for a moment, still deep in my half-sleeping stupor, I thought it was me, my own body. I'm still so unused to the bodies of others being nearby where my own senses can sense them.

I came to the cave mouth to stretch and to scratch, and watched the woman hiker—I could tell by her hair—burst through the tent's flap and crawl for the bushes. While I took my tea on the roof, while the sun climbed over the garden, she made three trips and he made two, but his purges sounded more comprehensive. I waited until they were both in the tent before making my way to the river; that was a change in routine, a disruption, but it seemed the right thing to do not to hobble on by while they suffered. And if they had been out of the tent as I passed, if I hadn't been able to see them... that could have been a sloppy collision.

I set off toward the water, but for once—the first time, I suspected, and my scribe informs me I'm right—I turned off the path halfway there, on a whim that may or may not have been mine, through the gap in the trees where I once tried and failed to erect a conical oven with dried clay and mud from the river. What I would do for a loaf of bread, or a slice, or even a handful of flour that hasn't been ground up from acorns or sun-dried potatoes! I veered into the brush on the slopes of the hill, and using the hum of the just-waking hives as a guide, I felt my way to a cluster of wild-growing herbs: dark velvet leaves like sage but not sage, curled like parsley, but not that, either. Not any parsley I know, anyway, which is only what the supermarket labels called parsley when I was a shopper; perhaps there are other kinds. I uprooted a fistful of mist-moistened stalks, then carried them back to my cave and stoked my fire and boiled those herbs to make tea. Then, following the sounds of uncomfortable bodies, I carried my cauldron and its verdant contents toward the bright blaze of the tent where those two hikers were, for the moment, contained, and I poured my concoction into their own pot where it hung over an idle but already blackened fire pit—when had they replaced their gas stove with a fire, I wondered?

They must have heard me, they must have known I was outside their tent, for I clattered not only to make myself noticed (and keep them away) but also because in that unfamiliar realm, on that expanding island of theirs, I was asea without sight. So they must have heard, but in the time it took me to return to my cave and replace my own cauldron, then walk past the tent once more toward the river and this time for real, I didn't see hide, hair, nor hurl of those hikers.

That tea I left them won't taste very good, not much better than what's coming out. But it will put them to sleep for a long stretch of hours, a deep sleep that will come as a mercy after how they spent last night and this morning, and they'll wake drained and diminished but well down the road to becoming themselves once again. Both their bodies and my potatoes will rest unmolested, and my garden will go back to its usual calm, back to as calm as it's been since they came.

23

As I sat by the river one afternoon soon after Jerome's arrival, digging with a stick in the sand just to find out how deep I could go, I heard something large approaching behind me. I turned to see him lumbering my way through the brush, tongue hanging from his mouth like a dog and dandelions and broken-off blackberry brambles tangled in the fur of his mane. He lumbered over and sat down beside me, like he was waiting for me to do something, so I thought maybe I should.

I decided to teach Jerome how to be more like a lion, to get him over his moping and loping and tumbling about, to get him to roar and to stalk and to act like the king of the jungle. He couldn't quite be the king of that forest while Mr. Crane was, but he could still stand to be more like he was meant to be and more like himself, more regal and roaring and rough. And I figured I knew as much about lions as anyone else in the garden—there didn't seem to be any lion tamers or zookeepers or biology majors around—so it might as well be me who showed him. If I got it a little bit wrong, who would know except us? He'd be as much a lion as my hand-sculpted cave is a cave.

I got onto my hands and my knees in a pose like a lion would strike, like I'd seen lions strike on TV, and I pulled air down into my lungs and let out the loudest, most leonine roar I could find. But it came out as more of a howl, too high-pitched, too keening and whining and wrong. I tried again with the same result, maybe just a little bit lower. Jerome, meanwhile, sat staring at me with his enormous head cocked to one side. He listened to my pathetic, weak roars, then leaned his own head back and—I swear it—tried to howl; not to roar, not to sound like the lion I'd hoped he'd become, but he tried to imitate me in my attempts to imitate him. And his howl was pretty convincing, not as a roar but as something else, the sound an overgrown house cat might make when his supper is late.

I tried again and so did he, and between the two of us we moved farther and farther from lionish sounds and instead began singing a song of a sort. I tried to harmonize, but every time I changed my note so did Jerome. I couldn't believe it, at first—a musical lion!—and, thinking back, I have to wonder if it really happened that way, but my scribe assures me it did.

Teaching him to roar was getting us nowhere, so I shifted gears and stalked around on all fours, trying to be my most fearsome and fierce, and Jerome fell right in step beside me as we stomped through the garden like lions. Well, not so much like lions as like two people pretending that they were lions, despite one of us being a lion.

My lioning lessons didn't go quite as I wanted them to, but expectations are overrated. Maybe I was meant to be teaching Jerome to be *less* like a lion, rather than more. Perhaps that was the Old Man's design—though I hadn't yet realized how much of a hand he had in these things—or perhaps I was screwing things up altogether. It's hard to tell, sometimes, in such a wild and tangled part of the world, whether I've left the path or am still walking on it. So I try to worry about only one step at a time, not where those steps are leading in accumulation.

Anticipation of what's to come, of what can be done, of what a life is bound to or meant to be worth—what's the use of all that? It's ego and it's self-deception to think we can plan our next steps and to think we might actually take the steps we have planned. Living a life without plans had rewarded me well, delivering me to the job I was meant for. I'd left plans behind with my voice and my pants and my shoes and my stifling apartment and ties. I'd left them behind with other people and their demands on my time— Mr. Crane made demands, of course, but those were different: those were demands I might have made of myself, they felt more like my own desires and dreams being pointed out by someone else. And I was getting paid for it, and I would be for the next several years, though those years began to look shorter and shorter the more full moons came and went, the more months I felt passing and the closer I came to my inevitable expulsion at the end of the term I had been contracted for.

So I tried not to think about that. I put it off, knowing the unwelcome moment would come but focusing instead on the moment at hand; I wasn't being paid to worry about what would happen in several years' time, or what I would do in the world when I went back to it. Like Jerome becoming the best lion he could, I tried to be my best hermit, as veiled from the concerns of the outside world and its pending problems as I could be. I became, bit by bit, day by day, self-sufficient and much more myself, the self I'd always wanted to be without knowing he might exist.

Instead of worrying about future or past, I floated day after day on the river, sensation streaming across parts of my body I'd never noticed before, every follicle and cilium tuned to temperature shifts in the water, each pore and inch of my skin fully conscious of fine grit and sand drifting in clouds underwater. Water striders skimming around me and dragonflies hovering an inch from my nose and, sometimes, some lucky mornings, landing on my face for a perch from which they could drink.

I'd say I was happier than I had been, but calling it happiness misses the point: it was more than that, so much more. To say I was happy, to use that hollow word, suggests I considered for even a moment whether or not I was, that I compared my new situation to how I'd lived and felt in the past, and I didn't have to do that: I'd moved beyond wondering whether I was happy, beyond comparing one day to the last or the next or to how I'd imagined my life might turn out. My experience had outstripped my dreams in degrees and directions I'd never realized were open to me.

Jerome, worn out by his lioning lessons, had curled up to sleep on the shore, his sides rippling and rising and falling as he snuffled and snored. So I left him behind on the sand and swam out into deeper water, toward the downed tree, but was barely halfway across the river when the quiet of the garden was broken.

"Finch," echoed through the air from the speakers, "come up to your cave. I'll be coming down."

At the first syllable of Mr. Crane's voice, Jerome had leapt up and run off, leaving me to climb alone from the water and shake like a dog—or as close to a dog as I could be without fur—to wick and whip water away. Then I pulled on my tunic—oh, how I loved every morning when I let that harsh cloth fall away on the bank before taking my plunge, and how I loathed pulling it on again in the evening for the walk to my glade, and the hours between drying and dreaming and sleep!—and set off up the hill toward my home.

When I got to the cave, Mr. Crane was halfway down the slope from the house, so I stood by my fire ring waiting, unsure if it would be rude to sit, so I didn't. I hadn't seen him since we'd spoken about painting—if that's what we had really been talking about; the paints showed up afterward, anyway—however long before that had been, and the only signs of his presence had been the sparkling of lenses up in his window and in his cameras down here on the ground. Had he traveled, I wondered, had he been away? But it wasn't my place to ask, it was my place to stand by the cave mouth and wait for him to arrive.

Mr. Crane approached slowly, hands in his pockets, in a blue shirt that fit him so well it may have been skin grown for him by a tailor. His hands were in his pockets, and though he looked ahead, toward me, toward my glade, I could tell at a distance that his thoughts were elsewhere. His stare reached past me and through the trees toward the river and the valley below, and perhaps to the ocean beyond.

When he'd drawn close to the cave he said, "Good morning, Finch," and I nodded, half-smiling (too big a grin, too much outward emotion, seemed at odds with why I was there; a wide smile didn't seem like a sign of serious contemplation to me in those days, though I've since changed my mind about that).

"The river's nice," he said. "I'm enjoying it." To hear him speak you'd think Mr. Crane had been swimming himself, as if I were the one responsible for discovering the river; it sounded like he was thanking me for pointing him toward some great secret I'd shared—that river I'd seen him stand beside several times, that river that had run through his estate for a long time by then. Like it was something he'd only just noticed. "Should be more fish, though. Bigger fish, enough to catch."

We stood side by side near my fire ring for a long time. I imagined the river filled with big, biting fish, filled with fish biting me, and wondered how I could talk Mr. Crane out of that without opening my mouth.

"I was talking to a contact in... well, that doesn't matter. The important thing is this contact of mine mentioned that he plays the cello. It relaxes him at the end of a day. Brings it along on trips, actually, and he practices in his hotel rooms, even in parts of the world that have never seen a cello before, I would imagine. Astounding."

He genuinely did look astounded, perhaps that this acquaintance of his brought a cello along on business trips, but he seemed most amazed that someone played the cello at all. As if it hadn't occurred to him before hearing it that this was something a person might do. I got a sense of where the conversation was headed and it turned out I was right: it was music, again, and me playing some, as if he'd forgotten about my wooden flute coming and going.

"I expect a cello would look a bit out of sorts here. A string quartet in a cave!" He laughed. "What else... what else... what are those things, like a harp, only sideways, or laying down, or... what are those called?"

A hammered dulcimer, I grasped, was what he had in mind, so I mimed playing one as if the twin mallets were in my hands, and I gestured with my fingertips the length of the instrument's invisible strings so he'd know it wasn't a xylophone or glockenspiel or—what's the other one like that?—marimba.

"Yes, yes, that's the one," Mr. Crane said. "Seems a little formal, though, doesn't it? A bit complicated. What else, though..." He turned on his heel, slowly, thoughtfully, and started back up the hill as smoothly and quietly as he'd arrived, but even from behind I could tell he was thinking still about dulcimers and cellos and who knew what else. I only hoped it wasn't tubas.

So it was no surprise the next morning when, along with my porridge and tea, my flute returned to the nook in my wall. Already my miserable music had gotten rusty in the time spent with no instrument, so it was like starting over—the first notes left me lightheaded, and I had to stop. But it came back to me quickly, to the extent that I'd ever had it, and floating on my back, feet propped against the tree, I spent the rest of the morning bobbing up and down on the water, drifting a bit to this side and a bit to that side but always anchored against the current by the log at my feet and the flute at my lips.

As afternoon shadows grew longer, as kingfishers fished for fish that seemed bigger than they'd been the evening before, as hummingbirds dipped and drank and even a bright orange fox crept down to the bank and dunked his snout for a sip, one wary eye kept on me as I tried not to be too insulted that he'd taken me for a threat (me, with no reason to hunt or to fish or to worry my shy vulpine neighbor at all). As all that was happening, rush hour in my garden, I huffed and I puffed, and my weak squeaks and squawks soon got me back to where I had been, noises assembled into tuneful order as if the flute had never been taken away. That felt like progress enough for one day, so I set the flute safely on the bank with my clothes and let my mind drift unfettered the way my body had been doing all day, savoring the last sunlit seconds of one more day like all others.

24

I kept at the painting, but I won't say I became any better. It always took me so long to find a subject, to choose the right leaf or best flower, that by the time I actually got around to opening my paints my energy and attention were drained, and it was time for me to swim. Over however many mornings my painting went on, I never completed one canvas. I only really started a handful—two or three tentative strokes, a preliminary swathe of background color, and that would be it. Maybe I set myself up for failure by seeking out perfect specimens every time. I might have been more successful painting flawed mushrooms, flawed flowers, birds and bees with only one wing; maybe their own imperfect nature would have allowed me to embrace my own, to get paint on canvas without worrying so much about how it looked and whether I was producing the painting Mr. Crane had in mind.

Or maybe—and this seems more likely—maybe I'm just a naturally, unavoidably terrible painter.

Mr. Crane must have noticed that I couldn't paint and that I wasn't improving from one day or week to the next, that my circles were getting no rounder and my apples looked no more like apples—though my pears did, in fact, look like green apples and my apples looked like overgrown strawberries and my strawberries... I don't think I tried painting strawberries, but perhaps they would have turned out like apples. Had I only known the fruit Mr. Crane preferred me to paint, I might have known which one to *try* painting in order to produce the one he had in mind. Would he have known that my apples were meant to be berries, or would he have been satisfied with the apples I offered so long as that's what they seemed to be?

Whether he recognized my fruited attempts as I'd intended or not, my days as a painter didn't last long. After a few weeks or a couple of months wasting canvasses on my mistakes, I returned to the cave after swimming to find that my paint box was gone. No note, no replacement, just gone—the canvases, the brushes, the works. And I can't say I minded much, either, because no painting meant more time for swimming and for my meditations, which had suffered between the time lost to art and the frustration of failure I carried to the water each day.

But painting hadn't passed from the garden, it had only passed from my hands. The next morning while I sat on my cave top and watched the sun, trying to work out how the whole scene came together as if it were paint—bands of purple and orange like leis I'd seen draped on the necks of arriving tourists on TV shows about Hawaii, against a blue background that was darker at the bottom and lighter up top somehow without seeming to change—Mrs. Crane walked down from the house, carrying a paint box and easel far more modern but also far more smeared and smudged and broken in than mine had ever been. Mine had come pre-rusted and worn, but hers had gotten that way over time. She wore faded, paint-spattered denim overalls, the most clothing I'd seen her in at one time.

"Come on down, Finch," she called up to me from the ground. "I'm going to paint you."

Once I was on the ground she explained that she'd studied painting and sculpture in college, an art minor to her theater and acting major. Though she usually painted still lifes in the studio Mr. Crane had built for her in the house, she'd come to do some painting outside after watching me fail at it so miserably from her window.

"Your pears look like apples, Finch," she said and laughed, "and I don't know what you've done to the apples."

I was glad not to have to reply.

She pointed toward a large, flat-topped boulder not far from my cave, and yet one I'd not noticed before. "Why don't you sit over there so we can get started," she said. "Try to look, I don't know, contemplative or something."

By the time I got myself perched on the rock, she already had the easel set up and a canvas upon it, and was mixing paints on her palette.

She told me to move this way and that, raise and lower my arms, stretch my legs, until at last I must have looked like some crumpled replica of *The Thinker*. Then she said, "Good, now don't move," and left me to sit there for what felt like hours with a sharp point of stone stabbing the left cheek of my ass.

As I sat I heard the distant shudder of the helicopter approaching, and watched as the underbrush bristled with the flight of small animals back to their burrows and dens, and the branches fell quiet but tense as every bird in the garden seemed to quiver and hide in the leaves. As if the helicopter wasn't loud enough on its own, it swallowed up every competing sound in the garden.

I watched it come in over the house, glinting and black in the sun, and its rumbling grew louder and louder until finally it spun and settled onto the pad and the rumbling whirred down to a whine. Several men in black suits climbed out, and Mr. Crane came from the back door to meet them, shaking their hands on the grass gap between the concrete of the back patio and the concrete of the landing pad. Once they were all out of the helicopter, I could see that there were six, plus the pilot in his black helmet, tending now to the machine. They stood where they were in that in-between space, apparently talking, and Mr. Crane pointed in my direction, and the men with him turned their heads toward me as one. Then they all followed him into the house.

Mrs. Crane didn't talk much on that first day of painting, which was a surprise because she always had so much to say, and I listened to the swish and the scratch of her brush against canvas, the soft slap of paint as she loaded bristles with color. A few of those black birds with red patches concealed on their wings had been hanging around a few days, and one of them spent that whole painting session perched on a branch just over my head (and, I learned later when I saw the canvas, found his way into her painting—maybe he'd perched himself there on purpose).

The longer I sat, the longer I posed, the more I was able to listen and look and think about things, and the more glad I became that I was no longer painting myself. I'd enjoyed it at first, but posing for someone else left me more time for the things I would rather be doing, which is to say no things at all. Even the posing itself was fascinating—how still could I hold, could I slow down my breathing, could I become so attuned to every quiver and spasm throughout my whole body that each follicle and muscle revealed itself? Could I be so inactive that body parts I'd never noticed made themselves as present to me as my eyes or my mouth? Posing for Mrs. Crane was, even on that first day, a lot like floating along on the river: the simpler it seemed, the more complex it actually was. It took great effort of will to do nothing, nothing at all, so completely for such long a time, and I was disappointed, though hungry and a bit sore, when she finally called it a day and packed up her paints and her brushes. I spent the rest of that day on the water, thinking about how much effort it took to hold still, and how much work it could be to do nothing.

She was back the next morning and the next morning, too, and most mornings after that for a long time to come. It became part of my routine, a new routine, I suppose: wake up and climb to my roof for the sunrise, get painted by Mrs. Crane, spend the afternoon

swimming. Between posing and floating, I spent the better part of
my day trying to hold my body as still as I could while my mind
wandered further and further afield—much of my daily movement
was only walking from one place in which I wouldn't move for a
while, to another place where I wouldn't move, either.

Mrs. Crane also found a routine to our work, and after the first
morning that routine involved talking to me while she painted.
The second morning I posed for her, she got me to climb to the
crook of an elm tree where two branches reached away from each
other. I perched in the seat of the vee, looking off toward the
house (which wouldn't appear in the painting, she said, because
her husband didn't like it when she included anything more than
the garden and me), and she stood below at her easel. I was pretty
high up in the branches, but when she spoke in her normal, quiet
voice I could hear like we were close together—perhaps the shape
of the tree helped to funnel the sound of her voice upward to
where I sat.

She said, as she had many times before, "You can talk to me,
you know. I really won't tell anyone. My husband won't need to
know. He already knows enough about everything else."

The first few times she'd invited that secret between us—a long
time before, when I was new to the garden—I had considered it,
at least vaguely. I'd thought how nice it would be to have a
conversation with her every once in a while, what I might tell her,
what I might ask, how I might share all the things I'd discovered
about myself and the world during my time spent in the garden.
I'd fallen out of the habit of imagining how my bloggers might
have described my new life—I hadn't thought about them in a
very long time, not since the day of the bee attack when I found
they'd gone quiet. Instead, without noticing at first or until it was
an entrenched part of my routine, I'd taken to imagining how I
might tell my story, picturing someone who followed me around
and took dictation the way I'd seen medieval scribes do on

historical reenactment programs. I came to imagine him as a monk in a dragging brown robe, rushing after me with a quill and a parchment at hand, to be called upon when I couldn't remember and always at hand to see what I saw and make a record I could return to. Arrogant, yes, and absurd, but sometimes, on some nights, it's a comfort even to imagine having someone to share all this with, someone else who knows my story like my scribe does—all that we've done here together and all we still have here to do. Imagining someone exists to record what I do, imagining that somebody knows—on days of great itching or illness, or when a toothache plagues me as they do sometimes—reminds me what my silence and occasional suffering are worth.

So I would be lying if I said I wasn't tempted to talk when Mrs. Crane offered. But I knew there were cameras, I knew there were microphones in my garden, and I knew I'd be found out whether it was her intention or not, and I wasn't going to lose my whole life only to utter a few worthless words. What could I possibly have to say to her that would be worth giving up all I'd found? I wouldn't be fired, I wouldn't be expelled from my garden, for the sake of casual conversation.

The only thing I really wanted to tell her was that I'd like a painting of myself with Jerome, perhaps of him curled asleep at my feet the way he so often was in the evening, while I ate my stew or drank my tea by the fire. But I had no way to ask without breaking my silence, and the request didn't seem important enough to do that.

So I smiled at her offer as I did every time, I shook my head no, and I didn't say anything.

"Fine," she said. "Suit yourself. But that doesn't mean I can't talk to you. Maybe I'll trick you into speaking. Maybe I'll get you so worked up about something that you can't help but talk. How about that?"

I smiled again, but I didn't want to encourage her plan by seeming concerned about it one way or another. Then I went back to concentrating on my pose in the tree, on trying to map the rough skin of the bark against my flesh in as much detail as I could, each ripple and bump, each broken-off piece of twig pressed under my thigh and each knot digging into my back. It was almost my own way of painting, perhaps, trying to develop a perfect mental image of everything touching my body, trying to capture the tree more fully than my inept brush ever could.

"So what should we talk about?" she asked. "Any suggestions?" She waited, with a smile that dared me to answer. Or dared me not to, perhaps. "No? I guess it's up to me then... Why don't you tell me about yourself?"

She waited again, and really seemed to believe I might speak at any moment. When I didn't, she said, "Honestly. Really. I'm not going to tell anyone—you can talk to me when we're alone. I'll let you know if anyone's coming. Besides, the boss man's not even around."

I must have made some expression of surprise, or of interest, when she mentioned Mr. Crane being away; probably it was my eyebrows—they'd developed a mind of their own, jumping up and down at things I didn't even know I was interested in, and the longer and shaggier they'd grown over time the more exaggerated their behavior became. They'd gotten so bushy I could see them myself just by looking up.

"You didn't know?" she asked. "Sure, he's in Afghanistan or Pakistan or somewhere like that. One of those places with more money than missiles, I guess."

My eyebrows and I both avoided asking that time, so she went on. "You're not going to tell me about yourself, huh? You really aren't going to talk? As long as you've been here, as long as we've been friends now, you still won't give me even that little thing?" I thought she might laugh, or else get up and leave.

I offered a sorry little smile and a shrug of my shoulders by way
of reply, which was more difficult than it may sound, considering
I was still perched in the tree and couldn't let go of the branches
for fear of falling, and was trying to hold perfectly still. She didn't
know what I'd given her, the sacrifice I had made for our
conversation and the risk I took making that gesture.

"Fine," she said. "Have it your way. I'll make it all up, then. I'll
tell myself all about you, and I'll get it so wrong you can't stand it
and you have to speak up to correct me. Sound good?"

She didn't wait for me to tell her whether I liked the idea,
which was smart enough, I suppose, because if I had spoken up to
answer it would have made moot her whole plan. Or made
mute—for once that linguistic error made sense, and I struggled
more than I had in a long time not to talk, not to share the joke I'd
made in my head, and not to laugh (which had been, over my
time in the garden, harder to avoid than actual speech; I wasn't
even certain that laughter was covered by my vow of silence, but
it was too late for me to ask, and I'd been stifling my smiles and
laughter for as long as I'd been in the cave). I remembered those
types of misheard words were called eggcorns, and I was thinking
about moot and mute and eggcorns and the acorns that were
growing and dangling all around me in that tree (so I suppose it
was an oak), and as my mind wandered off and away into all of
those topics so rich for reflection, Mrs. Crane painted quietly for a
while.

But when she started talking again she spoke about me, about
the me she imagined in place of the me who wouldn't speak to
satisfy her curiosity about himself. About myself, I mean.

She started right at the beginning. Not *my* beginning, but the
beginning of somebody's story. "So," she began, "you were born in
the shadow of a shipyard... no, wait, you were born in a coal-
mining town. Your father was a steel-drivin' man, and every
morning he hoisted his enormous black lunchbox and swung his

hammer as large as the hammers of two normal-sized men up onto his shoulder, and stepped into the stream of his co-workers flowing along the town's single road uphill toward the mine."

Where was she getting this stuff? It was exciting, it made a good story, but it wasn't mine.

"You were the quiet kid in school, of course. Not much to say, but watching it all—taking it in from the corner where you might be overlooked, and you knew more about what was going on in the lives of everyone around you than they could have ever imagined. The gossip, the secrets, the shared glances... no, wait. Hang on." She lifted her paintbrush away from the canvas and looked up at me in the tree with her head tilted and one eye closed.

"No, that's not it," she said. "You weren't quiet. Your mother always told people you were born talking because you had so much to say. Blabbing away as soon as you could, even before you could use any words. You were making up stories and rattling on about whatever it was you were saying. You talked to... to the plastic fish on the mobile over your crib, you talked to your stuffed animals and the, oh, what were they, the *cowboys* on your wallpaper. Talk talk talk, on and on and on."

She looked up at me, over her canvas. "That's more like it," she said. "That's more like you."

I listened for a while to the bristles of her brush splashing against the canvas, and it sounded like leaves falling from the trees above the river and landing on the skin of the water—the way they sound right up close, I mean, when they land beside your ear. Her paintbrush must have been louder than leaves, though, because I could hear it up in my tree.

She didn't say anything else for a while, just painted and smiled, and I couldn't tell if she was smiling at how the painting was going or at the story she'd told about me or at something else altogether. Whatever the reason, she wore a smile that would make clear to anyone looking that she, this woman, this actress who had been pretty famous and had given it up because her husband asked her to—so she'd said, on one of our berry-picking excursions— knew exactly who she was and what she was doing. That she was satisfied.

She had the kind of smile that would have made her a good hermit.

"And then all of a sudden," she said, "one day in, oh, maybe high school? Or was it later, in college? One day you were all talked out. You'd said what you had to say and didn't say anything else. Not a vow of silence like you've got now. It wasn't as dramatic as that. You still ordered food and answered questions, you still pleased and thanked when it was polite, but you stopped making conversation and you stopped telling stories and you stopped speaking for all but the most practical or pressing reasons."

She punctuated that with a broad, upswept stroke of her brush, from the bottom of the canvas to the uppermost corner with a snap of her wrist, the boldest, sharpest, most decisive gesture I'd seen her make all that morning. And I'd been paying attention, at least for some of the time.

"Your mother worried, of course. What mother wouldn't? Your father did, too, but not as much. He understood. He'd spent long years in the dark of the mines, don't forget." (I had, in fact, forgotten.) "He was used to days and nights without speaking because the mine was already so loud with all that clanging and clanking and the blasting of stone, and because he was so often tired—as tired as ten tired men, because that's how hard your father worked, remember. He deserved to be tired.

"He understood not needing to speak, and not having something to say all the time. So when your mother insisted you see a doctor about your new quiet, your father told her to wait, and he put his spoon down beside his bowl of soup—

remember how big his bowl was!—and he looked you in the eyes
and he asked if you needed a doctor. You didn't say anything, you
didn't nod or shake your head, so your father told your mother no
doctor was needed. And that was the end of that, wasn't it?"

And that was also the end of her work for the day, because Mrs.
Crane set the canvas against a tree trunk while she folded her easel
and packed up her case. I climbed down from my branch and tried
to look at the painting, but she turned it away from me and said,
"What do you need to see that for? I've already told you your
story."

25

It occurs to me sometimes that there must be goings-on going on in the world, current events more current than the ones I remember. The last news I knew of was Mr. Crane's downfall, if downfall is the right word. And even that, though it happened right here around me, I don't know much about, not much at all. Only that he was here and then he was gone. The whole story must have been larger, more lurid, played out across TV and papers and blogs. None of which reached me up here, and I can't say I mind. I can't say I've ever thought about it before, because my life went on more or less as it was; I had to provide my own food, set my own schedule, but I stayed in the garden and, if anything, my life became simpler once I was alone. I wondered, of course, where he'd gone, but only in the most general way—I never concerned myself with the specifics.

I might have felt a bit lonely, at first, in such a vast space without even Mr. Crane and his mansion, but lonely for what? Not for the life I'd left behind, a life no less solitary but far less satisfying than the one I live now. Lonely, perhaps, for some idea of what I had once expected my life would be like, or what I'd thought other people's might be. A useless, distracting loneliness, in other words, a longing for things that didn't exist. And what I had gained for giving up all of that, what had been granted to me in its place... I would have given up so much more had so much more been demanded of me. If all this hadn't come as a gift.

I lay in bed last night in the dark—the real dark, not the dark of my eyes—and asked the scribe if we knew anything more of Mr. Crane's fate, if there were clues I hadn't considered, but no, there was nothing. We only know what we know, the known knowns. Whatever happened to my employer, I knew as little of what happened right here at his home as I did of what was to come, the courts of law and of public opinion that must have held session, and for all I know he deserved what he got—I don't know what he was accused of, or if he'd done it, so perhaps it was something awful. Or not. I'd like to think that it wasn't, and that Mr. Crane is free somewhere else, away from these acres he left behind, perhaps living in his own cave in some other forest.

Should I have wondered? Should I have taken an interest when he was still here, an interest in him, in his wife? In Smithee? I wasn't being paid to take an interest in them—I was being paid for the opposite, even—but now whatever questions I may come to wonder about are never going to be answered whether I want them to be or not. What did I owe Mr. Crane, a job well done or more than that? Now that he's gone, now that he's given me this, I owe him a life well-lived, so that's what I've tried to accomplish in the years since his departure. I've thought, at times, that I knew just what that meant: a life of desperate quiet and sharp attention, of solitude and self-sufficiency, secure from the ups and downs of the world that are always, always the same however they change, and because of that are never worth knowing.

There was a war underway when I entered this garden, economic collapse on the horizon and the prospect of worse years to come. Maybe they have come, and maybe they haven't; the world for me is like that cat in a box that might be alive but might be dead, and until the box opens is somehow neither and both.

I don't want to know what's become of the world, but some days I wonder. I wonder in the safety of knowing I'll never find out, like playing a game. In the morning, most often, as I sit on my cave and watch the sun rise I imagine it glancing off clean cars and black top and tanning pale skin at the beach. I prefer to think it's all gone on the same without me, that my absence was swallowed like some lost explorer in quicksand—visible one moment, vanished the next, and the surface settled back into order as if it was never disturbed.

I suppose I imagine the world as a river in which I've settled onto the bottom, the Old Man's reach flowing from one pole to the other and around the equator and washing across everything in between. He taught me another way to be in the world, to be still and small and quiet in ways I never had been. Not that I'd ever been noisy or taken up very much space, but my insignificance had come from being anxious, being nervous or distracted or worried about looking busy, looking important, looking like somebody other than who I was. The Old Man, the days I spent afloat on the river, eyes open or closed, anchored by fallen trees or my toes in the sand, showed me that insignificance could be intended. That I was already dwarfed by the clouds and the trees and, most of all, by the river, so why pretend not to be? Why trouble myself to be something larger than I could possibly be?

I had the river, or the river had me; there was quiet and calm and there was the cave. There was the house on the hill and the appearance of food in the niche in my wall twice a day, and most of all there was time. Time enough, at last, for nothing at all. Time to think. And then the house and the meals and the Cranes were all gone, but I still had all that time. Maybe even more of it.

And it went on that way until the hikers arrived, but I know now—or I can admit what I've known all along—that it would have changed with or without them. Without my eyes, once they're really gone and not just slowly going, I will be swallowed up by quicksand, too. I will get lost some day or the next, and wander in circles with nothing to eat until I give up and lie down and die. Or go the wrong way and find myself out in that world beyond mine, which would be just about the same thing.

This morning I went to my garden as always, after my breakfast and after my swim. I crept past their tent quietly on my comfortable, much-improved crutch, thinking they were asleep—they seem to be recovered from their mushroom ordeal, but still sleeping more than usual, still healing perhaps. But when I passed the bright bulb of their tent and went behind the barrier of blackberry brambles—every year they grow thicker and creep closer up to my garden, and every year I spend more time breaking and trimming and burning them back from the edge of my field—when I moved past the bushes and past the strange, clean-scraped circle on the ground by their camp (something I hadn't spotted before, and noticed first with my bare feet), I heard them at work in my garden. One blur—him, I think—in the carrots, hunched over and weeding. And her with my watering can—I could tell because it was made from a dried and hollowed-out almost neon green gourd, and even its blur stood out against everything else—dowsing the thirsty young corn.

No one else has worked in my garden, no other hands have planted or weeded or watered my crops. No one else has even been in it, not since it was truly mine. Inside I raged despite myself, despite knowing in some smaller part of my mind that I need other hands if I'm going to survive. My hands balled into fists, then relaxed, then they tightened again, as confused as the rest of me was—it was clear they were helping, or thought they were. It was clear they were sharing the burden of work, but it was *my* work, in my garden, and not a task I wanted to share.

But maybe, I thought, as that quieter voice spoke up for itself, maybe the sharing, the intrusion, the arrival of these hikers into my garden, is what the Old Man has directed, and their work this morning is his loudest message to me. I won't know without more reflection, until I've spent more time on the river in thought, but in the meantime what could I do but go on with routine, do what I do every day? Go on, at least, with what I think I do every day— lately, with all these disruptions, it's been hard to tell and I often worry I'm getting things wrong, changing my routine from one day to the next because I'm unable to keep it all straight.

So I stepped into the rows of the garden and I firmed up the stakes for my beans and tomatoes. I guided the pumpkins on their prickled vines back into their corner and out of the peas they were chasing again. Always. Every year they roll into the neighboring patch, and every year I roll them out. And though my hands can work without eyes after doing this work for so long, I did everything slowly, as I always have. I savored each turned scoop of soil and each seed tucked into it and every pumpkin rolled out of the peas. And though I didn't ask the hikers to pay attention, I willed them to notice, to see what I was doing and how, and to learn how to care for this garden. I can't say if they were watching, or went on doing things their own way. But whatever they did, and however they did it, it dawned on me that the hikers weren't speaking any more than I was, and that I hadn't heard them speak at all, in fact, for a few days—not since their laughter while picking the poisonous mushrooms and complaining while they were sick. Did it mean something, I wondered, or had they just run out of words for a while?

And like that we worked through the morning, the three of us side by side in the field, each bent toward the ground and getting on with what had to be done for life to go on in this garden.

26

Every morning I emerge from my cave to stretch and scratch in its mouth and to present the performance of my regular wake-up routine to the world. First I lean left, hands on my hips, and push until my spine pops. Then the same to the right, before raising my arms up over my head and straining my body to reach as high as it can, up past the top of the cave's mouth toward the always blue, always untouchable sky. The ritual hasn't changed much over time, but the more mornings I've done it, the longer I've lived in this garden, the louder my body becomes: my back, my knees, my gas and my groans, everything is louder than it was long ago but my voice. I'm not sure I'd have a voice left if I tried to speak, or if it's atrophied over time and left behind little but a weak whisper. Perhaps someday I'll give it a try just to know, but not yet.

I went about breakfast as always, and climbed to my rooftop in time for sunrise and spent some time after the sky was lit blue with my eye on two squirrels who were chasing each other from branch to branch, from tree to tree, chattering and chirping and *tsktsking* each other before they finally got down to the business of mating far out on a thin branch that rose and fell so vigorously I thought it might break with the weight of their passion. But no, the branch held, the squirrels had their moment, and perhaps the next generation was secured for my garden.

They finished and went their separate ways—for the morning, I wondered, while gathering food, or had they parted for good?— and I thought back to another morning, other moments soon after sunrise, when Mrs. Crane came with her easel and paints. I moved to climb down from my cave but she said no, I should stay where I was, she would paint me there, in the first light of day. My face must have signaled that the sunrise had already ended, because she explained she would paint it from memory and imagination. Which was, I suddenly realized, what had been missing from my own paintings, and it seemed so obvious now—I'd been so caught up in giving Mr. Crane exactly what was in his garden that I never thought to paint the garden other than it was at the moment I painted. I'd been too caught up in the truth to get anything done.

"That's what I do, Finch, haven't you noticed? I pretend that things are what they aren't. I pretend everything is what I want it to be so I won't have to face what it is. That's what I'm told, anyway." She sighed, loud enough that it carried up to me on my cave. "It won't be hard to paint a sunrise not so long after it's happened, not for someone whose whole life is pretend."

She didn't seem quite herself, that particular morning, and in retrospect I suppose I knew something would happen. Her shoulders drooped, her whole body drooped—not really, of course, a body like that couldn't droop, but she carried herself like she was tired or bowed under weight. She painted quickly, with sharp, violent stabs of her brush. She didn't talk to me at all while she worked, which wasn't our normal routine. We worked a long time that day, and I found posing difficult because of her anger, the sour mood she radiated right up to me overhead. She kept me on edge, made me skittish and easily startled, and it was hard to fully focus on the nothing of what I was doing. She was still working when I became hungry for lunch, and when my body and mind both longed for their swim. She was still working as the sun blazed from yellow to orange; the ribbons of pollution in the sky to our west, out over the valley and ocean beyond, blossomed in purple and pink. It was the longest I'd posed at one time, the longest I'd ever held still, and as much as my body was screaming and sore and as much as I longed for my swim (and now wouldn't have it, as late as it was), I was pleased with myself and my effort, my effort at expending no effort at all and my accomplishment of sitting still for so long.

And Mrs. Crane had painted as long as I'd sat. She looked exhausted, her hair come undone and imperfect, one strap of her overalls hanging down on her arm, her face smeared with sweat and with paint, and the back of her neck badly sunburned—she looked a long way from the actress I'd seen on TV, or from the first time I'd seen her walking toward me down the hill, in the mist of the morning with a pail at her side. And I noticed now, at the end of our day and in fading light, that her toenails weren't even painted. I imagined the ways I might ask how she was, how I might ask if she was all right or if there was anything wrong. I imagined how Mr. Crane might ask her himself, and the conversations they might have that evening up in their big house, but then I stopped because I never liked to picture the inside of the house or to be reminded the big house was up there at all.

"What's here for you, Finch?" she suddenly asked, her old question again, and in thinning sunlight it was like her voice came out of the dark, disembodied. "What's here for any of us, except him? I don't know how you can stand it. I can't, not anymore, not all alone. It's too lonely here. Too far from town, too far from my friends. My family. My life. I should have gone back to my life a long, long time ago."

I think now, so long after the fact, that I knew she was telling me something. That I knew she was asking me something, or inviting me to ask her. When my scribe reminds me what happened, how that final conversation of mine with Mrs. Crane came and went, I can't help but think I knew there was more to it than I let myself know—she must have known she was leaving, she must have already realized that change was awhirl in the world, a tornado sweeping across the estate, but had I?

How could I know, in my cave, in my silence, deep down in doing my job? Then again, how could I not?

I wonder, too, if I could have kept her from leaving. Maybe if I'd made a sign, or offered a gesture to show I understood what she was telling me. Just so she knew I was listening. But why would I have done that, and why would she have wanted to stay? She said she had a life to get back to, and I wouldn't have kept her from that so she could hang around talking to someone who wouldn't talk back. She was right: I can't imagine what there was for her here, and there would be even less with her husband gone as, by then, she must have known he would be. And I don't think she understood what there was here for me, she never saw what I saw, and I wasn't going to speak; she'd said once she thought she would make a good hermit, and once I'd almost agreed, but I suppose both of us were wrong. I wasn't going to risk my place in the garden—if I did know that trouble and changes were coming, I wasn't aware that I knew it. I was living too much in the moment, living like there were no past and no future and focused only on spending each day in the garden as if my contract would never be up. She had a life to go back to, she said, but I had a life to preserve and a job to be done.

We stood in the half-dark of the garden as the lights of the big house above us came on one after another, like a fire was burning its way through one room at a time.

"Good night, Finch," she said, and I realized that while I'd been thinking she'd packed up her paints. And Mrs. Crane walked away up the hill for the very last time, though I didn't yet know it would be.

The evening drew the color out of her shadow in just a few seconds, and I watched her silhouette move off into the distance and dark. Then I climbed down and was surprised, but not really, to find my dinner steaming and ready to eat in my cave; it had arrived while I sat right above it, presumably by Smithee's invisible hand. More surprising was that Mrs. Crane's painting was in my cave, too, left behind and propped on my bed where I'd be sure to see it. It was dark in the cave, lit only by a small torch that stuck out of the nook on my wall where I'd wedged it, but I could make out enough of the painting to be confused.

It was me, on the cave as expected, but I didn't look much like myself. She'd captured my beard hanging over my chest, and my body looked accurately skinny and filthy and raw from all my scratching and scabs. But she'd painted me feathered, and crowned my head with a white plumage crest. And the sun wasn't rising behind me so much as it was bleeding, the colors the same as the ones in the sky, but somehow she'd made them look violent. And she'd painted the house, over my shoulder, but as she'd painted it had actually stood over hers. Mr. Crane was there, too, though we hadn't seen him that day. He was walking down the hill from the house in his usual gray suit, trailing a wake of money and blood, and leaving a dead, yellow swathe in the lawn.

I didn't know what to make of it. I didn't *want* to make anything of it, so I moved the canvas from my bed to the floor and into a shadow and went outside to my fire and dinner and a few cups of tea before going to sleep for the night. Had I known that was the last I would see of Mrs. Crane, I might have spent more time with her painting. But then again, maybe not, because it wasn't a picture I liked looking at. It wasn't something I wanted to see, so I went to sleep.

At some point in the night I was awakened, startled out of a dream that clung to me like a sticky film of sweat. Someone was talking outside my cave, close by and loud enough for me to make out two different voices but not quite what they were saying. I swung myself out of bed and padded to the mouth of the cave on my always bare feet—though they'd toughened to leather by then. I paused in my dark doorway to listen, and when I next heard the voices I could tell they were off by the blackberry brambles, and so I crept in that direction, keeping to the tree line to stay out of sight.

As I got close I saw the glow of two strap-on headlamps, bobbing around in the trees. Two men in black were making adjustments to one of the cameras badly hidden among the trees, two men in black like the one I'd spotted before, sneaking secretly over the river, but these two were talking, even laughing a little, not even trying to whisper, whereas the earlier intruder had made a show of his silence. Or hers. I crept closer, then stopped in the bushes to listen. Both of them were tall, and wiry-thin, and in their matching black outfits and masks I couldn't have told them apart if I'd needed to. They even sounded the same from where I listened.

"It's like they all fell for it," said one of the men. "All of 'em, every bastard in the world with more money than brains. You'd think they'd know better, you know? That it was too good to be true. I mean, come on. I could've told them you can't make money like that, and what do I know about money?"

"Looks like about as much as they do," said his partner, and they both laughed. As they talked, their headlamps ducked and wove across each other's masked faces.

One of the men held the boxy camera up to the underside of a branch, and the other tightened the metal straps that held it in place, whatever adjustment or repair they were making apparently made.

"No kidding. I mean, take this guy," he said and gestured up toward the house on the hill with his head and a thumb thrown over the shoulder. "More money than God, and he thinks he can get away with whatever he wants. Thinks no one notices what he's up to, thinks no one's as smart as he is. So arrogant he made it easy for our source inside."

The two of them crouched to repack a black bag of tools, and turn off then remove their headlamps. "Thinks we won't put it together. I mean, I've been working this case since you were in training. We've been on this guy since he was born. But I guarantee you, he'll *still* be surprised when it all comes down. They always are. The whole world'll see it coming, anyone who watches the news, but he'll be caught with his pants down and his head up his ass."

Tools packed, the two of them turned away from me and moved toward the river, walking quickly with no regard for the branches they broke with their steps or the noise they made with their passage. I followed, but being as cautious as I was to move quietly, I couldn't keep up.

The last thing I heard was one man in black say to the other, "Once I actually did catch a guy with his pants down, and he wasn't alone..."

It had been a long time since I'd heard a two-way conversation, and had heard someone talk about money or news or the world past the edge of my garden. I mean, Mrs. Crane had talked about going back to that world, but she didn't talk about what she would find. So hearing these two voices didn't sit well, it left me unsettled in body and mind, and before I could go back to sleep I needed a swim to calm down, to wash what I'd heard from my head—not the words themselves so much as the sound of words at all—and to get fully back to myself, to my garden and river and cave, as if those men in black hadn't been there for me to overhear.

After my swim, refreshed and washed clean by meditations under the stars, I went back to bed and dreamed about floating on the river as I had just done; I take it as a mark of success, a sign that I'm on the right path, that I often dream about my own life— like there's nothing more I could imagine, like there's nothing better for me to desire.

When I woke up again before dawn, my breakfast was of course in its nook, but Mr. Crane was in my cave, too. He stood with his hands clasped behind his back, wearing a gray suit and red tie (did he sleep in a suit?), with his head tilted forward to look at the painting left behind by his wife. His brow furrowed, his eyes alternated between squinting and opening wide, and he stared a long time at the canvas before releasing a long, heavy sigh.

I was still wrapped up in my blankets, awake but yet to move or to moan, wondering if Mr. Crane knew I was awake when he said, "It's difficult, Finch. It's difficult to rely on other people, however well paid they are. To count on them to do what you haven't time to take care of yourself. Can we be everywhere, Finch? Can we do everything? Of course, no, you're right. We must delegate. Share the load, yes. Rely on other people who are never, ever ourselves or even quite who we want them to be." He paused and leaned closer to the painting, then straightened up, turned to me in my bedding nest and said, "It's the nature of the thing, Finch. There's little we can do about it, as you and I know very well. We've been at this for such a long time, we know by now how the game works."

I felt like I was still sleeping, or at least like my mind was, because Mr. Crane made no more sense than most of my dreams. I thought about closing my eyes, seeing if I could wake up again, but the burning itch in my crotch and my bubbling stomach let me know that I was, indeed, wide awake.

"Self-sufficiency, Finch. That's the goal, isn't it? To avoid relying on other people, to avoid making them part of our plans. That's how we face things head-on. That's how we turn risk into advantage, of course." He stopped talking and looked in my direction, then scanned all sides of my cave. I think he said, "That's what you'll do," but he didn't say what "that" was. Then as abruptly as he'd started talking, as unexpectedly as he'd arrived—though who knows how long he'd been waiting before I woke up—Mr. Crane spun on his heel and walked out of the cave, hands still clasped behind him, fingers woven around one another, and he walked away into the morning. And a few minutes later I had stretched and had scratched and was full of my morning porridge, and was up on the cave with my tea just in time for another day's sun to arrive. For another day like all days to begin.

27

Time in Mr. Crane's garden usually passed in a seasonless stasis, one day and the next and the following month all blending into one another. I've asked my scribe if that makes it dull to record and retell, but he tells me no, that it's fine. Time here has no shape until something's changed, so I can only remember my life if I focus on disruptive moments, on events that stick out because they came as a break in routine. Of course there were many more days, days upon days, passing without variation except a chill or a warmth in the air and different thoughts crossing my mind as different shapes of cloud crossed the sky. But those kinds of days—the usual ones—are hard to pin down. It's easier on the exceptional days, on mornings like the one when Mr. Crane was in my cave when I woke up. Days like that were the boundaries around my routine, and the mileposts along which I marked time.

So after I woke to him considering the painting left behind by his wife, it was no great surprise that a day or two later a note appeared with my breakfast, another change to my routine, another strange season come into my world. It asked me to take up gardening, not of flowers but food, and said there were seeds and tools on the way and that I should begin by choosing a spot for my crops. It said, too, that my meals would still be delivered, as always, but I should make every effort to produce an amount of food that could sustain me, to make the endeavor more real.

Apart from a couple of abandoned window boxes and an apartment cactus that thirsted to death, I'd never done any gardening and didn't know where to begin. I had no idea what to look for in my garden plot, whether more or less sunlight was better, whether high ground or low, close to or far from the river, and on and on with questions I couldn't answer. I'd never stopped to consider—I'd never had a need—how many variables there might be in planting a garden, and how complicated it could be to get started. It was more work, though less painful, than gathering honey from the beehives on my hill, and I hadn't even planted anything yet. Part of me hoped Mr. Crane's interest in gardening would wane as quickly as some of his others, that this request would go the way of the morning I'd spent learning wood carving and gouged my hand open with an inexpert chisel, or the headstand morning meditations he'd requested between my periods of tai chi and of the lotus position, before the river was built and my reflections moved onto its water. And there had been other whims he had mentioned that never came to fruition, so perhaps the tools would never arrive and whatever spot I chose for my garden would remain moot.

But in the meantime I'd been asked to choose it, so I started with my own convenience: it should be close to my cave, as close as could be, so I wouldn't have to walk far to reach it. The closer it was, I figured, the faster I could be finished with what was required of me in the garden each day and the sooner I could get to the river. The stakes seemed low, I admit it: I'd already been told the garden wouldn't be feeding me, that my meals would still come from the kitchen, and not knowing how long I would have to maintain it—would I put in months of work, only to abandon it later?—may have sapped the earnestness of my effort.

Before wandering the estate, before walking from one possible plot to another, I sat on my cave with my tea even after the sun reached the sky, and I surveyed the ground around me. The open space near my cave, to the left as I sat on its roof—which must be north, if I consider the rise of the sun—had sunlight through most of the day, but part of it was in light shade. It was a flat patch of ground, and nearby to my cave, and that seemed to cover the bases. So I climbed down from my perch and walked the few steps to that open space where, to my quickly passing surprise, I found a selection of tools already waiting. A shovel, a hoe, and a rake, all of them superficially but not detrimentally rusted, all of them on worn wooden handles stained and patinaed and shaped by years of use—by whose use, I wondered, reminded of Mrs. Crane's blackberry pail: an actual gardener or a specialist in aging wooden handles and garden tools, an expert hired by Mr. Crane for the purpose?—and all of those tools were exactly my size, as I'd gotten used to things being, and honed to fit in my hands.

What else could I do but pick up the tools and start gardening, start going through the motions of gardening, at least, which were all I had at the time? I thought I might learn what to do by acting like I already knew what I was doing, by imitating what I'd seen farmers and gardeners do on TV. So I hoed and I raked and I shoveled throughout the hot day, my tunic scratching and scraping and dirt sliding down to collect in its wrinkles and folds and form extra blisters. My hands blistered, too, oozing all over the handles of my wooden tools, and I wondered if that was the source of their smoothness and shine—buckets and buckets of bloody and blistery pus—and then I tried to push that image out of my mind by working harder, by causing more pain to my hands and my back and my knees and other parts that hurt so much I couldn't tell them apart from one another. I was no longer a body but just ache and pain and just push and pull, up and down, back and forth, scoop and spread.

The soil, at least, was soft. It seemed soft to me. There weren't any of the roots and stones I'd been expecting because in movies when a fresh field is made, the farmers stack stones into walls around their edges and complain about all the rocks in the ground. My garden plot already had that much going for it.

And in time I'd turned all the soil. In time my green square had turned brown and I'd exposed the underground to the air. I'd known, of course, that there were worms and bugs in the ground, but I was amazed, astounded—aghast!—at how much had been happening beneath me; and it had been happening there all my life, I could only assume. Millions of pink squirming worms turned up to the surface, twisting and writhing and leaving soft wakes of soil as they stretched from one place to another, one body length at a time. I thought of the hyperefficient plants I'd been selling before all of this, how much time and money we'd spent making them look realistic, convincing the world they were real. We'd gone so far as introducing fake bees and apples and changing leaves, but all of that over the surface—so far as I knew, Second Nature had never, not once, introduced anything under the ground. And why would they have? Who looked in the cedar chips of an indoor garden bed? Who went digging for worms in the lobby of an office building downtown? The money and research would have been wasted, but now that I'd noticed, now that I knew, those plants seemed nothing but plastic. It wasn't the trees and the bushes themselves, they would still look real enough, they still did in my memory of catalog pages and websites and test installations, but they were all surface, no substrate. That word, "substrate," leapt into my mind, and I realized we'd used it in our catalog copy, not to describe the worms and the soil laid under our plants but instead as a name for the layer of netting and foam (made from recycled plastic, mostly our own flawed productions broken up and ground down) that we spread beneath all our plants to hold their woodchip surroundings in place.

By the end of the day my whole body hurt in ways it hadn't before. But my own substrate, the surface beneath my surface that held me together, felt strong and felt solid, felt alive and filthy with earth. My garden was ready, my earth was turned, and I hoped Mr. Crane's whim would survive—that his interest in gardening, *my* interest in gardening, wouldn't prove as fleeting as the hot spring I still hoped for, mentioned in my interview but never materialized.

I ate two bowls of beef stew with huge chunks of potato, and an entire loaf of bread in great bites, and fell asleep after only one cup of tea by my fire; I was so tired I hardly felt the itch of my blankets while drifting away, whistled off to sleep by Jerome's loud breath somewhere close to the cave.

And I woke the next morning with the usual creaks, cracks, and groans in my body—the usual but more of them and fiercer—though they felt better-earned than they had any morning before.

In my cave when I woke, along with my breakfast, was a basket filled with seeds wrapped in brown paper packets and labeled with only the name of what they would grow: pumpkins, beans, potatoes, carrots, and so on. No instructions, no pictures, nothing else. Just one abstract, empty word meant to tell me all I needed to know about growing that crop. I rushed through the sunrise, I wolfed down my porridge and tea, and carried my basket of seeds to the ground I had cleared.

What did I know about planting? I'd seen on TV that I should drag a hoe down the rows of the field, then scatter seeds into the trough, so that's what I did. A row of tomatoes, a row of potatoes, a row of carrots and one of corn; asparagus, parsnips, and something called kohlrabi I'd never heard of before. I planted cucumbers and cabbage and beans, and when all the packets were empty I planted a mixed row of all the spilled seeds left behind in my basket. The hollowed gourd watering can had appeared in the field overnight so I used it, filling it from the wooden pump that had sprouted from the ground while I slept; I supposed it drew water right from the river, as I had been doing, but I appreciated the ease and convenience of not hauling each bucket back and forth by myself. And it was easier to pump than to scoop errant fish from my bucket—they seemed to be breeding like the garden's rabbits, filling the river with fins and the shimmering motion of swimming more than I'd ever noticed before.

And when the whole garden was planted, when each row had been sealed by a long scar of turned soil, and each planted row had been watered, I went back to my cave. The whole day had passed, and I carried the basket of food delivered in my absence, containing that day's bread and stew, to the field where I ate it cold, in too much hurry to wait by the fire while it warmed. I watched my rows, anxious as if they might grow right away, and I chased off birds already pecking the ground after seeds—perhaps I had spilled some between rows, but in case they got into the habit of eating my crops I chased them away with my arms raised like a scarecrow.

After dinner, while the evening sky bruised as if its body, too, had worked a long day, I walked down to the river for a rare sunset swim. I wasn't in the habit of swimming at night, not for any reason except that I wasn't, but I hadn't been into the water since starting my garden had given me so much else to think about. As I floated the knots in my muscles untied, my back and arms and legs loosened as if they were water themselves, and my blistered palms soaked and soothed in the cool balm of the current. Fish glided past underneath, leaves and seedpods sped by on the surface and a rustling wind up above, and I lay between those three layers and thought about nothing at all.

28

I was afloat on the river this morning when the cracking and banging of stones struck together came to me on the air. It was the unmistakable sound of industry—its rhythm, its pace—if not quite the mechanized power of Mr. Crane's crews. And when I climbed from the water and onto my crutch, and began the climb back to my cave, I found my feet following a wide, flattened track of grass crushed on the slope by something heavy and flat with squared edges.

I hobbled uphill, wondering what the hikers were doing, but before reaching them something stuck to my foot and I sat down to see what it was. A sheet of white paper, crumpled and torn, but a sheet of actual paper like I'd never expected I might encounter again. I crumpled it in my hands, to feel its resistance and hear its soft crunch, then straightened and smoothed it against my knee, its wrinkles as fine and frequent as my own. Despite myself, I almost wept—not because I coveted paper, not because I even missed it, but there was something about feeling those textures I'd long ago forgotten that made the surprise overwhelming. There were words on the page, and a few pictures, so I held it up close to my eyes, but the text was still too small to read, or my eyes were too weak to focus enough to make sense of the letters.

I'd hate to think my eyes have forgotten how reading is done, even if they won't need to do it.

But I could see the pictures—a logo at the top of the page, and I recognized it as the mark of the same free email provider I'd used during those long ago lonely nights in my dark apartment. A bit updated, the logo a little bit different, but I could tell that this page was a printed-out email. An article, in fact, because at the top of the text was the logo of a movie industry magazine, or maybe its website; someone had emailed a clipping from that magazine to someone else, and someone had printed it out. And beneath those logos, the biggest surprise, was a photograph of a face I knew: there was Smithee, older now, out of his butler's suit, but the same strange man I'd once known with his notebook and camera and sneering eyes, creeping through the garden on quiet, professional feet. He must have had something to do with some film, something important enough to have his face there alongside the words.

I scanned the page, puzzled, amazed, wondering what it all meant. I held the paper so close to my face that I could feel the cool of the sheet on my warmer eyeball. But the letters all swam in a fog, or a soup. I nearly cried out, I nearly ran up the hill despite my knee, to beg the hikers for help, but I overcame those emotions and settled them down, I listened to the reassuring voice of the Old Man, lapping the banks with his calming and constant rhythm. And for a brief, fleeting moment—a couple of seconds—I somehow, by chance, perhaps not, held the sheet out at just the right angle, the light was just so, and I was able to read a headline, the largest text on the page:

"Anticipation for Hermit Film"

And I knew then what Smithee had done, what he'd been doing in all of his creeping and jotting and photography, and I knew how the hikers had come to be here. Unable to actually read it, I couldn't tell how old the email might be and how much older the article was. I didn't know if the film had come and gone or might still be coming. But I knew that one way or the other, in all this quiet time, some version of me, some part of my story, had made its way out of the garden and into the world.

I sat on the slope, on broken grass crushed by whatever the hikers had done, and for a moment I thought about nothing, and then my mind flooded with thoughts. What did I have left? What was my own? What did all this mean for me?

All those years ago at Second Nature, I'd sent out my emails and written my blogs and made my small impact on something much larger, just as here in my garden I grow my crops and harvest my honey and change the landscape around me in modest ways. But in the end it's all as fleeting as the bubbles I stir in the river—those websites will vanish if they haven't already, and when I'm gone the brambles will creep in to claim all the changes I've made. Someday, in time, they'll creep in to conquer my cave if I'm not still here to shear them. For so long I've thought of myself as self-sufficient, but I'm nagged by a new question now.

I pretend my solitude is isolation, that I've erased myself from the world, but I'm more in it than I've ever been. Which is to say, not very much, no more and no less than anyone else—we may have a more lasting impact on the world when we break down into nutrients and raw material that nourish a whole chain of life, insects and earthworms and grass, than we ever have when we're alive. Perhaps that's the closest any one of us comes to knowing how things fit together. But even before they arrived here, before I knew they existed at all, I was part of what those hikers were doing; however they learned about me, from a film or an email or an article, it made some difference for them like so many things made a difference for me, in bringing them here to this garden as I, too, in my time, was delivered. How could I keep that from them, and how could I know that I'm meant to?

I've been so busy wondering what I will give up by engaging these hikers, by making a gesture that invites them to stay. And I've worried, too, about what I might gain, so caught up in profit and loss that I only now realize both of those are the wrong questions. That the questions aren't mine to be asked—my life here, my life anywhere and like anyone's, is a sandcastle built on the edge of the sea. In my case a sea of blackberry brambles, waiting to rush in and wash what I've built here away. And that's a good thing. It's the way of the world. But to think of my life here as solitude, as self-sufficient, is my ego ignoring how much I depend on everything else: the river, the garden, the ground where my vegetables grow. Mr. Crane, whose presence is still here as much as my own, and these hikers, now, without whom I wouldn't last long in my present condition, a present that will be my future. Without whose mysterious intentions and unexplained willingness to help me, or so it seems, I would be lost in the dark sooner rather than later, I think.

Maybe self-reliance was never what I was meant to look for, and sustainability was: can I build something and have it continue without me, can my good works outlast my good life? That's what I should have been asking. What good comes of all I've done here if it rots and withers and vanishes with me, turning to dust along with my anonymous bones on some ever-still edge of the garden? What good is a story that doesn't get told, at least told in actions if never in words? Oh, it would be told by the worms, told in their devouring and digesting and divesting of me, but it's been told, too, by that movie in which Smithee played some major role, a movie that must have been seen by the hikers. Some movie somewhere has been telling my story for me while I've gone on thinking my story was no longer out in the world. And all the while that world was bringing the hikers right here to my doorless doorstep, the hikers and how many others to come, I now have to wonder—was the film a success, or will it be? Does anyone care? Part of me, I admit, wants my story to matter, and the rest of me knows that it would be disaster for this garden and the life I have built.

Does the Old Man have his hand in this, too? Is it just one more piece in the puzzle he's always assembling around me, or do these events far beyond the edge of the garden fall outside even his gaze?

Later on, back at my cave, while dinner bubbled away on the fire, I slipped that white sheet of paper, stained with grass and soil but bright as a supernova in the palm of my hand, into the flames. I heard it crackle and hiss, and I watched it flare in the fire, but before it was gone altogether a breeze blew and lifted charred feathers of paper out of the flames, brushing them hot against my cheeks and onto my legs and scattering them all over the garden in scraps too small to be gathered, or perhaps even burnt to ash in the air before landing.

29

My garden grew funny that first year, tangled and stubby and snarled. My tomatoes were too close together and my carrots were too far apart. My pumpkins rolled on long vines into the pea patch, and some of my potatoes were too deep and others were not deep enough. But I learned from my errors, I took mental notes and saved seeds from my harvest the way I'd heard could be done. And over time my planting improved, my vegetables flourished, though that first season strained my appetite, especially after the garden became my major food source. And I wasn't much better at fishing.

But I've gotten the hang of it, over the years.

And oh, that first harvest, those first fruits of my vines—the first bite of tomato I'd ever taken, in my whole life, that didn't come from a can or a store or the dank, dark dump of a truck. My God, that tomato. That carrot, that bean. Those peas. I could go on, but there's no use describing what needs to be felt to be known, what needs to be tasted and on the tip of your tongue to make sense.

Once my garden was planted, it took time to settle back into routine, into my *new* routine, because now I had more to do than float on the river all day. I had crops to water, I had weeds to weed. I had ladybugs and green worms and brown moths to keep an eye on and make sure they weren't eating my food, at least not too much of it. We'd made a silent agreement, the insects and I, that we could share my garden if we did it with mutual respect.

I would leave enough for them if they left enough for me, and from the start we found our balance.

The birds have been another story, right from that first day of planting. I chase them off, they return. I chase a bird in one direction and three others land behind me and have at my harvest. I tried making a scarecrow of sticks lashed with vines and my cast-off tunic to bulk up the body, but it worked no better than I'd expected it would—it looked too much like me, all bones and blanket, and the birds clearly had no fear of me, in the flesh, what little there was of it, so why would they fear a scarecrow in my image?

I've tried throwing rocks but I've never struck one single bird and, to be honest, I've never tried very hard—I'm not sure I want to hit one, because what would I do after that? I don't know how to butcher a bird, and they aren't big enough to be a meal in themselves. It took long enough to work out how to fish and what to do once a fish had been caught. Birds are a whole other warm-blooded ball game.

Once my garden was growing, once I'd reached a truce with the bugs and a stalemate with the birds—they were going to get some of my garden, and there was nothing to be done about that, so I'd just plant a bit more than I needed—my days took on the shape they still have. Breakfast and tea at sunrise, a short morning swim, a few hours weeding or planting or picking produce, back to the river in the afternoon before turning my crops into dinner. It didn't take long for my life to fall out on those lines. After the seeds and tools first appeared and after several days' wonderful backbreaking labor—backbreaking, veil-lifting, bodybuilding hard work—the garden didn't need me every minute so I headed back to the water as much as I could.

And one of those post-planting mornings, on the way from my cave to the river and passing the blackberry patch, I spotted something strange in the bushes—a branch out of place, too straight, too thick, with no offshoots or sprigs aspring from its sides. So I stopped to investigate, expecting another microphone poorly concealed or some other unwelcome device. But what I found was a bamboo fishing pole, leaning out of the bushes as if meant to be found. It had a hook and a round wooden float on the line, painted red and white, and there it was waiting for me. It was as brand new and antique all at once as everything introduced into my garden, but none of its hardware corroded by rust.

I held it in my hands, testing the weight, wondering when it had been delivered and placed in that bush. I practiced some baitless casting like I'd tried in a few fishing video games at which I'd never been good. I didn't know how to fish, I'd never cast a real rod or hook and I'd never baited one either, but I did know enough to use worms, and I knew where I could find some of those.

I wasn't sure, at first, that I wanted to fish, that I wanted the blood and bait on my hands. Later, of course, I would have to, but when I thought it was only a choice, when I still thought the fishing pole and garden were more of Mr. Crane's whims, I wasn't in a hurry to use it. So I spent that day swimming instead, the fishing pole on the bank with my tunic, and I carried it up to my cave when I went to lunch, to lean against my wall out of harm's way until I wanted to use it or until Mr. Crane told me to.

Only a few days later, some sprouts were beginning to emerge from the dirt in my garden—carrots, if I recall correctly, but those first shoots might have been something else. In all the excitement, my scribe seems to have missed making record of that. Buoyant on the thrill of having made something grow, of having actually brought life and green growth to the garden, I floated in the river and in my head all at once. As I drifted, eyes on the sky and two lion-shaped clouds in aerial combat, I spotted something at the edge of my eye. Turning, rolling on the water toward the far bank, I saw a brown wooden box up in the crook of a tree. So I swam toward the shore, and shimmied right up, and found a box built like my paint box had been: brass latches and corners, all looking aged.

It was heavy, and large enough to be awkward, so I had to haul it down to the ground before opening it to find what seemed to be a first-aid kit inside: not adhesive bandages or bottles of aspirin, but a crude (yet sharp) pair of scissors, clean cloth bandages, and a long, curved needle and thread. There were other tools and supplies that meant nothing to me, I had no idea what they were for, but I hauled the whole kit to my cave as I'd done with the fishing rod, too, wondering why I had found it. Was I meant to injure myself? Was it a request from Mr. Crane that I get hurt and play doctor? I wasn't big on the idea, so I waited to see what he said, if he said anything, rather than rush to break and splint a finger or gouge open one of my arms; I hurt myself often enough without doing myself in on purpose.

And my next discovery came a few weeks after that, I suppose, when the corn looked like stalks and the lettuce like leaves and I'd already eaten a bean and some peas—picked right from their shoots and their vines, straight into my mouth, and how did I go so long without knowing they tasted like that?

I was out in the garden pulling up weeds, which was tricky because I didn't know yet what all my plants looked like and had to wait for them to grow, to take on their shape, before I could identify the intruders hiding among them. I had nothing with which to make signs, and it was too late to make them after the seeds had already been planted. And I made mistakes; I pulled up ungrown carrots and left other things growing that later spread through the garden so I had to fight them right down to their roots. Sometimes I had clues, sometimes the insects I'd reached a truce with let me know what were weeds and what weren't, because they only seemed to spend their time on the plants that were something to eat. Anything with no beetles or butterflies on it, I pulled from the ground and dug out its roots, and for the most part that worked.

While I worked at the weeding, I found a long crate half-hidden under some flowering bushes (what they were, I don't know, but the orange butterflies seemed to enjoy them), as long as my legs and with a loop of rough rope at each hand as a handle. I pulled it out of the brush and pried the lid off with a flat, sharp-ended stone, and found a collection of hand tools inside: a hammer, a chisel, a saw, what I knew was a plane, and other tools I had no name for at all. Was I meant to build something for Mr. Crane? Was I meant to take on some new project?

Though after seeing the sharp edges on the chisel and saw, the first-aid kit I'd found made more sense. Mr. Crane must have noticed how clumsy I was—or how clumsy I was at the time; my hands have gained confidence over the years, and I've learned to trust them at work. But it's no wonder he might have expected me to find trouble with some of those tools, at whatever he meant me to use them for.

At the end of the day, when I was done gardening and swimming, I dragged the crate back to my cave. It was almost too heavy to lift, and the box was too long for me to comfortably hold it aloft—too wide for my wingspan, and holding it longways before me made it too heavy out front and made walking almost impossible. So I gripped one of its rope handles and hauled it over the ground, tearing a dark, damp trench through the grass of the garden that I regretted as soon as I turned around and saw it. But what else could I have done? The tools had to get to the cave, and there was no other way they would get there—not with me hauling alone.

When I arrived on my doorstep, out of breath and exhausted with sore back and arms, I left the crate by my fire ring and stepped inside. Where I found Smithee standing over my pallet, poking his camera into my niches, photographing my pinecones and feathers and all of the treasures I'd found. He wasn't touching any of them, I don't think he took anything except pictures, but when he saw me behind him a guilty look crossed his face, for a second, before it settled into a sneer.

"Who are you going to tell?" he asked me. "Yes, you've caught me, but you're not going to say anything."

Smithee let his camera fall on its strap so it bounced against his gray-vested chest and then settled. He stepped toward me, through the dim light of the cave, and something in his step made me think of a mugger, made me step back myself until I was almost outside the cave again. On the threshold, eyes both in the dark and the light all at once, I could hardly see for a second, and before my vision restored itself Smithee was right in my face.

"Am I scaring you?" he asked. "Am I making you nervous?" His voice wasn't professional any longer, it wasn't the tone of a butler. "At least I have your attention, for once."

I think my face showed my confusion, and asked the question my mouth never would, because he explained.

"You've hardly noticed me here. And I'm sure you've never spent a moment thinking about all the other people who make this estate run—the cooks, the cleaners, the landscapers who tend to your cave, for fuck's sake."

It was true, he was right: I hadn't thought about any of that. But I wasn't sure why I was meant to, and why Smithee expected that I would have been paying attention; that's not what I was paid for, it wasn't my job. Any more than he was expected to live in a cave, or to meditate on the shape of the clouds while going about his day's butling. I'd focused on doing what I was hired for and on doing it well, just like Smithee was doing his best at his job and, I assumed, all those others he mentioned were working at theirs. I worked for Mr. Crane the same as they did, and I couldn't help it if I liked my job better.

"You're as blind as he is," Smithee snarled. "You're as inhuman and cruel and self-centered. You're just as helpless without the rest of us behind the scenes, polishing the walls of your bubble. You people make me sick. You make all of us sick, people who work for a living. And you probably don't even know it."

I realize now that there was something to what Smithee said, though it's taken a long time to see it behind the screen of his confusing rage. Which was all I could see at the time.

Smithee laughed, a cold laugh, a laugh that sounded like resignation and revenge at once. Then he stepped toward me again and, despite myself, I backed away.

"I was going to say that it will all change for you now. But I've just realized it probably won't, not with all the money he'll give you. You'll go on playing your games someplace else while the rest of us go look for jobs."

Smithee advanced while he spoke, but he stopped at the crate of tools I'd dragged over and knocked open the lid with the toe of his shiny black shoe. He looked down, then reached into the crate and pulled out a hammer. "Maybe," he said.

I looked around, knowing that Mr. Crane's cameras were watching, wondering if he was paying attention or if anyone was. Hoping there was someone up there in the house who saw what Smithee was doing, or what I thought he was going to do. Hoping they'd come running down from the house to step in, and maybe they would be able to tell me what it had all been about. But if someone was watching, they didn't come.

Smithee kept moving closer and I continued backing away, and we could have gone on like that for a while, making our way around the garden hour after hour like some kind of boring performance. But he raised the hammer up to his shoulder, as if he was going to swing—or more like he was going to throw the hammer out into the grass, which turned out to be better for me, because in that instant a howling came from behind me, a long, low howl I knew well.

Jerome charged toward Smithee, his whole body bounding so hard that the ground shook and the tools rattled and clacked in their crate. He wanted to play, he'd seen Smithee's gesture and thought the hammer was about to be thrown the way I threw him sticks—he wasn't much of a cat, as I've said—and so here he was. But Smithee didn't know what Jerome's approach meant, and instead of throwing the hammer he turned and he ran, away from the cave toward the river with Jerome on his tail. I watched the two of them vanish over the hill, past the hives, and listened to Jerome's howl fading into the distance.

I'd been frightened, I realized after the fact, as soon as Smithee was gone. In the moment, when he was before me and threatening violence, I'd been too confused to know what I was feeling. I needed a moment to think about it, and as I sank onto the stump by my dormant fire ring my body quivered with all the leftover fear and adrenaline and whatever else I was feeling.

At the time, and for a long time after, I only thought Smithee was crazy, that his attack—does it really count as an attack?—had nothing to do with me, really. And once things had changed in the garden, once I knew what he must have already known, I assumed he was angry about losing his job. But now, after thinking about it for all these years, after asking the scribe to remind me what happened again and again, I know there's more to it than that. I know he was right, in some ways, about the bubble I lived in and the illusion of my self-reliance. But all that did change, and part of me wishes Smithee had been here to see it. And part of me is glad that he wasn't, because Jerome wasn't here any longer to intervene on my behalf. Because neither lion nor butler ever came back after running away down the hill, though I did find the hammer in the grass later on.

Losing Jerome as a friend was the bigger disappointment, perhaps my biggest in all the changes that came in those days. Even after I was alone here, I held onto a nostalgic image of Jerome and myself in the garden. It would have been poetic, the two of us side by side, never talking but always knowing the mind of the other. Had I been able to choose a companion, I think I would have chosen Jerome. He had his difficult moments, but in our time together we'd come to understand each other as well as I've known anyone in my life.

Then again, his medication would have worn off and run out, and he might not have behaved the way I recall—better to be left with the friendship I remember and have no doubt distorted, than to be shredded by the claws of a lion. Perhaps Mr. Crane knew that, perhaps he thought of it first, and had Jerome taken away. He might be in a nature preserve with other lions somewhere— that doesn't sound so bad for him. Or perhaps he chased Smithee down out of these hills, into the city, and is wandering the alleys somewhere like any other stray cat.

30

The last morning of my first new life, the end of my first life in this garden, began like every other morning had for a long time. Breakfast and tea, sunrise on top of my cave, my swim and reflections, and into my vegetable field for the day's labor. The day didn't feel any different, and I had no warning there would be change—no ominous weather or murder of crows the way I might expect if I were in a film, no heavy-handed music rolling out of the speakers that hid in the trees, none of that. Just the river, the garden, and me going about being me as always, as ever.

But it changed, it all changed, as I was re-staking a tomato vine that had shot up beyond the control of its too short post—I'd only recently realized that the plants might be staked, that they might grow better supported, but hadn't yet found the appropriate height for the sticks I shaved with my chisel and plane, and tied with braids of long grass from the banks of the river.

Then there it was, there he was, Mr. Crane's voice through the speakers, rumbling and buzzing and crackling out of the trees, shaking loose birds who burst into flight, up out of my pestered rows (and sometimes I wish now those speakers still worked, to drive the birds from my crops).

"Finch," he boomed from above and below both at once, from speakers in the branches and brambles. "Listen. This is important."

As if in that moment I could hear anything but his voice.

"I'm leaving. It's all over here. I only have a short time until I need to go."

Go where, I wondered, what was he talking about, but even if I had asked he wouldn't have heard (or maybe he would have—there were microphones, too, after all—but I didn't ask outside my head).

"My wife has already left, and so have the staff. Smithee went sometime last night, and he was the last." He sighed, and a few seconds of crackling hung in the air, tense like a record player had started up and the world was waiting for music. "I don't blame them," he said. "They did what I paid them for, and I gave them what they were owed. There's nothing left for them here.

"I've taken care of you, too, Finch. There's nothing to worry about. I've honored our contract. The full amount plus a bonus has been deposited into your bank account, the one we set up when you were hired. You can claim it whenever you want to, even before the rest of your seven years has been served."

My stomach sank like a rock in the river, and I fell onto my knees. I was being expelled from the garden. He was pushing me into a world that I didn't miss. I'd lived here as if I wouldn't have to leave, I'd found the place I belonged, and it was about to be wrested out of my hands.

"But listen, Finch. You don't have to leave. You don't have to go anywhere. I've called in some favors, and when they take everything else they won't be touching the garden."

The relief of those words made me almost more overcome with nausea than the first shock had done, but he went on, so I listened and held my quivering stomach in check.

"The garden, the whole estate, has gone into a trust. It can't be taken or altered in any way, unless it's by you. It won't be on maps, there won't be a driveway or road, and I've had my landscapers raise cliffs and create barriers on the edge of the property, to discourage any intrusions. And you have been assigned a legally binding lifetime right of occupancy. So it's up to you—you can stay for as long as you want to, or you're welcome to leave any time and be a rich man." He paused, and the whole world was silent except for the hum of his speakers, then the ratcheting rumble as he cleared his throat came like thunder.

"You don't have to decide now. You don't have to decide at all, Finch. You have the rest of your life. And thank you."

Then the speakers were as silent as everything else, for a very, very long moment. Then birds began chattering about what had occurred, and bugs buzzed again, and the wind returned to the trees. A soft splash fluttered up from the river and into my ears, and I sat on the ground looking uphill toward the house, at the dark upstairs window, wondering if he was behind it, where he was going and why, and what had just happened to me.

For once I had known what I wanted, exactly what I wanted, and I had—in my own idle way—worked as hard as I could to obtain it. And somehow, for some reason, it worked. The life I had found here would still be mine.

But why? I wondered if I should go up there, if I should knock on the door and ask. Or give him a handshake or hug. What would he do now, fire me for talking? The terms of my contract were broken, by Mr. Crane and not by me, and I supposed I could talk if I wanted to. I supposed I could do whatever I liked.

But he was my boss, not my friend. He didn't need questions or concern from me. Friendship wasn't the job I'd been hired for, and he had given too much for me not to do what he asked now. So I did what I had been doing since entering my cave, and what I have done ever since: I sleep and I wake and I garden and I swim, and I sit by the fire and I sleep again.

It was a shock the next morning when food didn't come to my cave. At first I thought breakfast was late, but it wasn't late, it was over. Like he'd said, the servants were gone and only I was still there—and perhaps Mr. Crane, if he hadn't left yet, though I didn't expect him to walk down with my breakfast even if he was in the house. But I was well-supplied by my garden, I had plenty to eat on my own.

In time, after a few weeks perhaps, I was disturbed at work in my garden by a great rumble from up at the house and turned to see wrecking balls knock it down. And in what seemed like no time it was gone, the hill bare as if it had never borne the concrete footprint of a mansion at all, and I was truly, completely alone.

The first thing I did was peel off my tunic, to parade my nude self through the grass and the garden and trees, past inert cameras and speakers and microphones, and I've never put that cursed garment onto my body again; it's withering now on the sticks of my useless scarecrow.

In my first days alone, I went through the motions. I climbed to my cave top and went to the river, I worked my garden because I needed to eat. I learned—slowly—to fish, and through trial and error, but mostly error, to clean and to cook what the river provided. But I thought constantly about Mr. Crane's words, about what he'd said through the speakers before he was gone: I was a millionaire now, I could leave, I could do almost whatever I wanted. I might have had enough money to build another garden like this one, another cave, in some other place if I wished. Anything I'd ever dreamed of was small, simple, and unambitious, and now I could afford all of it if I decided to leave Mr. Crane's... *my* garden.

If I decided to leave and go back to the world and the valley and city, with its traffic and TV and cubicles—not that I'd need to work in one ever again.

Without Mr. Crane's notes and directives to break up my days, they all ran together like a pool of still water, growing murkier the longer it sat. Sometimes it rained, sometimes I caught cold, but mostly the days ran together, and if not for the constant needs of my garden, which was really just my need to eat, I might have even grown bored.

Maybe I did, a little.

I spent the better part of a week weaving a welcome mat from reeds and rushes and grass I chose from the banks of the river, not for any particular reason, not because I expected a guest, but because having a project—even one as pointless as a welcome mat for a home without visitors—filled up my days.

Then one afternoon on the river, while I watched what might have been the nine hundredth lion-shaped cloud I'd seen since I came to the garden, a voice spoke to me. No, not a voice, that wasn't it... the words, or their meaning, were in my head, but even without being spoken aloud it was the voice of a very old man. And I knew right away that he was the river, that his was the comforting presence I'd felt that long ago morning trapped under the ice. The calm hand that had guided me through growing my first crop of beans and had taught me how to sit still. He'd been there all along, all over the ground and up in the trees and across the skin of the river, but he'd never once spoken until I thought I had been left alone and he revealed to me that I hadn't.

He told me I had more to do in this garden. He told me I wasn't done, that I should do more than just grow my carrots and beans and potatoes. I should create new ones, I should cross one vegetable with another, cross fruits with fruits, and bring something into the world. Something more than the boredom that had begun creeping in.

So I did. I took his direction and spliced carrots and parsnips together and slipped them anxiously into the ground. I wedged cloves of garlic inside small potatoes, in hopes of pre-flavored spuds. I tried to make blackberry apples and strawberry pears— and I thought back to my inept paintings—and most of my experiments failed to grow altogether. But there were exceptions, successes encouraging me to go on—the carsnip being the first—and there was the Old Man, my constant companion though he hardly spoke more than I did. He was always over my shoulder, he was always watching my hands at their work, and guiding me in my tasks. Revealing the world to me one secret after another. A mentor. A manager.

If I'd felt a few weeks of boredom, if I'd felt for a moment I'd seen all there was in this green world of mine, I was far from such foolish thoughts now. I could never grow tired of this place and the fresh mysteries it serves up every morning, arrayed in the soft light of sunrise and all within reach of my cave.

31

Those hikers I hid from have stayed, and it looks like they plan to keep staying. This morning I returned from my swim in the river to find them at work by their tent, on the round patch cleared of grass I spotted in their campsite yesterday morning. The circle seems to have been dug down a few inches or maybe a foot—I stuck an arm in to feel for its depth while they wandered away— and they've ringed it with the stones they dragged up from the river. They must have worked through the night, by the golden glow of the headlamps they wear (how I hope for those batteries to wane!), and I wonder why I didn't hear it. Now he's adding another layer of rocks while she encircles the inside of the ring with tall branches broken from trees in the garden—that explains the pile of bark and small twigs I came across on my way to the river, and I think those branches were also the base of the sledge with which they hauled stones up the hill and crushed that long stripe of grass.

So they're building a hut, they're going to stay, and who's to say that they shouldn't? There isn't another cave for them here, only mine, so I suppose they have to build something, and at least they have no power tools to tear up the quiet and calm of my home. Most of the time, those two are pretty quiet themselves. I haven't heard them speak since their mushroom hunting—have they given it up altogether, or is it only when I'm in earshot?

They don't appear to have brought any tools, except for a knife with a thick, heavy handle they're passing back and forth to share as a hammer. And here's me in my cave, sitting on top of a whole box of tools that I'll no longer be able to use once my vision has faded completely. All the tools Mr. Crane left me, revealing them to me one at a time as I built my life in this garden, all the tools those hikers will need to build here a life of their own. I've been sitting on this box most of the morning, waiting for the Old Man to tell me I should drag it out, share my tools with the hikers, or that I should push it back into the shadows of my own home and keep the secret all to myself.

I sit here as if he hasn't already answered, as if my mind is not already made up and is still mine to make. I won't be able to drag the tools to them, not with my knee as swollen and sore as it is. There's no way I'll be able to reach them without doing myself greater harm. But I'll pull the toolbox as far as I can, beyond the dark mouth of my cave and out into the sunlight where the hikers will see it. I'll find some way to get their attention and make them look in my direction, lead them to discover what I have to share— the tools they will need, and the tools I will need them to use if I am to go on with something at all like the life I've been living.

But not yet. First I'm going to sit here by myself, alone for another moment or two, before the brambles creep into my cave and the clatter of metal on stone and the clamor of building drowns out the hum of the bees.

ACKNOWLEDGMENTS

Big thanks to my parents and brothers, for indulging my daydreamer's mind, and to my wife, Sage, and daughter, Gretchen, for living with it. To Michelle Bailat-Jones and Laura McCune-Poplin, the best first readers and friends a person could want, and to Tom McCarthy, Rick Reiken, Michael Kindness, Peter Grandbois, William Walsh, Lise Haines, and Jessica Treadway for their support. To Nora Fussner at *Pindeldyboz*, Roxane Gay at *PANK Magazine*, Amber Sparks at *Emprise Review*, Laura Ellen Scott at *Everyday Genius*, Matt Bell at *The Collagist*, and Steven Seighman at *Monkeybicycle* for publishing excerpts, and to Jeanne Holtzman, Kevin Fanning, Rob Kloss, and Erin Fitzgerald for reading along the way. Also to Meng-hu, host of the invaluable *Hermitary.com*, Tony Robinson of *The Worst Jobs In History*, and AKM Adam for the inspiration, and of course thanks to Dan Cafaro, Libby Kuzma, Lindsey Kline, Jamie Keenan, and Angela Gabriel at Atticus Books. In memory of Checkers, who always knew when I needed a walk to think about the next bit of writing.

ABOUT THE AUTHOR

Steve Himmer's stories have appeared in numerous journals and anthologies, and he edits the online journal *Necessary Fiction*. He teaches at Emerson College in Boston, where he also earned his MFA, and he has a website at http://www.stevehimmer.com. *The Bee-Loud Glade* is his first novel.